Cherish Me Forever
The Maxwell Brothers
Layla Hagen

Copyright ©2023 Layla Hagen

All rights reserved. No part of this book may be reproduced or transmitted in any form, including electronic or mechanical, without written permission from the author, except in the case of brief quotations embodied in critical articles or reviews. This is a work of fiction. Names, characters, businesses, places, events and incidents are either the products of the author's imagination or used in fictitious manner. Any resemblance to actual persons, living or dead, or actual events is purely coincidental.

Contents

1. Chapter One . . . 1
2. Chapter Two . . . 11
3. Chapter Three . . . 18
4. Chapter Four . . . 27
5. Chapter Five . . . 35
6. Chapter Six . . . 48
7. Chapter Seven . . . 55
8. Chapter Eight . . . 65
9. Chapter Nine . . . 72
10. Chapter Ten . . . 79
11. Chapter Eleven . . . 89
12. Chapter Twelve . . . 101
13. Chapter Thirteen . . . 110
14. Chapter Fourteen . . . 121
15. Chapter Fifteen . . . 128
16. Chapter Sixteen . . . 136
17. Chapter Seventeen . . . 146
18. Chapter Eighteen . . . 157

19.	Chapter Nineteen	166
20.	Chapter Twenty	172
21.	Chapter Twenty-One	179
22.	Chapter Twenty-Two	187
23.	Chapter Twenty-Three	196
24.	Chapter Twenty-Four	205
25.	Chapter Twenty-Five	213
26.	Chapter Twenty-Six	219
27.	Chapter Twenty-Seven	227
28.	Chapter Twenty-Eight	232
29.	Chapter Twenty-Nine	240
30.	Chapter Thirty	251
31.	First Epilogue	258
32.	Second Epilogue	265

Chapter One
Reese

"You're a cutie. Oh yes, you are."

"Hey, I want to hold her too," my sister Kimberly protested. "You've got her the whole weekend."

"Girls," Gran said. "Stop bickering."

I kissed Rose's head before handing her to my sister. She was right—I could get cuddles all weekend long, so I could be generous right now.

Kimberly immediately took Rose in her arms, keeping her close to her chest. Our cousin Travis and his wife were on vacation, and I'd volunteered to babysit. I was good with babies, toddlers, *and* teenagers. I loved all my cousins' kids.

"Do you want something to drink, Gran?" I offered. "I've got coffee. Or something stronger?"

"Coffee is good," Gran said.

"So, how's married life treating you?" Kimberly asked our grandmother.

Our family was huge. We had six cousins, and everyone was engaged or married. When Gran tied the knot in June, we were all immensely happy for her. She'd been a widow for as long as I could remember, and it was endearing that she'd found a second soulmate.

"It's an adjustment. I've been on my own for decades, and now I'm learning to live with someone else."

"Gran, you sound like me," I said.

"I can't believe we've had so many weddings this summer," Kimberly added.

Our cousins Tyler and Declan surprised us when they announced they wanted a double wedding in July. They had both waited quite some time to get married, but all the pieces fell into place this summer.

I made three coffees—decaf for me—and returned to my dining room table. Rose had fallen asleep with her head on Kim's shoulder. All my instincts craved to ask to hold her again.

Get real, Reese. You'll have her all to yourself soon enough. Don't be too greedy.

As I sat down, we each took our cup of coffee and clinked them together.

"To more weddings in the Maxwell family," Gran exclaimed.

"We don't have that many left. Only Luke and Megan, and Kimberly." I looked at my sister, grinning and batting my eyelashes.

"We haven't set a date yet."

"Please tell me you'll give me more of a heads-up than everyone else is doing lately."

"Definitely," Kimberly said.

"I want us to plan everything in detail."

We both glared at Gran. We'd had three months to organize her wedding. Our cousins had given us even more headaches—we'd only had one month to put everything together for theirs. None of them had specific expectations, though, so they went along with most of the things we suggested.

"What are your plans for the weekend?" Kimberly asked.

"I need to finish up some spreadsheets," I told them. I had nothing going on. Usually I tried to set up a date, but ever since the guy I was seeing back in June turned out to be an ass, I'd decided to press Pause on dating. And here I'd thought he might be the one. Ha!

Gran frowned. "Darling, life's too short to work weekends. Please trust me."

"It relaxes me. And maybe I'll drop by The Happy Place too." Once upon a time, the Maxwell family was known for owning a chain of bookstores. Our dad, uncle, and aunt sold it successfully. But Gran had insisted on keeping the first-ever store—The Happy Place. I was beyond grateful because, as the name indicated, it *was* my happy place. I'd spent a large chunk of my childhood there, and now I worked right above it in the hotel I was running with Kimberly and Travis. The Maxwell Hotel was doing spectacularly, and I couldn't be prouder. We were opening a second one in Aspen and had lots to do. I loved keeping busy.

"By the way, the hotel received an invitation for the annual De Monet charity event. Want to join me?" I asked Kimberly. It was a local event for underprivileged children, and our family had been involved in it for years. Gran used to talk about the events growing up. They were black-tie and involved fancy dinners and sometimes even a weekend of activities.

"Sure. When is it?"

"Next weekend."

She scrunched her nose. "I can't. Drake and I plan to fly over to Aspen again."

Drake also worked at the hotel, and the two of them were very hands-on with the Aspen location.

I waved her off. "That's okay, I'll go by myself. Or maybe I'll rope someone else into joining me." I was good at that. "Let me just check what time it is."

I looked at the email, scrolling to the end. They'd attached two lists, one with the details and one with the attendees. Of course, I clicked the wrong list. I went to close it as soon as it popped up on my screen, but then a familiar name made me freeze.

Malcolm Delaware.

It couldn't be.

I swallowed hard, but the name I below nearly choked me.

Francisca Delaware.

No, no, no.

I took in a deep breath. I thought they'd moved away from Chicago, but the names weren't coincidental. My ex-fiancé and my former best friend. I swallowed hard. *What are they even doing here?*

"Reese?" Kimberly asked. "What's wrong?"

I cleared my throat. "I clicked on the wrong list." Was my voice shaky? I hoped not. I didn't want Gran and Kimberly to notice something was off. "It's at seven thirty in the evening."

"I'm sure someone will be able to join you."

I looked up at her, confused for a second, before remembering what we'd been talking about.

"Actually, I changed my mind. There's no need. I'm representing Maxwell Hotels, and I know Travis is leaving next weekend, too, so I'll go there on my own."

The last thing I wanted was for any of my family to run into Malcolm. He'd caused enough headaches for me and my family. He was my problem to deal with.

Kimberly lifted a brow. Damn it. I'd changed my mind far too quickly. She'd figure out I was hiding something.

"Stop by the house before you go, and I'll feed you something good," Gran said. "At those fancy events, they usually put out some crumbs and call it dinner."

"I'll do that." I was grateful for the opportunity. I would need to soak in some family love before facing my ex.

Years ago, Malcolm and I were engaged. I bought this apartment right around that time. I had so many dreams about it, and about us. I thought we'd start a family here.

I'd even crossed one of my personal boundaries, because he'd asked me to. I agreed to do a spread in *Vogue* highlighting the wedding. The Maxwell name was a big deal in Chicago, though we rarely spoke with the press. I was generally a very private person, but I'd wanted to do it for Malcolm and make him happy.

Just before the wedding, I found out that he was sleeping with my best friend, Francesca. I felt an ache in my chest, just remembering the way they both betrayed me.

Shake it off, will you? It's been years. Your family can't see you like this.

After Gran and Kimberly left, I was restless. Rose fell asleep, so I put her in the mobile crib.

I went to the egg-shaped swing hanging from the ceiling. I liked to curl up in it with my Kindle and read for hours; it made me feel safe, like I was in a cocoon. I threw a fuzzy blanket over myself, even though I wasn't cold, and settled into it.

I couldn't believe I had to face Malcolm and Francesca. Though maybe it would do me good. As my therapist liked to say, "Sometimes we have to come face-to-face with our demons in order to put them behind us."

But I'd come face-to-face with him several times since we broke up. After every encounter, I was in shambles. He'd come after my family and me repeatedly. Last time, he blackmailed me into giving an in-depth interview to the press. My cousin Declan threatened him and made sure no firm in Chicago hired him. Malcolm moved away after that. Was he back?

I couldn't believe I'd have them together.

Maybe it would be just what I needed to put everything behind me.

Rose woke up at seven o'clock. I was going to have trouble putting her to sleep later, since she'd had such a healthy nap. To be honest, I still hadn't mastered the art of them. I was trying my best to follow the instructions Travis and Bonnie had left me, but the naps still eluded me. I always messed up and let her sleep too long.

"Come on, baby girl. I've got a delicious puree for you. Oh yeah, Aunt Reese is going to spoil you all weekend long. And we're going to spend some quality girl time with your cousin as well."

I was taking Paisley, my cousin Tate's daughter, out and about tomorrow. Initially, I'd offered to take her baby sister as well, but I knew my limits. I hadn't yet mastered the art of juggling two toddlers at the same time, but I was a fast learner.

My mind circled back to Malcolm and Francesca. Maybe I could bail.

But deep in my heart, I knew I couldn't. The charity event itself was planned as a few separate activities overall, and I'd even helped organize one of them. I couldn't let them down.

Besides, I was no chicken.

Dom

"Mr. Waldorf, I have everything covered," Dora, my father's caregiver, said.

"Let me know if there's an issue with his medication or anything else," I replied.

"I will, but so far, we're good. He's in the living room. The chessboard is already prepared."

These days, Dad could barely get around without help, but his mind was still as sharp as ever.

Dad still lived in the same house I grew up in—a historic home near Irving Park. It was like walking back in time. He'd kept everything as it was when Mom was here. Even the outside was painted the same blueish color with white windowsills and trim.

I'd tried to talk him into moving into a condo or a bungalow—something without stairs—but he insisted that he belonged here, so I didn't argue. I went right into the living room.

"Looking sharp, son."

"Thanks, Dad."

"Where are you going?"

"Charity event."

"Always those charities, eh?" Dad said. The board was right in front of him. "Come on. Give me your best."

He turned the chess clock the second my ass hit the chair. That was Dad to a tee; he didn't like to waste his time.

"Now, don't you dare let me win."

"Never," I said.

He looked at me suspiciously. I might have done so over the past few months, especially if he was having a hard day.

"How's the company?" he asked.

Waldorf Fashion was my life's work. We were a force to be reckoned with in the industry.

"The last quarter of the year is always a busy time."

"Don't forget to take a break now and again."

"I won't."

Dad usually didn't give advice, but since my divorce, he'd slipped one or two words of wisdom in here and there.

"Dad, you're winning again," I exclaimed several moves later.

"Yeah, because you're distracted. Thinking about that ex-wife of yours?"

"No," I said truthfully. "Just about the shit show that followed."

"Son, you'll get over this. Now come on, give me a real game. I prepared for this all week."

A pang of guilt rose in my chest. I was a lousy son. Sure, work kept me busy, but I could find time to drop by Dad's house more than once a week. It was one of the only times he got human interaction, aside from Dora. Most of his friends were the same age and not as mobile as they used to be either.

"When does your charity thing start?"

"I have plenty of time."

"I know you. You're trying to weasel your way out of it."

I held up my hand in despair. "I dislike events as a rule. And the ones for charity even more. I prefer to simply write a check. Just the fact that they're organizing a party for it means some of that money's going to be swallowed up by the event itself."

"Yes, but being able to boast about the celebrity attendees will likely attract more people. They'll pay good money to rub elbows with the likes of you."

I laughed. "Right. It still doesn't make me keen on going."

"It'll do you good to get out. And checkmate. Want a drink? Some sage advice?"

"Nah, you don't need to commiserate with me."

He rolled his eyes. "Yes, I clearly do. I just beat your ass. Third week in a row. Come on. I need you to bring your best game."

"Want to play another one?" I asked.

"No. One time's the charm. It's when all the adrenaline happens. The game is boring without it."

We spoke about my week for another twenty minutes, until it was time for me to leave.

"All right, then. I'll go," I said.

"See you next week, son."

"I'll drop by before that," I replied.

"No, no. I don't want you coddling me. You've got enough on your plate running Waldorf Fashion."

"I'm good with time management, Dad. I just don't like events."

"Son, make the best out of it."

That was his motto in life. To his credit, he always made the best out of every situation. He could have been crippled by pain at Mom's passing, but he wasn't. He was housebound and yet still full of life. I had plenty to learn from my dad, and I was glad to have him as an example to look up to.

I'd started Waldorf Fashion fifteen years ago, and he and Mom cheered me on from the get-go. Obviously, neither of us expected it to take off the way it did. I'd worked hard, yes, but I also had luck.

As I got into the car, my driver looked in the mirror. "Straight to the event, sir? Do you want to drop by the office too? We could still swing by, although that wouldn't leave you much time."

I considered this for a moment. Headquarters was above the flagship store on the Miracle Mile, and traffic was a nightmare at this time of the day.

"No. Let's head straight to the event." Punctuality was my forte. I might not be a fan of charity events, but I'd agreed to attend, and I was going to do it properly. I never did anything half-assed.

We arrived thirty minutes later.

"Good thing we didn't drop by the office," my driver said, looking at me in the rearview mirror. "Do you need me to pick you up, sir?"

"No, it's going to be late."

"I know a good restaurant around here. I can eat dinner there while I wait for you."

I considered this. I liked the convenience of having someone pick me up and drop me off at a whim, but I didn't want to keep him overtime. "Let's do the following. Have dinner at the restaurant. Text me when you're ready. If I'm done, too, you can pick me up. If I have to stay longer, you can go home." I liked to treat my employees with respect.

"That's great, boss. Let's do that." He smiled in the rearview mirror.

I stepped out of the car, immediately thinking I should have brought a coat. It wasn't very warm for the middle of September.

I took a good look at the building. I had to give it to the coordinators of this thing: they'd chosen a good venue. We'd had company events here, and they'd always run smoothly. Even so, I would have preferred to write a check rather than attend.

I stepped inside, heading straight to the young woman who stood next to the door with a list in her hands.

"Dominic Waldorf," I said.

Her eyes widened. "Welcome, sir. I hope you have a great time tonight. You're at table seven."

"Thank you."

"May I get you anything?" she asked. "I can ask the servers to take extra care of you tonight... or I can do it myself." Her smile widened. "I'll give you my number. In case you need anything later."

This sort of attention had been happening ever since the press published that damn article: "Chicago's Most Eligible Bachelor Is Single Again."

"I can find my own way to my table. But thank you."

Tonight is a mistake. I shouldn't have come here.

Chapter Two

Reese

"Good gracious, girl, you didn't eat anything," Gran said.

"I'm a bit nervous," I admitted. As promised, I'd stopped by her house the evening of the charity event, not just for food but to get some cuddles from Rose. Gran and her husband, John, were babysitting her this weekend. Rose was sitting in my lap, playing with the belt on my dress. John wasn't home right now. Pity, as I would have liked to say hello.

"You've been to events like these hundreds of times," Gran exclaimed. "What's there to be nervous about?"

Oh, right. I cleared my throat. "I don't know." I hadn't told a soul that Malcolm was attending as well. Knowing my big mouth, I was about to ruin it any second now. But I was determined to keep myself in check. Even if I asked Gran not to tell the rest of the family, she'd worry, and that wouldn't do. And besides, I'd given myself several pep talks at home about this evening.

Spoiler alert: none of them worked.

I was a basket case.

Rose held up her hands, and I helped her to her feet. She was barefoot, pressing her little feet on my thighs. God, I loved kids. My heart ached every time I held one. She opened her arms wider and leaned forward. She knew what I needed.

Rose put her tiny arms on my shoulders and the side of her face straight over my boobs. Then she straightened up and pushed herself onto her toes even more. I lowered my cheek to her tiny mouth, and she placed a wet kiss there, probably also wiping away three layers of foundation. I immediately grabbed a napkin and tried to get it off her lips.

Gran tsked. "Oh, she made a mess of you."

"It doesn't matter," I said. "I'll just reapply if needed."

"Chop, chop, off you go, or you'll be late. Unless you want to actually eat?"

I looked at Gran apologetically. She'd made her specialty—apple pie. *Wait a second.*

Gran only made apple pie when she wanted to get information out of someone.

I looked up from my plate. Gran gave me her knowing smile. *Oh shoot.* She knew there was something off with me. But why was I surprised? Gran had practically raised Kimberly and me, after all.

"I'm sorry I didn't touch your apple pie." And good thing I didn't, because one thing was for sure—if I had as much as a spoonful, I'd totally run my mouth. Kimberly and I were certain it had magic powers.

"Whatever it is, Reese, you're strong enough to face it, my girl."

I completely mellowed. Even more so when she opened her arms. I willingly stepped into her hug.

"Thanks, Gran." She knew me better than anyone else—except perhaps Kimberly.

"And I'm also here to talk if you need to."

I winked at her, chuckling. "I don't right now, but I'll keep it in mind."

I ordered an Uber and paced in front of Gran's bungalow. While waiting, I was tempted to run back inside and spill my guts.

No, Reese, come on. Be strong. You don't want to worry Gran. You'll be fine.

I arrived at the venue twenty minutes later. As soon as I stepped out of my Uber, I tensed up. I was on high alert, looking for my ex and his wife. Thankfully there was no sign of them outside.

I was surprised by how efficient everyone was at the entrance. The friendly hostess informed me that I was assigned to table seven. As I took in the room, I noticed the modern decor with metal-and-wood light fixtures. There was a table with sweets but no buffet or chafing dishes, which meant dinner would be served at the table. I'd attended several charity events here over the years but had never been inside this particular room.

"A glass of champagne for you, miss?" the waiter asked. He had a tray of flutes and was making his way around the tables.

"Yes, please." I needed some liquid courage. I accepted the glass, then walked quickly to my table.

My phone vibrated in my small evening bag. I made to remove it with my left hand, but then several things happened. I lost my footing and my right leg stumbled, and although I recovered quickly, I still managed to spill champagne everywhere—mostly on the only other guest sitting at table seven.

"Oh my God, I'm so, so sorry," I exclaimed, dropping my purse on the chair, then salvaging the rest of the contents in the glass. That's when I realized I'd poured half of it on the poor guy.

Holy shit!

When he looked up at me, the disgust was obvious in his dark green eyes. He was so handsome that I forgot where I was, what my name was, and even how to breathe. It was simply not possible for anyone to be so attractive. He looked vaguely familiar, but that wasn't a surprise; everyone here was famous in one way or another.

"I'm sorry. I'll get some more napkins. I'm not even sure what to say. I'll pay for dry cleaning. Or you can give your shirt to me, and I'll take it to the cleaners," I babbled.

Why would I offer that? That was the most ridiculous thing that has ever come out of my mouth. What's he supposed to do? Strip?

"I can't believe it. Can no one give it a rest tonight? This is really not the best way to get my attention."

I straightened up at that. *Hot guy is a douchebag.*

"I'm sorry, what? You think this was a ruse to get your attention? I'm sitting at this table. And I lost my balance."

He glanced at my dress. "And yet you didn't spill anything on yourself, just on me."

"Have you ever lost your balance before? You can't plan which way you land."

He snorted. "Right. I'm off to the bathroom to clean this mess."

I took a step back as he lurched up from his seat.

Damn, he was tall and well-built. Pity he didn't have his temper under control. Whatever. I had too much on my mind tonight to try and second-guess why my tablemate was such a grumpy ass. That was none of my business.

I sat down before my nerves got the better of me. I glanced around the room again. I still couldn't see Malcolm and Francesca anywhere. Maybe they weren't going to come tonight after all. That would be wonderful.

So much for not being a chicken.

As I sat here, I was sure that seeing them together wouldn't help me heal. Quite the contrary—it would reopen an old wound.

But just in case, I needed reinforcements. I grabbed a plate and went directly to the table of sweets.

They had plenty of goodies, but what I yearned for was one of Liz's brownies. My cousin Declan's wife was a very talented baker.

As I pondered over which sweets to take, I thought this would be a good venue for her to expand her business—catering events. She'd gotten into weddings lately, but this could be another great revenue stream. I made a mental note to talk to the host later; maybe I could pull a string or two for Liz. She would definitely appreciate it.

"I knew I'd find you here."

I nearly dropped my plate when Malcolm's voice came from behind me. I gripped the edges until my knuckles turned white and turned around. Francesca was right behind him. My vision faded at the corners. I swallowed hard and blinked three times, trying to clear my eyes.

Come on, Reese, don't faint. It's not so bad.

It *was* that bad. I felt as if I had a stone crushing my chest. I cleared my throat. "Malcolm?"

"We saw your name on the guest list," Francesca said, "but didn't know if you'd actually come."

"Why wouldn't I?" I asked.

Malcolm set his jaw.

"Well," Francesca replied, "with the two of us attending."

She'd been my best friend. Who did this to their best friend?

"What are you two doing in Chicago, anyway?"

"You Maxwells don't rule Chicago," Malcolm said in a stern voice.

Dread prickled at me. "I think you know better. I thought Declan made it clear last time."

He took a step closer.

"Malc!" Francesca exclaimed.

That sliced right into my heart. *Malc.* I used to call him that.

"You and your family will stop intimidating me," he sneered. "Do you understand? Or you'll be in serious legal trouble. You got away with it once. You won't again."

I breathed deeply, trying to calm myself. I didn't want to cause a scene.

"If you'll excuse me, I have better things to do." I walked straight past him.

What was I thinking, coming here tonight? God, I hope they aren't at my table.

I put the plate with sweets down and looked around the room. They were at the table in the opposite corner. Thank heavens for small miracles.

I took in another breath and then exhaled. *I have to leave this room. Right now.*

I went into the lobby, straight to the hostess. "Hey, are any parts of the premises off-limits?"

She frowned. "What do you mean?"

A light bulb went on in my mind. "I have to make a phone call, but I'd prefer some privacy." I hated lying, but I needed to be alone.

"There's a second coatroom in the back. We won't need it tonight, so no one will bother you there, and it gets a good signal. It's straight ahead." She pointed me toward it.

"Thank you," I said. All I needed was a few minutes to myself. I'd always been a bit of a loner, except when it came to my family. I could be surrounded by them all day long and not get enough. But other than that, I liked to be on my own, especially when shit hit the fan.

I headed to the coatroom with determined steps, praying Malcolm or Francesca wouldn't pop out and find me. I needed to get myself together before facing them again or I might end up causing a scene.

The nerve of Malcolm. He was the one who threatened us first. He tried to blackmail me. Why was he back in Chicago?

It didn't matter. He wasn't part of my life anymore. Even if our paths were bound to cross at some point again, I'd have to learn to deal with it.

I stepped into the coatroom, closing the door and taking a deep breath.

"You've got to be kidding me."

I startled, then opened my eyes wide. My asshole of a tablemate was leaning against the wall, glaring at me.

"Here we go again."

Chapter Three
Dom

I unhitched myself from the wall. What had gotten into this woman? No way in hell had she not spilled that drink on me on purpose. No one could be that clumsy. I'd half expected her to ask for my number so she could "return" the shirt after she took it for dry cleaning.

"You want to convince me that this isn't a coincidence?"

She stared at me. "I have no idea what you're talking about."

"You followed me in here."

She blinked, stepping away from the door. "You think very highly of yourself, don't you?"

"Okay, I'll give you the benefit of the doubt."

"Why, thank you. I didn't know I needed it. I'm so eternally grateful." Her voice was full of irony.

"What *are* you doing here, then?" I asked.

"It's a secluded room. I wanted some time to myself. Why are you hiding in here?"

I exhaled sharply as I took in her body language. She seemed different than before. Sad.

Don't even go there, Dom.

She was a fucking beautiful woman, but that was beside the point.

"Who said I'm hiding?" Though I was. The event was beginning to get crowded, and on the way from the bathroom to the ballroom, I'd been hit on by four women.

"Well, *I* am," she said. She'd been full of fire before. And although now she tried to give me shit, too, something was different about her. I was certain of it.

"Why?" I asked.

She raised her hands and dropped them again in resignation. "My ex-fiancé and the best friend he cheated on me with are attending the event tonight. When I saw their names on the guest list, I thought I could face them. Spoiler alert: I was wrong. I hoped that drinking some champagne would help. But even that didn't work out in my favor, since I poured it all over you. They cornered me before I had the chance to grab another glass."

That completely took the wind out of my sails. There was no way in hell this woman was lying. No one could come up with this story on the spot.

She glanced away, and I realized she was tearing up.

"Fuck," I exclaimed. "You really didn't do that on purpose?"

"No." Her voice shook. She dabbed at her eyes.

"I apologize for being a total asshole to you." I replayed the whole scene in my mind. "Damn."

She looked up at me again, a wide smile on her face. "Well, this is quite a way to meet someone. I'm usually running my mouth, but I think this is a first, even for me. I didn't even introduce myself before telling you my life story." She stretched out a hand. "Reese Maxwell."

I shook her hand. "I'm Dominic Waldorf."

She gasped. "Oh, that's why you look familiar. From Waldorf Fashion, right?"

"Yes."

"You've gotten some press lately. I can see why you thought I might have tried to latch on to you."

I laughed without humor.

She looked at the door and then back. "That's why you're hiding in here? You don't like women throwing themselves at you?"

I stared at her.

"You're not in the mood to joke. Got it. I'm sorry. When I'm out of sorts, I tend to quickly change between sad and extremely happy and making a fool of myself and being inappropriate. I think you're getting to see all sides of me tonight." She sighed and stared up at the ceiling. "God, why didn't I show up here with a hot date? That would take Malcolm off my back for sure."

Is this woman for real?

"Reese, I think you need this room more than I do."

She laughed. "Oh God, yes, I do. I think I might never come out of it."

I frowned. "I can get you a cab, or I can have my driver drop you off wherever you want. He's nearby."

"Hmmm... no matter how out of sorts I am, I definitely wouldn't get in a stranger's car."

"Hardly a stranger," I said, my tone harsher than I intended. "The whole country knows me and my story. Anyway, I'm going back out there."

Her eyes clouded for a moment. "I'll be out in a few minutes too."

I nodded, heading to the door and opening it, then looked at her over my shoulder. "You have even worse luck than I do. I couldn't even imagine running into my ex here. Reese, give them hell."

She laughed just as I closed the door.

I went into the ballroom quickly. Heading to the table, I took two glasses of champagne from a tray, putting one at Reese's spot.

As more guests arrived, a guy stopped dead in his tracks at the table. He didn't even attempt to sit down, so I figured he wasn't assigned here.

"You're Dominic Waldorf, aren't you?" the guy asked. "Man, I've been meaning to meet you for years. I can't believe I'm finally lucky enough to run into you."

"That's me," I confirmed.

"Look, I want to pitch you something."

I flashed my PR smile. I was told it was more of a grimace, but it would have to do.

"I don't conduct business at charity events," I said. "Now, if you'll excuse me, I need to catch up with someone." I got up from my chair, looking to the left and then to the right. Where to escape to? Ah yes, the bar.

As I waited for my drink, I looked at the hostess, Monika De Monet, searching for a sign that they were beginning the event soon.

She caught my eye and walked right over to me. "Mr. Waldorf, what a pleasure to have you here."

"Always happy to contribute to noble causes." I might not like the process, but I liked knowing the money would be used for a good purpose. "When are you starting the show and taking donations?"

"Oh, not for another two hours. I want to spoil you all a bit first," she said with a wink. *Fuck me.* "Experience has taught me that people are more generous when they're fed and happy."

She was right. I just didn't like the prospect of spending hours here.

Over her shoulder, I noticed Reese. That woman was truly a work of art. Her curves were stunning. She went straight to our table. She didn't even get to sit down before a couple walked up to her.

"I'll catch up with you later," I told the host, grabbing the glass of whiskey I'd ordered.

I headed to the table and was only a few steps away when I caught wind of the conversation.

"Really," the guy said with a sneer, "you're going to do what exactly?"

"Why are you even here? I thought you didn't like these events," Reese said.

"None of your business."

"This is not your table. Why don't you go back to yours and leave me alone?"

"Or what? You'll cause a scene?" he asked.

His question made me wonder if that was what he was after. I stepped right up next to her. "Do we have a problem?"

Reese looked sideways at me. "Malcolm and Francesca were just leaving."

"Actually, we just arrived," the Malcolm dude said. He glanced at me and froze. I recognized that expression on his face—he realized who I was.

He tried to school his features, but his expression was hungry. "Dominic Waldorf. The man of the hour. I saw your name on the guest list but assumed you would send someone in your stead."

Instead of telling him to fuck off, I glanced at Reese. She had a hardened expression.

I had no idea what possessed me to do it, but I put an arm around her shoulders, pulling her close to me. "Couldn't leave my woman here alone tonight, could I?"

Reese's eyes widened as she parted her lips.

The question she had was obvious: *What the hell are you doing?*

I turned to look at Malcolm and Francesca. "So, why don't you two get the hell back to your table and leave my woman alone? She doesn't need to deal with any more of your crap than she already has."

"Dominic," Reese said in a low voice.

"What do you think, beautiful? You want to go outside to get some fresh air?" I asked, looking at her. Fuck, she was even more attractive up close.

She licked her lips, and all my instincts demanded I lean forward and capture her mouth. "No. The food is going to be served soon. I think we should stay."

"You two are dating?" Malcolm asked.

"Yes, we are," I said, and Reese pressed herself into me.

"So really, I have nothing more to say to you, Malcolm," she said with a smirk.

Reese

How was this happening? I had to be imagining all this.

When they accosted me again, my first thought was *Why can't I just flaunt a hot date?* I had no idea what got into Dominic, but my God, seeing the expressions on their faces was worth it.

And being pressed against this wall of muscle that is Dominic Waldorf is no hardship either.

"Well then, we'll see the two of you around. We'll have a lot of fun, especially next weekend," Francesca said.

Crap. I'd forgotten. The charity was organizing various events for fundraising, and the next one was a weekend trip outside the city.

Could this evening get any worse? Wait, don't ask yourself that, Reese. As a general rule, things can always get worse.

Dominic pulled me even closer to him. I could smell his cologne, which reminded me of winter. It was fresh and crisp and 100 percent manly.

"See you around. And by the way, man, maybe we can talk business sometime," Malcolm said.

It took me a few seconds to process his words. The nerve of him! I couldn't believe it.

"Or not," I retorted. "I've warned Dominic not to get involved with the likes of you."

"Come on, Reese. It's unlike you to hold a grudge."

"I've changed," I replied icily.

"You heard her. Now fuck off," Dominic said.

It felt good to have someone else tell him to fuck off. But I was pissed that Malcolm heeded Dominic's words when he'd ignored my request.

The second they were out of earshot, I glanced at Dominic. "Want to step outside the room and talk a bit?"

He flashed me a smirk. "Right now? When they're about to serve food?"

"Yes."

"Okay then. Let's go."

How was he suddenly in such a good mood? He'd seemed like a royal grump earlier. Then again, I *had* spilled a glass of champagne all over him.

Luckily, there was almost no one in the corridor as we headed to the coatroom. Once inside, he closed the door. I took in a deep breath, biting the inside of my cheek as I focused on him. I couldn't get over how attractive he was.

"What was that about?" I asked.

"You inspired me when you said you wished you'd brought a date." He shrugged. "Honestly, I can't explain it. Just saw him being a jackass and went with it. Clearly he didn't expect that."

"I didn't either. Thank you. That certainly took them by surprise. I'll just have to think of an excuse to ward them off from now on. The fundraising includes a weekend event too."

He grunted. "Fuck. I forgot."

Ah, there he was, back to his grumpy self. "Don't worry, there's no need to take this any further. I just didn't want you to think I'd expect that."

There, that'll let him off the hook. He didn't say anything.

"Anyway," I continued, "Malcolm's going to find something to rub in my face, I'm sure of it. So don't worry about it. I appreciate your help."

He stared at me, then said, "You don't have to go back in. Or attend the weekend event."

I shook my head, standing straighter. *Is that a dimple in his left cheek?* "No, I'm representing Maxwell Hotels, and I promised I'd attend. I don't like to go back on my word."

He narrowed his eyes and then opened them wider as if he were conversing with himself.

"They're going to raise even more money with the weekend event. It's for a good cause," I added.

"You're seriously going to put up with facing that asshole for a good cause?"

I scoffed. "You're one to talk. You clearly don't want to be here either."

"It's a minor inconvenience for me. It's—" He hesitated, staring at me for a beat. "—more than that for you."

"*That* is an understatement. Anyway, thanks again for earlier. It certainly was worth seeing that expression on both their faces."

"I won't be attending the next events."

Didn't I just let him off the hook?

"Don't worry. I'll figure something out. Should we go back to the table?"

He nodded. "If you're ready."

"I am."

He opened the door and gestured for me to walk in front of him. I got another whiff of his cologne as I walked past him.

Damn, the man was hot!

Pity I'd probably never see him again.

Chapter Four

Dom

"Dom, they've sent you menus for the charity weekend so you can pick out your favorite food. Should I do it for you?" my assistant Charlene asked.

"I'm not attending. I'm sure I told you that."

"Damn it. I'd hoped you'd change your mind."

I looked up at her. "Why?"

She shrugged. "It's good for you to go out in the world and not stay holed up in here all the time."

I leaned back in my chair, pushing a stack of papers to one side. I could look at them after Charlene left the office.

"Who in PR has time to attend?"

"I've made you a list." She immediately put it on the desk. "If you tell me by the end of the week who you want to go, I'll make all the arrangements."

"Anything else?" I asked.

"No, that was all."

I surveyed the list. It contained four names—the usual suspects. I was going to decide by the end of the day; I didn't need to drag my feet.

Last night had been insane. I couldn't remember the last time I'd done something as spontaneous as pretending to be Reese's date. It felt good to save her from that asshole, and I was glad the douchebag backed off. He hadn't approached Reese for the rest of the evening.

After Charlene left, I began reading through my stack of papers again. But after I read the first three sheets twice, I realized I wasn't focusing.

I tapped the pen against the desk. Reese said she could get that guy off her back by herself, but it hadn't seemed that way last night. He was damn persistent. When she spilled that champagne on me, she'd seemed like a no-nonsense woman who wasn't going to take shit from anyone. That's why I'd been so shocked to see her cower when her ex popped up. But some people knew our vulnerabilities, giving them the power to hurt us. We all had our weak spots. And Malcolm was obviously Reese's.

Damn it. I have more important things to focus on than someone else's drama.

I opened a blank email on my laptop screen and began writing to Charlene. I'd intended to tell her to send Paul to the charity weekend. Instead, I wrote one sentence: **Get me Reese Maxwell's number.**

After that, I returned to my stack of reports. Surprisingly, it was much easier to focus. At least until Charlene burst into my office one hour later.

I looked straight at her. "You got it?"

She smiled nervously. "Uh, no."

I straightened up. "Why not?"

"She's even more private than you."

I frowned. "What do you mean?"

"She doesn't have any social media profiles."

"I don't care about social media profiles. I need her number."

"See, the funny thing is, if people don't even have a social media footprint, they're not likely to leave their number lying around."

"She works for... or owns Maxwell Hotels. Follow that lead."

"I tried to. No one is giving out any numbers."

"Try following the lead through the charity's coordinator."

She gave me yet another nervous smile. "I tried that too. She's under strict instructions not to give Ms. Maxwell's number to anyone else."

I was intrigued. Why the need for privacy? The Maxwell name was an important part of the city's past. I'd heard it a lot growing up. They were royalty in Chicago even today, but most people with that kind of notoriety basked in it. It was a shock that the Maxwells didn't.

"Fine. I'll get to the bottom of it."

"I know you can do whatever you put your mind to, but I think this might be beyond even your powers."

"Leave it to me," I repeated. I already had a plan. "Close the door when you go. Thanks, Charlene."

"Sure."

I could let this drop, but that wasn't my style. Then again, I couldn't understand why I was obsessing over it. What did it matter if I went to the charity weekend or not? I didn't know Reese Maxwell. I'd only met the woman yesterday, for God's sake. But I couldn't let it go. I had this odd need to protect her.

I looked up the hotel's contact information. There was a general phone number, and I immediately called it. I'd probably have to fight my way to Reese, but I wasn't going to let this go.

"Maxwell Hotels. How may I help you?" a friendly female voice said.

"Hello! I'd like to speak to Reese Maxwell."

"I can take a message."

"Not a message. I want her direct line."

"I'm sorry, that's not possible."

How the hell did they get any business done if they were so hard to reach?

"I'll wait on this line or any other line while you check with her. Tell her it's Dominic Waldorf."

A little gasp followed my sentence.

"How do you know Reese?" The woman got points for not immediately fawning over me.

"I met her last night at the charity event. I sat next to her. If you tell her my name, she'll confirm it."

"Sure. Is the number you're calling from your personal one?"

"Yes."

"Are you sure you want to wait? I can just have Reese call you."

"I'll wait." In my experience, people moved faster when they had the additional pressure of someone waiting.

"I'll put you on hold."

I put my phone on speakerphone when the background music began and set it on the desk. A few minutes later, the line disconnected. Then my phone rang. I answered immediately.

"Dominic?" Reese sounded incredulous.

I took the phone off speakerphone, putting it to my ear. "Hello, Reese."

"I was shocked when they told me it was you. Why would you even go through reception?"

"It was the only contact information I could find. I think your number is more guarded than the president's."

She laughed, and I wondered what Reese was like when she wasn't stressed out from having her ex hovering around.

"Yes, we do make it hard to reach us. So, why are you calling? Oh my God, I forgot. I offered to pay for your dry cleaning yesterday."

It took me a few seconds to remember what she was talking about. "Don't worry about it. It's taken care of."

"I feel guilty about it."

"Forget about it." My tone was almost cutting.

"All right, so then why are you calling?"

That was a good question. Why had I gone through all the trouble of getting to her?

"I want to talk to you about the charity weekend."

"Really? Because I'm just trying to forget it's coming up."

I rose from my chair, leaning against the desk and glancing out the window at the Miracle Mile. "Someone from my PR team will show up instead of me."

"I figured that. You mentioned you wouldn't go." She sounded confused. "There's no rule saying you can't have someone attend in your place."

"Then why aren't you doing that too? I get that it's all for a good cause, but if you send a PR person, you're still contributing."

She sighed. "The organizers say I have a knack for making people part with their money. And, well, why not use my skill for a good cause?"

Reese Maxwell was a fighter.

"Listen, I have an idea. Why don't I show up for the weekend, too, and we can continue the ruse every time your shithead of an ex is around." Yet another impulsive moment. It seemed to be a thing where Reese was concerned. It was frankly disconcerting.

"You're not serious," she said. "Why would you want to do that?"

"I don't know. Seeing him talk to you like that rubbed me the wrong way."

"You don't even know me, Dominic."

The hesitancy in her voice challenged me. Suddenly, I really wanted this weekend with her.

"You can call me Dom."

"Dom, hmm? That sounds much better."

Fuck me. I liked the sound of my name coming out of her mouth.

"This is insane," she continued. "I mean, I'd obviously like to see Malcolm's face when he sees us together again, but what's in it for you?"

"Honestly, it'll help me too. The press, the women, people in general will get off my back if they think I'm seeing someone."

"But how will they know?"

"Trust me, word spreads. I promised myself that I'd never date anyone with a high profile, but they don't know that. If people see me around you, they'll back off. The season for Christmas parties is approaching pretty fast. It'll do me good if word gets around that I'm seeing someone."

"This is the most bizarre conversation I've ever had. I'm not even sure what to say." *Just say you want it.* "I mean, if you're sure. I loved the look on Malcolm's face. And the weekend is going to be fun. I actually looked over the program. There's going to be an archery contest and—"

"You're joking!"

"Oh, you didn't look at it?"

"No. That doesn't sound appealing in the slightest."

She laughed. "I can't decide if you're a knight in shining armor or a total grump. Or maybe you're both?" She seemed to be talking more to herself than to me, or so I hoped. Because what did that even mean?

The more I thought about going, the more sense it made. I had invitations to a few Christmas parties this year where I couldn't send a representative, so being seen with Reese this weekend would benefit me too.

"Okay, you know what? Let's do this. I was trying to think of excuses as to why my hot new boyfriend wasn't there, but now it seems I won't have to."

"You think I'm hot?" I asked.

She snorted. "Um, hello, of course you are. Why do you think all those women are accosting you?"

"Because I'm Dominic Waldorf."

"Yeah, that too. But you're also sexy as hell. As your fake date, I'm more than entitled to say that—from an objective point of view, of course."

I burst out laughing. Talking to this woman was the highlight of my day.

"Want to drive together? It's two hours away," I suggested.

"Sure. And on the way we can hash out the details."

"What details?" I moved back to my chair.

"We need a story."

"For what?"

"How we started dating, how we met, and so on," she explained.

"I didn't realize this would be so involved."

"Well, if we're doing this, I don't want it to blow up in my face. I couldn't live with Malcolm knowing I made up a boyfriend."

"You didn't. Technically, I did."

"Same thing."

"Sure. We can sort it out on the drive."

"Great. This is your number?" she asked.

"Yes."

"I'll save it."

"And I'll save yours."

"Oh, this isn't mine. It's one of the hotel lines."

"You're joking, right?"

"No. I thought there might be a possibility that someone was posing as you."

"Why?"

She sighed. "Everyone knew you were sitting next to me. The press has deceived me often enough. I'll text you my number."

"Great. Have a productive day, Reese."

She laughed again. "That's how you say goodbye to people?"

"That's as good a goodbye as any," I retaliated.

"Oh, Dom. Well, I wish you a great and happy day."

"That works too." I shook my head, laughing as we disconnected the call.

Two seconds later, my phone beeped with an incoming message.

Unknown: This is my number. Reese.

I felt triumphant. Reese Maxwell didn't give her number to anyone, but she'd entrusted it to me.

Chapter Five
Reese

On Saturday morning, I woke up at seven, even though Dominic wasn't picking me up until nine. I was on pins and needles. I'd finished packing my bag last night, but now I was having second thoughts. Did I choose the right outfits? Was it too much? Was it too little?

Why was I overthinking this? I'd attended a lot of charity events over the years; I had nothing to worry about. But honestly, the thought of seeing Malcolm again made my stomach churn.

And then there was Dom. I couldn't believe he'd offered to continue the ruse.

Not that I minded.

I'd already figured out our story. I just had to check if Dominic was okay with it. Just thinking about him made my mouth go dry. He was definitely the most handsome man I'd ever seen. No wonder women were clamoring to get his attention.

Since I woke up so early, I put the time to good use. Instead of staying home and fretting, I decided to go by Liz's bakery. I could double-check if she wanted to get into catering charity events and also treat myself to something delicious. I grabbed my bag, then texted Dom as I got in my Uber.

Reese: Change of plans. Please don't pick me up from home anymore. This is the new address. It's a bakery.

He replied a few minutes into my car ride.

Dom: Sure. See you later, Reese.

I arrived at Liz's place ten minutes later.

"Hey, girl," I greeted. She was behind the counter as usual. Even though she'd hired a team, she enjoyed waiting on customers. My cousin Declan always grumbled about the long hours she put in at the bakery.

"Reese, why didn't you tell me you were stopping by? I would have made a batch of your favorites."

I pouted. "You already ran out?"

She nodded sadly. "The brownies are popular."

"Doesn't matter. I'll have anything. And a coffee, please." She'd gotten an Italian espresso machine six months ago, and it was the best coffee in town.

"Where are you heading?" She pointed to my bag. "Oh wait, I think Declan told me you have that charity weekend."

"Exactly. Listen, I got an idea. Having a table with sweets is very popular at charity dinners. Is catering events like that something you're interested in?"

Her eyes lit up. "Yes. We certainly have the baking capacity."

I narrowed my eyes. "Do you also have personnel capacity? Because the last thing I want is for Declan to accuse me of giving you even more reason to overwork yourself."

"I'll manage," Liz said.

"Okay, then I can give your contact information to some of the organizers I trust."

She grinned. "Thanks for thinking about me, Reese. So, would you like some hazelnut cake? If people give me good feedback, I might even try to make brownies with the flavor."

"Ohh, sounds delicious."

She put a slice of cake on a plate, then grabbed an espresso cup. I stepped to one side, waiting for the coffee machine to do its thing. The bakery was far too small. I devoured the cake immediately.

"This is truly fantastic."

"Want another slice?"

"Oh, no. One is enough."

"Are you driving there?" she asked.

"No, another participant is picking me up," I said while devouring the cake.

"Declan didn't mention that."

I flashed her a huge I'm-not-hiding-anything smile. "It was a last-minute thing. Not really something to bother the family with."

Liz frowned. "Bother?"

Why did I think I could pull off my fake dating? This was exactly why I needed to get all the details of our story right; otherwise, everyone was going to see right through this.

"I'll just wait for him outside."

Big mistake. Liz's eyes widened when I said the word *him*.

"Right," she drew out. "Want me to prepare another coffee for him?"

"Great idea. Thanks," I said. "And please don't mention any of this to the family."

She glanced around, leaning over the counter as she handed me the first coffee. It was futile because the place was too small to have a secret conversation.

"You're dating someone?"

"No," I said. "It's complicated. Just please don't mention it to the family."

"No one? Not even Kimberly?"

My sister would hand me my ass if she knew what I was up to—especially because I didn't tell her.

"No."

"Are you in trouble?"

"No, Liz." Now she was worrying for me, and I didn't want her to do that. On the other hand, I was grateful that my cousins were so lucky in the romance department. They'd chosen wonderful women, and that made my heart happy.

"I'll fill you in once I'm back, okay?" I promised.

"Sure. Can't wait. Here's your second coffee."

"Thanks! Now, take care of your customers. Wouldn't want any complaints that you're making them wait."

She sent me an air kiss before I stepped out of the bakery with my tiny carry-on, thankful that I'd mastered the art of packing outfits and shoes in small bags over the years. Liz had put the coffee cups in a cardboard tray so I could hold it in my left hand and drag the carry-on with my right one.

Once outside, I let go of the bag and took out my phone, checking if Dom had texted me. He had indeed.

Dom: I'm driving a Range Rover.

Reese: Okay.

I fidgeted in my spot. My stomach somersaulted, and I knew myself better than to think it was just nerves. I was looking forward to seeing him.

My heart started racing when the Range Rover turned around the corner. He stopped the car right in front of me and got out.

I shook my head. "Don't get out. You're not allowed to stop here."

" I won't let you load your luggage by yourself."

"It's small and easy."

He just shook his head and took my bag in one hand, opening the trunk with the other one.

He was even hotter today, wearing a shirt and jeans. Casual clothing looked good on him. He'd seemed uncomfortable in that tux. Sexy, but uncomfortable.

"Thanks for picking me up from here," I said.

He opened the car door for me. "No problem."

As he closed it, I noticed Liz's face in the window of the bakery. She was grinning. Oh, God. Would she keep this a secret? I hoped so.

As soon as Dom got inside, he started the engine, and the car lurched forward.

"And by the way, I got you a coffee," I said, putting the espresso in the cupholder between the seats.

"Thanks, I need one. I've only had two today."

I looked at him closely. His eyes were a bit unfocused and swollen with sleep. He had a five-o'clock shadow, which meant he hadn't shaved. Somehow that increased his sex appeal tenfold.

"Not a morning person?"

He shook his head. "Not at all."

"Right," I said, opening the Notes app on my phone. "I've made a list of things we should talk about. Do you want us to start right away?"

He burst out laughing. "Let me have a few sips first. Otherwise, only half my neurons will cooperate."

"We wouldn't want that," I murmured.

He took a sip and then grinned sideways at me. I was fiddling with my fingers. "You're nervous?"

"Yes."

"Then let's start. What do you have on that list?"

"First things first. When and where did we meet, and did we know right away or not?"

"I have a feeling you already have some answers."

I cleared my throat. "I did prep something, but I think it should be a collaborative effort so it's realistic for both of us. Made-up scenarios always work better when they're anchored in truth."

"You often deal with made-up scenarios?"

"No, but you know what I mean. Let's start with a very simple one. How long have we known each other?"

"I signed my divorce papers two months ago, so it can't be longer than that."

I felt a pang deep in my chest. "I'm sorry. I didn't know it was that recent."

"The breakup wasn't, but the divorce stretched on and on. I sometimes thought it would never end."

"All right, so let's say we met three weeks ago. That would mean we knew each other well enough to attend a charity event, but not too well." I was fumbling my words. Why was I so nervous? "Or maybe we should make it six weeks? And then we can say we started dating three weeks ago."

"Let's go with three overall. We met and immediately started dating. Do you actually anticipate anyone asking us this?"

"Malcolm might," I said quietly. "So, three weeks it is. And where?"

He nodded, narrowing his eyes. He'd been right about the coffee; he actually did seem more awake, and he'd only had two sips.

"The gym?" he suggested.

"I don't think anyone would believe that, and especially not Malcolm. I work out at the hotel in the morning before anyone else starts their day," I explained. "And the gym isn't open to anyone else except guests at the hotel. Before we opened the hotel, I worked out at home. He knows that."

"Okay, the gym's out."

Now that the subject had come up, it was obvious he had to spend a lot of time at the gym.

"You like shopping?" he asked.

"Hell yes."

"Then it's easy. We met in my shop."

"That's smart. See? That's why I figured it would be better as a collaborative effort. We've got this," I exclaimed. "You often go to your shop?"

"Daily. Mostly in the evening to check if there's anything out of the ordinary."

"That's very committed."

"I always ask the sales associates for any feedback they've got for me."

"But you have stores all over the world."

"I know. I get written feedback from the other places too. But I like to go to this one personally, since it's local."

"All right, then that's our story. I came in to try one of those gorgeous dresses."

He looked sideways at me. "Have you ever shopped in our store?"

"You're kidding, right? It's one of my favorites. We can say that I came looking for a dress that had a velvet corsage with organza sleeves and skirt. I love that combo. By the way, you have an excellent talent for picking out designers."

"Thanks. They're the most important part of the company. I can run it, but I can't create anything."

I liked that he owned up to that. A lot of CEOs thought people around them were disposable and replaceable.

"All right, so I came in the store. What next?" I held my breath. *Why is this so exciting?*

"I was talking to my sales associate, asking for feedback. You came in right at closing and said you desperately wanted a dress for the next event. And I was so smitten with you that I decided to keep the store open for a while longer."

"Smitten at first sight? I like it," I said. My heart was beating faster.

It's not real, Reese.

"But wait... remember, we said we'd try to keep it realistic? During our first meeting, I poured champagne all over you, and you thought I was hitting on you." I snorted at the memory.

He chuckled. "Now that I think of it, 'smitten at first sight' doesn't sound like me. How about this: you came in, and I thought you came on purpose to try and pick me up. I got annoyed. Then you clarified that you just wanted a dress."

I considered this. "It sounds realistic. But I also like the smitten-at-first-sight version. I've always thought there's something dreamy about the idea of love hitting you out of nowhere. Or at least lust. Feeling that spark before you even know the person."

He laughed without humor. "That's a recipe for disaster because you only judge a book by its cover."

"I know, but I still like the idea of it. Soulmates and all that."

He turned to look at me and seemed confused. "You believe in...soulmates?"

"Yes," I said.

"Your fiancé cheated on you with your best friend."

I winced.

"Fuck. Sorry, I shouldn't have said that."

"No, you shouldn't," I murmured. "I get what you're saying, though. I should probably forget about romance. Reality is cruel." I frowned. "But maybe that's why I believe good things do exist."

"Right. So we have our meeting set in stone. I honestly don't think anyone's going to ask details about how many times we've been on dates and stuff like that."

"They might. We should probably know things about each other, just so we're not blindsided."

"All right. You go first."

"I grew up in Chicago. I went to college here."

"Did you ever work in the chain of bookstores?" he asked.

"No. That was sold before I was old enough to work. I was in finance for a long time, and then my ex and I wanted to open a spa in the building where my grandmother still runs The Happy Place."

"What's that?"

"It's the first bookstore she and my granddad ever opened."

He nodded. "Right. I'm assuming the spa didn't work out?"

"No, not at all. After I broke off our engagement, the whole project fell apart. I did wind up working at The Happy Place for a while at that point. Then Travis, my cousin, bought the buildings adjacent to Gran's and opened The Maxwell Hotel. I'm the CFO."

I hesitated, unsure how much more of my past to unload, but knowing Malcolm, he'd bring it up.

"Malcolm didn't take it well at all that the business fell apart. He'd been working for an investment fund, and the fund would have invested in the spa. But after I backed out of the agreement, they fired Malcolm."

"Serves him right," he sneered.

"He tried to sue my family for it repeatedly." I swallowed hard. "And last year he decided to blackmail me. Said he'd give a little interview about why our relationship ended if I didn't get him his old job back."

Dom turned to face me again.

"Hey, eyes on the road."

"Continue. I'm shocked."

"Yep, so was I."

"Please tell me he didn't get away with it."

I shook my head. "He didn't. *I* gave the interview instead. That way, no publication would be interested in his side of the story. He'd get no money for it."

"Sounds like a nightmare."

"It was. The press didn't stop hounding me after that. They've lost interest lately, thank God. Anyway, that's enough about me. Actually, wait... I mean, you probably know about the family, right?"

"Just bits and hearsay."

"Well, there are eight of us."

"Eight?"

"I have a sister, Kimberly, and six cousins." A*nd also a baby half sister in London, but I didn't want to get into that right now...*

"And you all work together at Maxwell Hotels?"

"No, no. My cousin Tate runs Maxwell Wineries. Declan is a lawyer. Luke owns Skye Designs."

"Tyler Maxwell plays hockey," he said as if he'd just remembered that tidbit of information.

"Exactly. Sam is a doctor. Travis is the one with the hotel. Kimberly and I work with him."

"Got it."

"We're all very close. Malcolm knows that. By the way, in case it comes up, you've already met my family. That will kill him. I waited a long time before introducing him to them."

Dom said nothing for a few seconds, then asked, "Are you trying to make him jealous or just get him off your back?"

"I don't know. I just want to annoy him right now. It feels good."

"Fair enough."

"What about you?"

"I studied at Harvard and lived in Boston for a few years before moving here and starting Waldorf Fashion."

"You grew the company exponentially in just a few years. I think that's fabulous."

"All I did was use the knowledge I acquired from business school."

Humble! Yet another thing I wouldn't have pegged him for.

"I married one year ago," he continued. "Worst mistake of my life."

"Can I ask what happened?"

"I don't think that's going to come up."

"Fair enough." The wound was obviously still fresh. And even though I'd felt an instant kinship with him, I remembered those early days after Malcolm's betrayal. I walked around feeling physically in pain, so I understood Dominic's reluctance.

"Anyway, I think we've covered the basics," I said.

He looked at me briefly before focusing on the road again. I noted a glint in his eyes.

"Not yet. We should clarify what attracted us to each other."

"You think that might come up?"

"You never know. So…you go first."

"Other than your great looks?" I laughed. "Let's see… your voice. It's deep and rich and sounds sexy even when you're a total grump."

He stiffened, his eyes wide. Clearly he hadn't expected me to run my mouth like that. I wasn't even sorry.

"Your turn."

He didn't hesitate. "You're hot as hell. You have a great sense of humor and an enormous capacity for caring."

I stilled. "How do you even know that?"

"Because even though you have to face that moron, you're going to this stupid charity weekend because you want to raise money."

I licked my lips. "It's not the poor children's fault that my life is so complicated. Oh, I was also very attracted by your tattoo."

"What tattoo?"

I tapped my temple. "The one I'm imagining here."

He smirked. "You spend a lot of time thinking about my body, Reese?"

I swallowed hard, deciding to ignore the question. "In my mind, it's in a super-private spot. That way, no one will be able to check my story."

"What spot?" he asked.

I blushed. "Never mind."

"I'm sure you thought about it in great detail. You're very thorough."

I looked out the window, feeling like I was about to spontaneously combust. "On your left ass cheek."

He burst out laughing, the sound filling the car. I glanced at him and started laughing too.

He took one hand from the wheel. Before I realized what he was doing, he undid the button of one of his sleeves, rolling it up before switching hands and unbuttoning the other, then pushing it out of the way. I gasped when he revealed inked forearms.

"I wasn't expecting that."

He grinned. "It's one of the reasons I always wear long sleeves in meetings."

"You shouldn't hide that ink. It's beautiful."

"Glad you think so. Anyway, you were right with that guess."

"Which one?" I asked.

"A tattoo in a private place."

My jaw dropped, and I swallowed hard. *Holy shit. Where else does he have tattoos?* I had a sudden urge to map his body—and not just with my gaze. I wanted to touch and kiss and lick.

My imagination going wild, I licked my lips. "So where is it?"

"Why do you want to know?"

"You're right. I don't have to know that. Pretty sure it won't come up."

"It's in a very private spot, but I'll give you a hint. It's not the left ass cheek."

I had never blushed so much in my life. I looked away again, but the air between us was charged.

I immediately changed the topic. We made small talk for the rest of the drive and arrived an hour later.

"Welcome," the receptionist greeted us when we entered the venue.

"We're here for the charity event," Dom replied.

She took out two papers and pens. "Just put in your names and signatures. We don't need the rest."

Dom nodded. "Fair enough."

The receptionist smiled and then disappeared into the back.

"We probably should have booked one room," Dom said.

"What? Oh, I never thought about that." I bit my lip. "We can say we signed up for this before we got together."

"That sounds good." He wiggled his eyebrows, leaning in. "Or I can say I snore so much that we need separate rooms."

I thought I couldn't blush more than I had in the car. Turned out I was wrong.

Chapter Six

Dom

I couldn't remember the last time I was so relaxed. The whole weekend seemed over-the-top to me. I'd only glanced at the list of activities without reading it through. The first was archery. Damn, wasn't being here good enough? I had no idea why they wouldn't just accept a check for this. Why it was necessary for us to participate?

The best thing about this weekend was spending some time with Reese. I couldn't explain the connection I felt to her. It was a combination of kinship and attraction.

I grabbed my keycard and left my room, intending to knock on Reese's door. We'd been given adjacent rooms. The receptionist thought we were together, which suited me fine.

I chuckled at my own story. I wasn't usually a humorous guy. If you believed my ex-wife, I was the exact opposite. But being around Reese had an interesting effect on me.

I knocked at her door and got no answer. Maybe she was already outside. We hadn't talked in detail about how we would handle this. We had to make enough appearances to give the impression that we were a couple, but we were going to play the what and where by ear.

On my way out, I took stock of the hotel. It was one of the most recommended for a getaway near Chicago. It got on my nerves that the charity was wasting money housing us all here, but I appreciated the lodgings.

I went outside, following the signs for archery, remembering from the listed activities that it was going to start soon. I crossed the open field, looking around. In the distance, there were already a few people gathered. One of them was Reese, and my body instantly reacted to her.

Pull yourself together. You're here to take a few people off her back—and yours. That's it. Don't complicate matters... even though she is the most interesting woman you've ever met.

As I approached, I realized her ex was there. The guy wouldn't give her a break. *What is his deal?*

"Reese, you have to wait for me, babe," I said, deciding to lay it on thick. I didn't know this bozo from Adam, but I wanted to wipe that smirk off his face.

Reese glanced over her shoulder. Was it my imagination, or did she seem happy to see me? Not just relieved but *happy*?

"You could have just joined me in the shower instead of coming here early," I continued.

She laughed nervously, but I noticed a light blush on her neck. "I thought I'd check out the premises. I texted you. Didn't you see it?"

"No." That was the truth. "I've put my phone on Airplane Mode. I don't want anyone disturbing our weekend together."

I looked at Malcolm with fake interest, putting an arm around Reese's waist. "You're alone?"

I could practically hear my words stirring in his head. He first looked at my hand on her hip and then between the two of us as if trying to put two and two together.

"No. My wife is going to catch up with us later."

Reese stiffened under my touch at the word *wife*.

"How long has this been going on?" the douche asked.

I kissed the side of Reese's head. She was a genius for preparing a game plan before we arrived.

"Three weeks," I said.

Malcolm frowned and then looked incredulous. "That's not long at all."

"Feels like we've known each other forever." I took Reese's hand, kissing the back of it. I turned it around and planted a kiss there too. Then I held her palm against my cheek, tilting so I could make eye contact with her. The smile on her face wasn't fake. Not even one bit.

I looked back at Malcolm. He seemed stricken.

Tough luck, pal. You let a good woman go, and now you can suck it.

"And how exactly did you meet?" The guy was unbelievable.

"Reese, you tell the story. You always tell it better. I was too preoccupied thinking how to ask you to go out with me to pay attention to what was happening."

That wasn't even a stretch. If she had indeed walked into my store, and I hadn't been idiotic enough to think she might want to fish me, I would have definitely asked her out.

"I went into his store because I needed a dress for an event. It wasn't for this one... I don't think. I can't actually remember. Anyway, we started off on the wrong foot. He thought I was a gold digger. Then one thing led to another, and he asked me out." She was good at this—the pretend pauses, the frown.

A weight pressed on my chest. My ex was good at telling stories, too, and that didn't sit well with me. But Reese wasn't my ex. And even if she turned out to be like her, it wouldn't matter. We'd get through this weekend, and that would get us what we both wanted.

"I see," Malcolm said after Reese finished talking. "Dominic, are you good at archery?"

"No, but I'll cheer Reese on." I needed to get rid of this guy.

We were putting on a good show, but it was taking a toll on Reese. I knew exactly how to get him out of the way. "Isn't that right?"

I turned her slightly to me. She pushed her tongue out, licking her lower lip. I followed my instinct, tilting over her and capturing her mouth. She was soft against my body, and it just fueled me on. She gave me access, molding herself against my chest.

I didn't need any further invitation. I cupped the back of her head and deepened the kiss, exploring her. I'd fantasized about this exact moment, and it was even better than I'd dreamed up. She tasted delicious, like cinnamon and an underlying sweetness I liked too much. Her body was soft and on edge at the same time.

A light buzz filled me. It was electrifying. Could she feel it too?

I wanted to touch every part of her. I wanted to make her mine.

Reese

How was this kiss so amazing? It wasn't fair. I was putty in his hands, my body more alive than it had been in years. I felt the thrum of his heart in his chest. All I wanted was to sink my hands into his hair.

Oh, why not? We might be pretending, but this kiss is so good that it can't be anything other than real.

I rose onto my toes, needing to get rid of some of the vibrant energy filling me. I wrapped both hands in his hair, threading my fingers through it. He groaned, a deep, guttural sound, and lowered his hand from the middle of my back down to the small of it, pressing me against him.

"Now, I think everybody is here," a voice cut through the air.

Noooo! I didn't want this to stop.

Reluctantly, I pulled away. Dom and I made eye contact for a split second, and then I quickly looked away.

It was only a few seconds later that I remembered Malcolm was next to us. His face was a few shades paler than before. Hell yes! We'd managed to stun him. Good. He'd always said I was a stick-in-the-mud because I wasn't into big public displays of affection. Truthfully, I usually wasn't, but that kiss had given me *life*.

"Reese, I was hoping you'd be here already," Monika said.

She looked from me to Dom and sighed. My God, he hadn't been joking. He was truly a magnet for women, and they didn't even know he was a fantastic kisser. And a good person. Maybe he wasn't as grumpy as I initially thought? He certainly was playing his part as the devoted boyfriend well.

"Reese is a very good archer," she said, speaking to the group at large.

I didn't even dare look up at Dom. Could he tell how much I enjoyed our kiss? Had he?

I took in a deep breath and finally risked a glance at him. Holy shit! I all but melted. His gaze was fixed on me as if he wanted to read my every thought. I fidgeted in my spot, taking a deep breath and flashing a smile at the host.

"I can show everyone how to use the equipment," I said. "For those who need instructions, I mean."

Dom walked right behind me as we headed to retrieve our bows and arrows. There were several targets laid out, each at a different distance. I'd learned this useless skill at a camp years ago and aced it.

"I invoke boyfriend privilege," I heard Dom say from a distance. "I'll get closer to take a look and maybe get some pointers."

I looked over my shoulder. A lot of people had joined us. Dom seemed even sexier to me than before as he strutted down the field with all the confidence in the world, coming over next to me.

"Come on, Reese, show me what you've got," he said.

I double-checked that there was no one around, then leaned into him. "That was surprising. Very unexpected. And we didn't get to discuss..." My voice faded. What could I say? Kissing, touching, tearing each other's clothes off?

No, Reese, that's completely out of the question.

"Did it bother you?" he asked. His voice sounded different, though I couldn't tell why. When I glanced up at him, his expression was unreadable.

"No, not at all. I wasn't expecting it, but that was a nice touch."

His expression turned from unreadable to smug. "Since we're doing this, we should do it well."

I was tempted to ask exactly what he meant by that. More kissing? Could I jump him in public and pretend I just wanted a kiss? Could I insist we practice behind closed doors?

Get a grip on yourself. He isn't doing this because he's attracted to you. He's benefiting from this too. And he pities you.

There was no mistaking that. I'd seen it in his eyes when I told him my life story in the coatroom.

"Now, pay attention," I instructed. I picked up the bow and held my hand over the arrows. They were all identical, but I wanted to get a feel for them. Plucking one that took my fancy, I positioned it and pulled at the bow, putting the forefinger of my left hand on the flexible part of the arch and setting the arrow on top of my finger. "Your finger, the arrow, and the target must be in line."

"I heard you're the top scorer," he said.

I grinned without moving from my position. He stepped up behind me. If he touched me, I wasn't going to be able to focus.

"He's watching," Dom whispered. His hand went to my waist and slid around to my belly. He splayed it wide, and I felt every finger press against my muscles.

I swallowed hard, trying to focus.

This was the easiest target, and I was a pro. I never missed.

Positioning my fingers, I blinked a few times and then opened my eyes wide. I let the arrow go. It went spectacularly off course. There were cheers behind me. I blushed furiously. Dom started laughing.

"Well, that was shit," he exclaimed, and I started laughing too.

"My God, it really was. My focus is shot." I wasn't sure if it was from the kiss or the way Dom held me. Either way, I wanted more—of Dom, not archery.

Chapter Seven
Reese

After an hour, we moved on to darts. Turned out I couldn't focus on that either. But still who cared? I'd been thoroughly kissed by a sexy man. My ex was livid, and the fact that I lost seemed to motivate everyone to try harder to win. All in all, we were going to raise a lot of money for the kids, and that made my heart happy.

"All right, everyone, we'll wrap this up in thirty minutes. Then you have an hour time to change before dinner. It's nothing fancy, but I think you'll like it nonetheless," Monika said. Then she came up to us. "Hey, you two." Next to me, Dom stiffened. "Word on the street is, you've been an item for a few weeks."

I looked at Dom, who whistled. "That was fast."

"Hey, good news always spreads quickly. I'm happy for you." She didn't sound happy at all. In fact, she was glancing at me as if trying to figure out what he'd seen in me.

She raised a brow. "Funny! Neither of you mentioned anything when I made the seating arrangements. I actually thought the first time you met was at the party."

My jaw ticked, and Dom took my hand, intertwining our fingers and squeezing in assurance. The contact electrified me.

"No, that was a happy coincidence," I said, trying to sound nonchalant.

"Well, I'm glad to hear the good news." She turned abruptly and walked away without a backward glance.

When dinnertime rolled around, I changed into an evening dress. Nothing too flashy, just a classic little black dress paired with my favorite turquoise Manolos. When I stepped out of the room, I hesitated in front of Dom's door. We should have coordinated this—it would make a better impression to arrive together. Or was I overthinking this? Even real couples didn't spend their whole time glued to each other. Mind made up, I headed to the main restaurant and bar area on my own.

There were quite a few people gathered at the bar, including Dominic. He stood at the counter, his gaze moving down my body and then slowly back up. Was he doing that on purpose, or was it just his reaction to me? I walked straight toward him.

"What can I get you?" he asked once I reached him.

"A Negroni, please."

He narrowed his eyes. "I'll have the same," he told the bartender, and I watched him intently as he mixed the drinks.

He added a lime, which I hadn't seen before. I didn't know it was part of the recipe.

"It's my favorite cocktail," I told Dom.

"I haven't had it before."

"I think it's the perfect way to unwind after a long day. And maybe listen to jazz music."

He wrinkled his nose.

"You don't like jazz music?" I asked.

"Can't say I've listened to it too much."

"It's one of my guilty pleasures, along with fries and dessert, but I don't order those too often. Usually when I go out with my sister, she's the one who orders them, and I just steal from her plate."

Monika came up to us. "There you are. Reese, you look stunning as usual."

"Thank you. You as well, Monika."

"Would you like to say a few words to the crowd? You always rally everyone to open their wallets."

I rolled my shoulders back, standing straight. "Of course."

I didn't like to be the center of attention, but this was for a good cause. I was the type of person who liked to organize things behind the scenes. Kimberly and I loved to plan family events for our cousins, birthdays and the like, but I never wanted to be the focus of anything. It wasn't my thing.

"I don't think you need a microphone, right?" she asked.

"No, the room isn't that big."

Monika turned, speaking to the attendees. "All right, everybody. Before we begin, Reese Maxwell would like to say a few words."

The group clapped as I looked around the room, happy that Malcolm and Francesca weren't here yet.

"Welcome, everyone," I said. "Thank you all for giving your best today. I'm pleased to announce the De Monet charity is now $300,000 richer. But I'm sure we can get that number higher before the weekend ends." Monika had messaged me with the total sum as I was getting ready.

I spoke more about what the funds would be used for, and then a few people asked some questions about donations.

Then a guy asked, "What happened to winning at archery all the time, Reese?"

I couldn't remember his name, but he'd attended last year's event too. I wasn't sure if he was heckling me or just teasing, but I decided to play along.

I glanced at Dom, wiggling my eyebrows. "Oh, I've been distracted." It wasn't even a lie. "Now, I'll match the biggest bid for tonight. I encourage you all to be as generous as possible. As you know, it's for a great cause. We're making kids happy."

"Hear, hear," the same guy said.

Everyone clinked glasses before going back to their conversations.

"That was short and to the point," Dom said. "And I'll match the donations too."

I whipped my head in his direction. "That's a lot of money."

"I know. Your speech won me over." He leaned closer to me. "And your kissing skills." He smiled wholeheartedly, and it melted all my defenses. Did he mean it? Did he say it just to get a reaction from me to make this seem more real to onlookers? I couldn't tell. And I wasn't sure I cared. I was enjoying this evening much more than I'd thought possible.

I leaned even closer so I was practically speaking against his cheek. "You're one to talk. I almost swooned out there earlier."

"Great. That was the reaction I was going for."

For a split second, I thought he might kiss me again. He turned his head toward me, and I felt his exhale against my lips, but instead of sealing his mouth over mine, he straightened up.

"Come on, let's go," he said.

"Where?" I asked.

"You didn't hear Monika saying dinner is starting?"

"No, I guess I was distracted again."

He took my hand, and we headed to our seats.

Dinner wasn't as bad as I'd feared. Francesca and Malcolm didn't approach me. I made conversation with a few other participants I knew from previous years. No one was in the hotel industry, so there was no business talk. Although I always kept my ears open for any information that could help any Maxwell family member. You never knew when an opportunity might pop up.

The food was arranged buffet style, and they'd put the pans on chafing dishes, so everything stayed warm throughout the evening. There were drinks after dinner, too, but I was in no mood for that. I kept glancing behind me at the clock. I hadn't brought my phone with me and was ready to head back to my room.

Where is Dom? He'd wandered off a while back to talk to some of the others in attendance, but I had a feeling we should probably be on the same page about this. Finally, I spotted him by the window, deep in conversation with a woman I didn't know, and walked over that way. She seemed familiar, but I couldn't place her.

"Anyway, I was so sorry to hear about the two of you. I thought you made a nice couple," I heard her say when I was close enough.

Oh shit. Was she talking about his ex?

"Hey, I was looking for you," I said, and Dom glanced up at me. His eyes were cold, but I could see life coming back to them when he realized it was me.

I looked at the woman he was speaking with and asked, "Do you mind if I take him away?"

"Not at all." Her response was indifferent, which was fine with me.

I walked a few steps away, and Dom joined me a moment later.

"Who was that?" I asked, then realized I didn't have to know everything he was doing. This fake weekend was just that—fake.

But he cleared his throat and answered me anyway. "Someone who knew my ex and me."

"I should have come over earlier."

"It's fine. I can look out for myself."

"Yeah, but this weekend is all about having each other's backs. Anyway, I know everyone's going to head for drinks, but I'll just call it a night and go to my room. In case anyone asks," I clarified so he didn't wonder why I came over like a lunatic to tell him my plans.

"Sure. See you tomorrow morning, Reese."

What was that in my chest? Was it disappointment? Yes. Yes, it was. I think deep down, I'd hoped he'd offer to come back to my room to... to what? Spend the evening talking?

I was ridiculous.

"Okay, see you," I said, hurrying out of the room. I was beyond lucky that Malcolm and Francesca had stayed away from me this evening. I went through the narrow corridors, yawning. I just needed a good night's sleep, and tomorrow I could do this all over again.

Once I reached my room, I locked the door behind me, kicked off my shoes, and removed my dress. After a quick shower, I changed into my nightie and went to lie in bed, then opened my Kindle.

I typically only read one chapter before I fell asleep. Two chapters later, I accepted that it simply wasn't going to happen tonight. I'd always had problems sleeping, but I'd gotten better at keeping it under control lately. My insomnia came back whenever I was stressed, though. And having to deal with Malcolm yet again definitely counted as stress.

I got up and began pacing a bit. My doctor had instructed me to get out of bed when I couldn't sleep; if possible, I was supposed to get out of the room too.

Much easier when I was at my apartment. I didn't want to run through the hotel like a weirdo.

I glanced out the window. The moon was huge. It wasn't full yet, but it gave a lot of light. I could go for a walk. Most people were probably still at the bar, but I bet there was no one on the back porch where I'd noticed a seating area earlier today.

I changed into jeans and a sweater, putting on a jacket as well, and headed that way.

Dom

I only stayed at the bar for one drink before realizing this wasn't for me. I didn't want to go back to my room. I knew I wouldn't be able to sleep. For sure, I'd fantasize about Reese. It surprised me how obsessed I'd become with her in such a short amount of time.

I needed to clear my head, so I went outside. It was cooler in the evening than it had been during the day, but it was just what I needed. I had to get my thoughts straight and my libido under control.

I walked around the corner, remembering there was a sitting area there. Right now, everyone seemed to be busy schmoozing inside, so with any luck, it would be empty.

I turned around and stopped in my tracks. It wasn't empty. Reese was sitting there, holding her phone. No, wait. It was bigger than that. It had to be a tablet. The light was illuminating her face, which was scrunched up in concentration. She looked fucking adorable.

What was it about this woman that disarmed me so quickly?

Get your shit together, Dom. You need your guard up. Remember what happened the last time you let it down.

"You didn't go to sleep after all," I said.

Reese gasped, straightening up and placing a hand on her chest.

"Sorry. I didn't mean to scare you."

"I was so immersed in my book that I didn't even realize you were here." She pressed a button, and the light on her tablet went dark. But the moonlight was strong enough that I could still see her perfectly.

I went up the steps, and she tucked her feet under her, making space for me. The small couch was like a swing, and when I sat down, it moved a bit.

"What were you reading?" I asked.

"A thriller. It wasn't my best idea considering how dark it is around here. I was wondering how I'd manage to go back to my room."

I leaned closer. "Don't worry. I'll be your escort."

She pressed her lips together. I repeated my last sentence, waggling my eyebrows, and we both started laughing at the same time.

"Not my best line," I admitted.

"No, it was just what I needed," she said, holding her belly as laughter shook her. "I didn't think anyone else would be out here."

"It wasn't exactly my scene. And I knew I wouldn't be able to sleep."

"Oh, a fellow insomniac?"

I frowned. "No. I just didn't feel tired yet. You have trouble sleeping?"

She nodded, running her hand through her hair. I barely held back from reaching out and wrapping my fingers in it. I'd been close to her all day, and now it felt unnatural to push down my interest.

It's all for show, I reminded myself.

"I've had trouble sleeping since I was a little girl," she said. "It started after we lost Mom. I kept searching for her in the evening."

"I'm sorry for your loss."

She was quiet for a beat before adding, "Thanks. I don't know why I brought that up."

"I don't mind." I was interested in her story. Reese was a beautiful woman with a huge heart, and I'd never met anybody like her.

"Anyway, I tried a lot of therapists over the years. I even have a sleep schedule. I try to avoid screen time for a few hours before I go to bed. I couldn't resist reading, though. But they've all told me that if I can't sleep, I shouldn't stay in bed. If possible, I should get out of the room, walk a bit. I saw this place earlier today and wanted to enjoy it by myself."

"That makes two of us," I replied. "Want us to just sit quietly?"

She laughed softly. "We can try."

For a few minutes, neither of us spoke, and it was perfect. This moment was just what I needed, and I thought it was exactly what she wanted too.

"Thank you for today," she said eventually.

"What do you mean?"

"The show you put on was very helpful and very convincing."

"Oh, yeah." The fucking show. I was starting to wonder if any of it had been for show at all. I'd used every opportunity to be close to her, and I had zero regrets.

"You still have feelings for him?" I blurted. It was none of my business, but I needed to know.

"That's a loaded question. I want to slap the shit out of him every time I see him. Does that count as a feeling?"

I chuckled. "Hell yes."

"But it also hurts every time I see him with her, so maybe somewhere deep down, I do still have feelings for him. Even my therapist hasn't been able to work that one out."

Fuck, that stung. But why? I wasn't looking for a relationship. Hell, I just got out of a nightmare of a marriage, for God's sake.

"But I couldn't ever see myself getting back with him," she continued. "He's hurt me and my family so much over the years."

"What do you mean? He physically...?" I was going to punch that moron.

"No, no." She shook her head. "But as I told you, he tried to cause a lot of trouble with lawsuits, general harassment. But my cousin Declan, the lawyer, put the fear of God in him. At least that's what I thought.

Malcolm moved away from Chicago for a bit after that, and I don't like that he's back."

"Want me to find out why he's here?"

"Don't worry. I'm sure my cousins are already on it. Even though I didn't tell them a word about him."

"Then how would they know he's in Chicago again?" I asked.

"They know everything."

"And you don't mind?"

"No, not one bit. They've always been protective of me and my sister. Anyway, it's been a while since we had to deal with Malcolm. I hope he won't cause any trouble. Maybe he just wanted to come back to Chicago because it's where he's from." She seemed to be talking more to herself than to me.

"How long ago did you two split up?"

"Years ago."

I jolted my head back. *He's been hassling her ever since? What an asshole.*

She dipped her head. "I've been working on getting myself back on track ever since. But I still haven't healed completely."

"Go easy on yourself. Your fiancé cheated on you with your best friend. There's a lot of trauma to deal with from that."

"Yeah. And it's not like I haven't dated in the meantime."

That got my attention. So she did date.

Reese cleared her throat before continuing. "It was just all so shitty—what happened, I mean. It kind of took the fun out of dating."

I could work with that. Why did I suddenly want to prove to her how much fun I could be?

Chapter Eight
Dom

"How about you?" she asked.

"I haven't been on any dates since my divorce."

"Do you want to?"

I sat still for a few seconds, looking at her intently. "If the right person came along," I replied. "But the whole thing left a sour taste in my mouth."

"I can't blame you. Are you still in contact with her?"

"No. There was no point. I like to rip the Band-Aid off completely, so to speak."

"That's the best way—if you can do that, of course. Are you being hounded by reporters? Though, come to think of it, I only found one article where they proclaimed you're the hottest bachelor in town."

"No, not at all. That article came out of nowhere. People know who I am, but I'm not a person of interest to the general public. I've always been extremely private, though apparently not as much as you Maxwells are."

Reese laughed. "Oh yeah. We do our best. Unfortunately, we found that if you open the door, even a little bit, you can't get rid of the press. My interview didn't help. It simply renewed interest. But we learn from our mistakes."

"Speaking to a reporter about what happened sounds awful. I could never do that."

"Did you talk to *anyone*?" Her voice was tentative.

"You mean a professional?"

"Yeah." She frowned. "I know it's a personal topic, so I can stop if you want me to."

"No, go ahead."

"I think it helps to talk to someone you don't know, or at least who you don't know well. It can help you get perspective on things."

"I don't like the idea of talking to a stranger."

"If you want, you can practice by talking to me."

"Reese. I don't want to unload my drama on you. You've got enough going on." I'd swept it under the rug since it happened, focusing instead on Dad and Waldorf Fashion. Those two things were enough to occupy my life and fill my time. Whenever someone asked me what happened, I'd just placate them. I could do the same with Reese, but I didn't want to.

When she just stared at me, obviously waiting for me to share, I added, "I never imagined someone could marry me and not care one bit about me."

"I'm sure that's not true," she protested, then held up a hand. "Sorry, I shouldn't have said anything. Go on."

"She told me as much. Said she'd hoped it would pave the way for her in the fashion world." The idea of being used weighed on me. That she'd fooled me so easily. I'd always thought of myself as a good judge of character.

She gasped. "Oh my God. That is horrible. I'm so sorry." The look in Reese's eyes was real, and I appreciated that.

"Yeah. I'm still in disbelief myself every time I replay it in my head. I wonder how I didn't see the signs."

"How did you find out?" she asked.

"We were at an event. She was flirting with a guy. I confronted her about it, and she just threw it in my face. I thought she might be drunk, but when we got home, she laid it all out. She *had* been drinking too much, but that didn't mean she wasn't speaking the truth. The next morning, she tried to patch things up, but there was nothing to salvage. When she realized she'd lost me, she turned vicious. I filed for divorce the next week. It was a shit show."

"I don't understand how someone can do that."

I shook my head. "Me neither."

"Ummm... well, I thought I'd have words of wisdom for you, but I don't. Sorry I can't be of any help." She turned her head away, her eyes downcast.

"Reese." I reached for her hand, squeezing it. She startled for a few seconds but then relaxed. At the back of my mind, I realized I was probably crossing a line, but I didn't care. This felt right: touching her, talking to her. I didn't feel the need to hide anything from her. "You were right about one thing. Talking to you helped."

She brightened a bit at that. "Okay, that's good. I'm happy to give you a recommendation—"

"No, I'm not going to talk to a therapist. It's just not how I do things."

"I respect that. Just so you know, you can call me at any time to talk about it. Your conversations are safe with me."

"Why would you offer? I'm practically a stranger."

"I think we know enough about each other to stop pretending we're strangers," Reese said.

She was right, and I did want to call her after this weekend. But not to talk about my ex-wife.

A gust of wind blew past us, and she shivered. "Oh, it's getting chillier. I wish they'd put cozy blankets out here."

"Here." I took off my jacket, wrapping it around her shoulders. She already had a jacket on, but it seemed far too thin.

"Dom, you're going to be cold."

"No, I'm not. I have a shirt on and an undershirt."

She made a small sound at the back of her throat.

"What was that?" I asked.

"Nothing." Reese blushed. "Thank you for the jacket."

The wind intensified out of nowhere. It looked like a storm might roll in.

"I think we should head inside," she suggested.

"Yeah, come on. I'll hold you close and warm you up."

We descended the porch steps, taking a left turn toward our bedrooms, but then I felt Reese pull to the side before she yelled, "Ouch!"

"What happen—"

She lost her balance, falling to the right. I was so surprised that I didn't have time to brace myself, and I went down with her. Before I knew it, we were both on the ground. I managed to stop myself from landing on her, but only just barely.

Reese was shaking. A few seconds later, I realized it was with laughter. "Oh my God, I'm so sorry. I don't even know how I did that. I must have put my foot down the wrong way."

"Are you hurt?" I asked.

"No. Are you?"

"No. I'm glad I didn't crush you."

She looked beautiful like this, her smile unrestrained. There was a lamppost a few feet away from us, and I could see her much better than on the porch. The impulse to kiss her was so strong that I leaned in a bit closer. She swallowed hard, biting her lower lip. Her entire body seemed to pulsate under mine, her chest heaving up and down at a rapid rate.

I felt her breath on my cheek, but I knew she wasn't ready for this. I also didn't want to pursue something that I had no idea if I'd be able to continue.

"We should go back," I said, pushing myself up to my feet. I grabbed her hand, helping her up.

"We look like we just rolled around on the ground," she said.

She had little twigs and a few leaves in her hair. I picked out a handful, but I knew she must have more.

She brushed my hand away. "You can leave it. I need to wash my hair anyway."

We walked side by side with quick steps. The wind was turning to a damn tornado. And then we heard thunder.

"Oh no," Reese said. "The last thing we need is to get caught in the rain."

I could already feel a few drops on my face, but we managed to get inside before it picked up. Just as I opened the door, the sky let loose. We both burst inside, laughing so hard, we almost fell over again.

"Oh my God. What are the odds of that?" she asked once she'd managed to catch her breath. "Today was absolutely beautiful, and now there's a storm. I love storms, though."

We walked down the corridor that went to the bedrooms, then turned left... where we came face-to-face with Malcolm.

"Oh," Reese said as she took a step back. We were both still smiling.

"Where have you two been?" His voice was sharp. I didn't like it.

"We felt like doing our own thing tonight," I replied.

"That's right," Reese laughed. I was surprised because it was genuine. "But the rain and the wind had plans of their own, so if you were going outside, I suggest grabbing a jacket with a hood. An umbrella won't do much."

Malcolm swallowed hard.

"Now we're going to continue what we started outside," she added.

We moved past him, both laughing again. She was funny as hell. I didn't even need to look back to know Malcolm was stunned.

Serves him right. How the fuck did he let this woman go? Why didn't he appreciate her?

We took another turn, heading down the hall to our rooms. When we reached our respective doors, Reese pressed her lips together, clearly trying to stifle more laughter.

"Good night, Dom. Thanks for the laugh, for the company this evening, and for being here."

"You have more leaves. And a—" I cleared my throat, cutting myself off, but Reese seemed to know what I was about to say.

"Oh my God, tell me I don't have a critter. Just take care of it really, really quickly."

"Stand still."

"Don't tell me that, because I have this crazy urge to shake my hair all around."

"Don't do that." There was a worm in her hair. I reached for it, but the damn thing went deeper inside her gorgeous mane.

"Is it gone? It's not gone. I can see it on your face." Her eyes bulged so much that I thought they might pop out of her head.

"Please relax."

She breathed in and out and then in again. Before long, I had to use both my hands to try and untangle the worm. This was not how I imagined I would end up running my hands through Reese's hair.

"That's it," I said, finally getting the thing out, squeezing it between my fingers.

"Thanks. I hope I don't have any more."

"Want me to check?"

She shivered, shaking her head. "No, that's fine. I'll do it myself. Good night."

Before I could reply, she handed me my jacket and headed inside.

Yeah, she was definitely adorable, and I was screwed. I brushed a few twigs from my clothes as I stepped inside my room.

I chuckled, imagining what Malcolm must be thinking.

We were both disheveled and looked like we'd been rolling around on the ground. Like we'd been intimate.

And in many ways, we had been. Reese Maxwell now knew me better than half the people in my life.

Chapter Nine
Reese

The next morning was a shit show. When we woke up, the storm was still raging. The rain was so heavy that you could barely see a foot in front of you. There was no way we could go back outside to continue the activities, so I wasn't surprised at all when Monika sent everyone an email.

Subject: Activities canceled.

I'm sorry to spring this on you, but the weather forecast will not improve today. You are, of course, welcome to stay at the hotel for the rest of the day. My team and I will plan another event to replace this one.

Before I had a chance to reply, there was a knock at the door.

"Who is it?" I called.

"Dom."

I scrambled to my feet, taking the bathrobe from the hook on the bathroom door and throwing it over me—I was wearing a shirt but was commando downstairs. I secured the robe around my waist before opening the door. "Come in. Did you read the email?"

"Yes. What do you want to do? Want to stick around here?"

"Hell no. Can you imagine anything worse than being trapped with Malcolm in a hotel?"

He snorted. "Yes. Being trapped with him *and* everyone else."

I grinned. "All right. I don't need a lot of time to pack."

I didn't know why I was so nervous. Last night it felt like something had passed between us, an understanding of sorts. Something more real than anything I'd experienced in years.

I loved that he'd opened up to me. After we fell on the ground, it felt like he was about to kiss me. Of course, I was probably projecting because I would have loved that... even though I knew it would just complicate matters.

"My bag's already packed," he said.

"Wow. When?"

"I woke up too early and didn't have anything to do."

"I can join you in the reception area in—" I glanced at the clock on the nightstand. "—let's say fifteen minutes."

"That sounds good. I can hunt down some breakfast if you want."

I nodded. "Yes, please."

We were such a great team. But I was relieved that we didn't have to put on a show today. Yesterday had already been more complex than I'd anticipated... and more confusing. I didn't think I could do one more full day.

I'd put my bag on top of the armoire, which was super high, so I shoved the desk chair over to it. I'd practically fallen off the dang thing when I'd set the bag up there in the first place.

"I can do it." Dom obviously saw the precariousness of it all.

"No, that's fine," I said with bravado.

I stretched my leg up to the chair, and then I heard Dom suck in a breath. I glanced at him, noticing his eyes were fixed on my center.

My entire body was on fire, and my stomach turned into a tight ball. I'd forgotten I wasn't wearing any underwear. And Dom had a direct view to my lady bits.

I gasped, quickly putting my leg down and wrapping the robe around my thighs.

He cleared his throat, turning to one side. "I didn't see anything."

"Yes, you did. Don't lie to me."

"I was trying to be a gentleman."

I was *so* embarrassed.

"I'll just wait for you at reception," he said.

"Great idea," I muttered as he went past me. I put my palms on my cheeks, closing my eyes and drawing in deep breaths, trying to calm down. It was no use.

How am I going to spend the next two hours in a car with him? Why did I think it was smart to ride here with him?

A few seconds later, I got a grip on myself. I'd focus on packing and just take it from there. I accidentally flashed him. So what? These things happened.

Though I didn't know in what universe.

I threw my things in the bag quickly. Since I'd washed my hair last night to get all the debris out—no more creepy-crawlies, thank God—I didn't bother with a shower. I refreshed my face, brushed my teeth, and applied some makeup.

Now I just had to face Dom.

I'd been through my fair share of embarrassing situations in my life. I could handle this.

Five minutes later, I was having second thoughts when I spotted Dom standing near the doorway in the reception area. This was going to be awkward. Since everything was paid for, there was no need to line up at the desk; we simply dropped our keycards in the box designated for them.

Taking a deep breath, I rolled my suitcase toward him. He looked immensely sexy in his polo t-shirt. His ink was on full display, and I approved. He should do away with shirts altogether. When you had forearms and biceps like that, why hide them?

"We can go," I said, my voice squeaky.

"I'll take your luggage for you. This is our breakfast, by the way."

He held up a large paper bag.

"I'll carry that." I took the bag from him. They'd obviously packed hot beverages, too, because the paper was warm.

He didn't seem embarrassed at all about my little scene earlier. *Should I bring it up?* That had been my initial plan, but I simply couldn't.

"Okay, let's go." Holy shit, my voice was even worse than before.

"We have to run to the car. I have my jacket here for you. The hotel won't lend us any umbrellas, though they wouldn't help anyway. The wind is too strong."

I tilted my head at him, confused. "I already have a jacket on."

"You can put it over your head, or your hair will get wet."

"That's no problem." I waved my hand, then grinned. "Let's see who gets there first. Race me."

"With your track record, you'd just manage to hurt yourself." He smiled, then started laughing.

"Catch me if you can," I called over my shoulder as I ran out the door.

I had to make an actual effort to see where I was stepping and to locate the car.

We weren't the first ones to leave, as the parking lot was significantly emptier than yesterday. I only realized I'd passed his car when I heard the sound of the engine starting and turned my head.

Dom was quite a bit behind me, but he'd clicked on the remote, starting his vehicle.

"I'm so cold," I muttered to myself when I got inside the car. My clothes were sticking to me. It wasn't awful, but it was uncomfortable. I took off the jacket, putting it in the back. The bag with our breakfast was soaked.

Dom joined me a few seconds later. He wasn't in any better shape, water dripping from his hair.

"Want me to turn on the heat?" he asked while he got rid of his jacket.

"Yes, please."

I opened the breakfast bag. It contained toast, bacon and coffee. I didn't care much for the bacon, but I did need something to warm me up.

Grabbing one of the cups, I took a sip and then sighed. "Oh, this is good. I can feel life coming back to my limbs. By the way... I won."

He winked. "You're here in one piece, so I consider that *my* win."

There was a playful glint in his eyes. I had to address the elephant in the room.

"I'm sorry about... before... in the room."

His eyes glinted even more. "As I said, I didn't see much."

"Right, just the essential parts," I filled in for him.

He grinned. "Something like that. Don't worry about it, Reese. It was just unexpected, that's all."

"You don't say. I'd be shocked, too, if someone flashed me their pussy."

He swallowed hard and then covered his mouth with his hand, stifling a fit of laughter. Then he started to choke.

Well, today is off to a good start.

"I'm sorry, my humor is way off this morning. It usually is when I'm nervous."

He cleared his throat. "There's no need to be nervous, Reese."

I handed him his coffee and breakfast so he could get things situated before we started our drive home, then grabbed my phone.

"Let me just text my gran that I'll be back earlier. Maybe she has time to meet up."

"You're really close to your family. How about your dad? You mentioned your cousins but not him."

"He moved to London after they sold the bookstore chain. He remarried recently, and now we have a half sister. I wish I could be closer to them, but it's hard, even with all the technology. I try to make up for my absence with presents, and I'll shower her with gifts on Christmas. She'll love everything that's on my list."

"You already have a Christmas list?"

"Oh yeah. I have many people to shop for, so I always start early."

We spoke about Christmas shopping a bit longer, and then about everything under the sun. It was so easy talking to him.

"Where do you want me to drop you off? Home?" he asked when we entered the city.

"No. My grandmother texted me that she's at The Happy Place."

"Then I'll take you there."

The city was surprisingly empty, but then again, it wasn't even lunchtime. I was disappointed that the storm had interfered with our plans. It meant I hadn't seen the last of Malcolm.

When we arrived in front of The Happy Place, I moved to take my half-full cup of coffee from the cupholder and nearly knocked it over. I was jittery again.

He squeezed my hand. "You're still nervous."

"I am."

"I thought we cleared the air about what happened in the room."

I widened my eyes playfully. "I wasn't even thinking about that, but now I am. Thanks for reminding me."

He chuckled. "My bad. So what is it?"

"I'd hoped to put the charity events behind me this weekend, but Monika said she'll make new plans because of the weather today. Now I'll have to figure something out."

We both got out of the car. He took my bag out of the trunk, frowning.

"What do you want to figure out?" he asked.

"What to say when people ask why you're not there."

"I *will* be there, Reese."

"Oh." My body started buzzing. "Are you sure? I mean, that's more than you signed up for."

"No, I signed up for being your fake date for the duration of the event."

"Are you sure? They'll probably suggest a few days for the next event, but I'm sure not everyone will be able to make it. It won't be suspicious if we say you already have plans on all those days."

"Reese! I don't want you alone anywhere near that moron."

My insides warmed up at that. His voice dripped authority and maybe even a hint of protectiveness. "I don't know what to say."

"You don't have to say anything. We'll be in touch. And judging by how this weekend went, the next event will be explosive."

I didn't know what that meant, but I instinctively knew he was right.

Chapter Ten

Reese

I rolled my suitcase in front of The Happy Place. I'd expected to see Gran at the counter, but Kimberly was here too. There were a few patrons inside, browsing books.

I loved the bookstore. I'd spent hours upon hours here as a kid, when my aunt and uncle had too much going on at the house. That happened often, considering they had six boys. Kimberly and I would come here after school. My grandmother set up a corner for us where we did our homework. If she wasn't here, one of the employees took care of us. I grew up surrounded by the smell of books and, in winter, the cozy fire.

"What are you doing here?" I asked Kimberly.

"Gran said you were stopping by. I thought that was interesting. You usually come to The Happy Place when you need extra love."

I bit back a laugh. That was 100 percent true. I was surprised my cousins didn't "accidentally" show up too.

"Kimberly," Gran exclaimed. "Don't rush the poor girl. Let her tell us what's on her mind in her own time."

I stepped behind the counter between my grandmother and my sister.

"We heard you dropped by Liz's bakery yesterday."

My face exploded in a grin. "I knew it. She spilled the beans."

"Don't blame Liz. She tried to keep it a secret, but she didn't stand a chance. I fed her my apple pie," Gran explained. "I could see right through her. She did put in a good effort, though."

Kimberly crossed her arms over her chest. "Why you didn't you tell me you're seeing someone?"

"Who is he, and since when are you dating him?" Gran grilled me.

I sighed, leaning against the desk. "I'm not dating him."

"Then what's the deal?" Kimberly asked.

I took in a deep breath. "Don't panic, but Malcolm is also participating in the charity event."

My sister turned white.

My grandmother gasped. "When is that man going to leave you alone?"

"He hasn't done anything. He was just *there*." I wasn't going to tell them about the semi-threatening conversation. Knowing Malcolm, he was just trying to make himself feel better by putting me down. "On the evening of the first event, he was there with Francesca."

Kimberly lightly gripped the edge of the desk. "I'm so sorry. Reese, why didn't you say anything?"

"I didn't want to worry you. Anyway, long story short, Dom pretended to be my boyfriend that evening."

Kimberly's eyes bulged, and then she burst out laughing, "You're joking."

"No."

Gran said nothing.

"Wait, why would he even do that?" Kimberly asked.

"It doesn't matter. One thing led to another, and he offered to keep helping me with the ruse this weekend. That's why we drove together. I thought we could use the road trip to get to know each other a bit and set up a story."

"Oh my God, you're serious?" Gran asked, sounding shocked.

Kimberly pointed at me. "All right. I'm going to need to know exactly why he offered to be your fake boyfriend and all the details from the weekend."

"Want to go for coffee later?"

"Girl, we have coffee and cookies right here," Gran cut in.

"Yeah, and we're both extremely curious," Kimberly added, bouncing from one leg to the other.

"Let's go sit down," Gran said.

We sat on a small couch at the far end of the room. There were several spread throughout the shop, encouraging readers to sit and thoroughly inspect the books before buying them.

"What's his full name?" Kimberly asked, grabbing her phone.

"Dominic Waldorf."

"That name is familiar. Let me google him." She tapped the screen a few times. "Holy shit. Waldorf Fashion. They just named him the city's most eligible bachelor."

"Kimberly, since when do you read gossip magazines?" Gran asked.

"I don't. I got wind of him because he's a respected CEO. Usually they grant that distinction to athletes or actors or something." She turned to me, an eyebrow raised. "You sure about the fake part? Because the man is hot."

I laughed nervously. I wasn't sure how to explain everything. "Look, I simply wanted..." I sighed. "Honestly, it was kind of childish, but I wanted to flip off Malcolm in a way."

"Ha, the revenge date. I approve," Kimberly said with a grin.

"Revenge date? What do you mean?" Gran asked.

"Malcolm was there with *her*, and I couldn't bear facing them. He thought I was single and was trying to make a joke out of it. Or possibly pity me. I'm not even sure what it was. I think Dom just... well, he probably pitied me, too, but it all turned out for the best."

"Right," Gran drew out, obviously unsure of my explanation.

"That explains the charity evening. But why would you pretend for a whole weekend?" Kimberly asked. My sister was nothing if not thorough.

"Look, it's hard to explain without sounding ridiculous. I'm not even sure why Dom went along with it. But I'm grateful he did. The weekend would have been excruciatingly painful otherwise."

Kimberly moved next to me. "You should've just backed out of the weekend or sent me instead."

Gran nodded. "Reese, life is far too short to go through unpleasant moments. Especially when it comes to that asshole."

I was stunned. Kimberly just blinked. I couldn't remember a time when Gran had openly sworn.

"Why are you girls looking at me like that?" she huffed. "Of course, I know how to swear. I just try not to do it around Paisley."

"Or around us," Kimberly said.

That settled, they both looked at me intently, obviously waiting for an explanation. But I didn't have a good one.

"It felt like if I chickened out, then he would win, you know?" I murmured.

"Why is Malcolm back?" Kimberly asked, and the hair stood up at the back of my neck.

"I'm not sure," I admitted. "Maybe he just wants to live in Chicago. He's from here, after all."

"Let's talk to Declan. Clearly he didn't scare him enough last time."

"No. I mean it, Kimberly. That's one of the reasons I didn't tell you."

Gran shook her head. "Reese, you can talk to us. You don't have to keep things to yourself. We won't tell anyone if you don't want us to."

"Thank you. I would appreciate it if you didn't. You should have seen Malcolm's face when Dom was next to me...tall and so much more attractive than him."

Kimberly and Gran glanced at each other, and then Gran narrowed her eyes, pointing at me. "I will say just one thing on this topic. This man makes you light up, and we haven't seen that in a while. Not even when you were with that asshole."

"Gran—" I began.

"Just let me finish. If there's any chance, any at all, that you have real feelings for him, see if it leads to something."

I shook my head vehemently. "No. That's out of the question."

Gran sighed and then looked at Kimberly, who shook her head. "No, don't look at me. I'm supporting my sister no matter what she says." Then she turned to me. "But for the record, I agree with Gran."

"Of course you do. All right, well, I came by to say hi to both of you. But since I'm here, I'll go upstairs and take care of a few things."

"But it's Sunday!" Kimberly exclaimed.

"I know, but I had some to-dos on Friday that I didn't get to. And I want to start the week with a clean slate."

"If you change your mind, we'll be down here for a few more hours."

"Okay."

They both waved me off, and I headed upstairs.

I loved coming into the office when it was empty. I wasn't an early bird, but I often stayed after everyone left, especially if I had numbers to crunch.

Gran and Kimberly's words kept spinning in my mind. Why were they giving me ideas?

I started by looking over the projections for this quarter and moved to checking the bookings for the rest of the year when my phone pinged.

Dom: I tried to make myself a Negroni, but I forgot the steps. Do you have anything going on?

All of a sudden, I found myself grinning from ear to ear, and my heart sped up. What did it say about me that my pulse was erratic just because he wanted to talk to me?

I replied right away.

Reese: No.

He called me in a fraction of a second. In my haste to answer the phone, I nearly dropped it on the floor.

Oh, if Kimberly and Gran could see me now.

"Hey," I said. My voice was a bit shaky.

"Am I interrupting anything?"

"Yes, but it's a welcome interruption because I've been glued to my chair for hours."

"Doing what?"

"I'm checking the financial projections for this quarter."

"On a Sunday?" he asked incredulously.

"Oh, stop being so judgmental."

"I'm just surprised. You didn't seem the type who works on weekends."

"I'm not, but I spent Friday thinking about the questions we should discuss prior to the event, and I didn't get my work done."

"I see. So... the steps for the cocktail?"

I seriously doubted that he didn't remember them or couldn't at least google them. For some reason, that made me intensely nervous, and I stumbled over my words as I gave him the recipe.

"Mmm. This tastes good," he said a few minutes later. Hearing his groans sent a tendril of heat through my body, and my nipples perked up. "But it's missing something."

"They put some lime in it as well," I said, just remembering that moment. "It's not actually part of the recipe that I know of, but it fit."

"I don't have any limes. And you have a good taste for cocktails."

"I like to play around at the hotel's bar from time to time. Actually, you know what? I'm almost done with work. I can do the rest tomorrow. I'm going upstairs to have a drink too."

"Or you can join me."

I swallowed hard. "Oh?" I asked noncommittally, playing with a strand of my hair.

"Yesterday, we spent a lot of time together, but at the same time, it felt like we didn't spend enough," he said, completely taking my breath away.

"Dom," I whispered.

"Last night on the porch was real. I want more of that."

"So do I."

"Tell me when to pick you up, and we can go for a drink."

I swallowed. "God, I love the sound of that... but I'm terrified."

"Of what?"

"Getting hurt."

"Reese, I wouldn't hurt you."

"No, I know, or maybe not intentionally, or... God, I'm babbling."

He chuckled. "That's okay. Let's take it easy and share a cocktail over the phone, like you suggested."

I laughed nervously. "Right! Yes. Let's do that."

But now that he'd brought up the idea of spending time together, this felt different, more intimate. I didn't want to hang up.

I probably looked a bit stupid walking up the stairs to the bar, holding the phone to my ear. We weren't even talking, but I could feel him on the other line. I heard him take a few sips and two deep breaths as I went to order—we couldn't carry on a conversation if I slipped behind the bar to prepare my own drink.

"Wait a second, this place is packed. I'll just ask Tom to make me one."

I held the phone to my chest and flagged the bartender. "Tom, make me a Negroni, please. You know how I like it."

He nodded, and I went to the table we usually kept for ourselves. It had a permanent tag on it that said Reserved. I liked to come here from time to time. The building wasn't very tall, so I only had a view of the rooftops of the nearby homes and other smaller buildings. A few trees peeked up from between the buildings—a smattering of green among reddish and brown tiles.

One of our servers brought me the drink only a few seconds after I sat down.

"I like the service in the hotel. It's so fast," I said into the phone.

"Got your drink?" Dom asked.

"Yes."

"Then cheers, Reese."

"What are we toasting to?"

"A completely unexpected friendship. No, that's not the right word. Acquaintanceship?"

"I never even knew that was a word," I replied, laughing as I took a sip.

"I'm not sure it is."

"So what did you do today?" I asked him.

He hesitated for a bit, then said, "I visited my dad."

"Oh, that's sweet. So he also lives in Chicago?"

"Yeah." His tone was a bit quiet.

"You don't want to talk about it?"

He seemed to hesitate again. "No, I do. He's housebound and doesn't get much social interaction. Since Mom passed away, the only person who's around him full-time is his nurse. We play chess once a week."

That was even sexier to me than those muscled and tattooed arms.

"Who plays better?" I asked.

"Lately, I do. But I let him win from time to time. Not too often because then he catches on."

Oh, be still my beating heart. "That's incredibly thoughtful," I said.

"So you've been working since I dropped you off?"

"No. I was downstairs at The Happy Place with my sister and my grandmother. We were... chatting."

"Your voice changed. Are you hiding something?"

I blushed from head to toe. "N-No." And now I was stammering. Good God, I was a wreck when I talked to this man. "I told them about you and our game of pretend. They were shocked and then proceeded to tell me that I should go ahead and act on my instincts if there was something between us."

Why in the name of all that is holy did I tell him that?

"Good to know your grandmother and sister are on my side."

I snorted. "Dom, there are no sides here."

"What did you tell them?"

"That I didn't want to confuse things."

"Reese." His voice was dangerously low.

I sipped from my drink, needing the liquid courage. It was loosening my tongue. I wondered if Tom made it stronger than usual. Then I remembered that I didn't eat much today. Yep, that would do it.

I couldn't believe it. I was tipsy while talking to a guy I was attracted to but wanted to stay away from. That was going to work out in my favor for sure.

"I haven't eaten much today, so I'm blabbing even more than usual. Just ignore me if I say something stupid."

"Not at all. I like knowing you intimately."

Tendrils of heat curled through me before pooling between my thighs. I swallowed hard.

"Did you see the email from Monika?" Dom asked, and my stomach bottomed out.

"Oh no. I haven't checked my emails. When did she send it?"

"A few hours ago. She's got it all mapped out."

I grinned. "Let's hear it."

I braced myself as Dom went on. "She's proposing another evening event instead of a day of activities. She could only find one space on short notice, so she can't offer more than one option. It's Friday in two weeks."

"Let me check my calendar." I pulled it up on my phone and scrolled to that date. "Friday is good."

"For me too. Though she pointed out that it's understandable if someone can't make it."

"So we'd have an easy way out," I said.

"Do you want that?" His voice was now a whisper, a little apprehensive.

"No, I don't," I replied just as tentatively.

God, what am I doing? What are we both doing?

I wasn't ready, and he clearly wasn't either.

So why couldn't we stay away from each other?

Chapter Eleven
Dom

I'd never been ashamed to look at my own actions with a critical eye and admit when I was right or wrong. I never lied to myself.

I was attracted to Reese Maxwell; I wasn't going to deny it. After the divorce, I'd set rules for myself. I wouldn't date any time soon, especially not someone who was a public person in any way, shape, or form. And yet I couldn't stop thinking about Reese. But I wanted to respect her boundaries, so over the next two weeks, I kept the contact to a minimum.

But I knew tonight was going to be challenging.

The event was taking place at a gallery in Bucktown. Monika had included a lot of details in the email. I'd skimmed over it; I didn't care because I wasn't going to engage in any silly activity tonight. I'd write a big fat check and be done with it. I was here for Reese and Reese alone.

And just like that, I was breaking yet another rule. I was chasing a woman who wasn't ready. What the hell had gotten into me? I wasn't ready either... was I?

Over these past weeks, I'd also done something I'd never done before: I had Malcolm investigated. I knew what he'd been up to these past few years. He was working at an obscure investments firm. They likely paid a good salary, but not enough for him to be attending charity events.

"Ms. Maxwell, you're here," a voice said behind me.

I turned around and nearly choked on my breath. *Is this woman trying to kill me?*

She looked absolutely stunning. Her dress was light pink with some sort of spaghetti straps that were bunched together on one shoulder. I walked straight to her. I heard someone call my name, but I couldn't have cared less.

"Good evening," I said when I reached her.

"Hey." She sounded shy.

I gave her my arm. "Ready for another fake date?"

"Oh yeah."

"You look fantastic, by the way." I towered over her and had a glorious view of her breasts. I took in a deep breath, instantly looking elsewhere. Fucking hell, I was going to pin her against the nearest wall and kiss her if I didn't get myself under control.

"I know, right? I wanted to pick something tonight that would make everyone look. My revenge dress, so to speak."

I felt as if someone had thrown ice cubes at me. She'd dressed like this for *him,* not for me.

"Now, did you get your auction stickers?" she asked.

"I did. What are we supposed to do with them?"

She giggled. "You didn't read the instructions, huh?"

"No. Figured I'll just write a check."

"Well, it's easy this time. We're betting against each other by placing stickers on the paintings we want."

"I'm not an art collector," I said flatly.

"You can put it in your office or donate it." That was a good idea. "Anyway, the highest bidder wins."

"That is straightforward. Thank fuck for small mercies."

"I can't believe they closed off the gallery for us. Monika has skills.," she said as she kept looking around.

I knew exactly what she was searching for. "I haven't seen them anywhere."

She relaxed. "Maybe they're not here."

"I'm willing to bet money on it. We would have run into them by now. He seems to make a habit of getting in your face."

"That's true."

Suddenly her body language changed. She wasn't hanging on to me for dear life anymore; she was simply lacing her arm through mine. Her shoulders rolled back. Her smile was easy. Even her eyes seemed lighter. I wanted to remove that asshole from her life completely since it clearly weighed so much on her. It should be illegal to make anyone suffer. Reese didn't deserve this.

We walked around the perimeter once while Reese placed stickers on half a dozen paintings. I put some on three paintings that weren't impossible to look at. I really wasn't a fan of art.

"I can't believe people call this art."

She snickered. "Oh, you're such a grump. What can I do to lift your mood?"

"We could grab a drink."

"They arranged a bar in one of the rooms."

"We're good at bars," I told her with a wink. "Lead the way."

She laughed. "Yeah. It's like they inspire us, huh? Thank God Malcolm isn't here tonight. I'm so much more relaxed without him."

"I was going to mention that. You completely transformed when I mentioned he isn't here."

We walked through two more art-filled rooms before entering one that was dimly lit. There were paintings hanging on the brick walls, too, but the focus wasn't on them. Everyone was hanging around at low tables dispersed throughout the room. The bar itself was a pop-up.

People were staring at us, and I knew why. Reese looked stunning and deserved to be ogled.

Once we reached the counter, I looked at Reese. "Our usual?"

Something flickered in her eyes. She cast a glance downward and then at the bartender. "Yes, our usual is Negroni. Two, please. With lime if you have it."

"Right away," he said.

"You're getting me hooked on it," I whispered in her ear.

"It is addictive, huh?"

"And so are you."

"I am?" She smiled.

"Yes."

And then I kissed her.

There was absolutely no need for me to do it. Her stupid ex wasn't here. But I wanted her, and I needed this kiss. I needed to know that she felt the connection between us just as strongly as I did.

I was greedy, and she responded in kind. Something unfurled in my chest when she wrapped a hand around my neck and then ran her fingers through my hair. I kissed her so hard that she stumbled backward, but I held her by the waist. Her breath quickened, and she released the most delicious sigh. This kiss was real; I knew it in my bones. Nothing else was, but I was going to change that.

I only came to my senses when she moaned against my mouth. It wasn't loud, but it reverberated throughout our bodies. She pulled back, glancing around.

"I like how your lips look right now," I said.

She covered her mouth. "Do you think anyone heard me?"

"No, it was a soft sound. Relax," I murmured as I put my hand at the small of her back.

The bartender looked like he was about to burst out laughing as he shoved our cocktails in front of us. We clinked glasses, but Reese kept looking down as she sipped her cocktail.

"Reese, are you avoiding me?"

"No, I'm just..." She put her glass down, finally making eye contact. Her mouth wasn't red anymore, but her cheeks were. "I'm not sure what that was. I mean, Malcolm isn't around."

"No, I didn't do it for anyone's benefit. I told you, you're too damn irresistible and addictive."

She narrowed her eyes. "I believe you only said 'addictive' before."

"That statement needed amending," I said with a wink. "I just wanted to kiss you."

"Oh." She put her hand to her stomach and took another sip, then swallowed hard. "I'm flattered, but I..." She looked around. "Should we go somewhere else?"

"Find an empty coatroom?"

She laughed. "Something like that."

We took our glasses and looked around. There was no need for a coatroom, though. We went to one of the tables in the corner.

"Tell me what's on your mind, Reese. I can feel you thinking," I said. I barely refrained from reaching out and pulling her closer to me, holding her by her lower back against my body. I couldn't explain why I always wanted to be touching her.

She pressed her lips together, then parted them. "I really liked the kiss."

Fuck me. "That wasn't what I thought you were going to say."

She shrugged one shoulder. "Neither did I, but it's the truth, and that's the only thing I'm sure of right now, Dom. But..."

I liked hearing my name in her mouth. I wanted to hear it while her legs were wrapped around me when I was buried inside her.

"What? You sound like you want to add something."

"Oh, so many things, but I'm afraid to voice them."

"I can help with that."

She laughed. I liked seeing her relaxed around me. "Dom, I'm not even sure I know how to flirt."

"No problem. I'll take the reins."

"I think you already did that back at the bar."

I wiggled my eyebrows. "I have zero regrets."

"Neither do I." Taking a sip, she added, "Sometimes I overthink situations, but I'm not sure if that's the case here. I'm just not sure if this is a good idea."

"Want another kiss, just to see if that clarifies things for you?"

Her face opened up in the biggest grin I'd ever seen on her. "Don't tempt me. I might take you up on it."

"Happy to sacrifice myself for a good cause."

She snorted. "So generous of you."

"Always."

We both downed our drinks, and then Reese bit her lip. "What do you say we get out of here?"

"Fuck yes. Thought you'd never ask," I said.

Being impulsive wasn't in my nature, and I figured it wasn't in Reese's either, but we brought that side out in each other. I grabbed her hand, interlacing our fingers as we strode toward the exit. The lines were blurring. I wasn't even sure what was for show and what was real, but it didn't matter. She didn't pull her hand back.

We made a big deal of saying goodbye to Monika. She wasn't surprised to see us go, but I caught her fixating on our intertwined hands a few times while we spoke.

Once we were outside, I said, "I'm here with my car. You?"

"I came by Uber."

"Then I'll drive."

"Where are we going?" she asked.

I turned around, tipping her chin up. "Wherever you want, Reese."

"Okay."

I guided her to my car and opened the door for her, but she avoided my gaze when she climbed in. This wasn't a good omen. I hurried to get into the driver's seat. She swallowed hard, and then I heard her stomach rumble.

"I have a proposition," I said.

"I'm all ears."

"Food?"

"God, yes. I'm starving. I didn't even look at the canapés. Were they any good?"

"I don't know. I didn't see them. What are you hungry for?"

"There's a Taco Bell drive-through."

I turned to her. "Reese, I can take you out somewhere."

"But Taco Bell is much faster. And my guilty pleasure."

"Got it. Tonight is the night for guilty pleasures, huh?"

"Or just pleasure," I heard her mumble, and my cock twitched. I needed to get myself under control.

I put Taco Bell into the GPS and took the route to the nearest drive-through. I could practically feel Reese tense up on the way.

Once I entered the drive-through line, I really looked at her. She was fiddling with her thumbs and starting to shift her weight from one buttock to the other. I held my palm open, and she put her hand in mine.

"Reese, talk to me."

"I'm nervous. This seemed like a good idea back at the gallery."

"Do you want me to drive you home after picking up food?"

She glanced at me abruptly. "You wouldn't mind?"

"Of course I wouldn't mind. What kind of moron do you think I am?"

"I don't know. I didn't want you to expect something and be disappointed."

I shook my head. "I'm not fucking disappointed. You're a human being, Reese, with emotions. And I understand that. Now, what do you want to order?" I asked her once we reached the speaker box.

She immediately leaned over to my side of the car and spoke loudly. "One crunchy taco and the cheesy gordita." She said it quickly, in one breath.

"You didn't even look at the menu."

She smiled. "Told you it's a guilty pleasure."

"Two orders of that, please," I said into the speaker.

"You can pick it up at the next window," the sales associate replied.

"Oh, and two Pepsis." Glancing at Reese, I added, "Unless you want something else."

"No, that's good."

I finished ordering, and by the time we got to the next window, everything was ready. I glanced at Reese, pointing at the parking lot. "Want to eat it on the way or...?"

"No, let's stay here in the parking lot. Otherwise, you won't be able to eat at all, and it tastes best when it's hot."

"Good thinking. Let's see what the fuss is about. I've never been—" I stopped, thinking I didn't want to sound like a food snob.

She gasped. "You've never had Taco Bell?"

"No."

She narrowed her eyes. "How about Chipotle?"

"Also no."

"Kentucky Fried Chicken?"

"No."

"Are you an alien?"

"My parents never took me when I was a kid, and I guess I never got into the habit."

"Huh," Reese exclaimed. "Dad didn't take us either, but guess who created that habit by stopping by after school? That's right. This girl right here."

I took a bite out of the gordita. "This is good." I frowned. "Really good, actually."

She grinned. "Yeah, welcome to the world of cheap but super-delicious fast food. It'll probably give me a coronary by the time I'm fifty, but nothing makes me feel better than this."

I stole a glance at her. She was busy with her food, but something about the way she'd phrased the sentence bothered me.

"You needed a pick-me-up after tonight?" I asked her. "Reese... I know I crossed a line."

"It's not about you," she said so quickly, the words almost ran together, but I picked up the gist of it.

"Talk to me," I urged, turning to face her even though it was dark in our corner of the parking lot. The nearest lamppost was at least five cars away.

"I liked tonight. I like you. I liked the kiss." I was sensing a *but* coming, so I didn't interrupt her. "But I'm afraid of liking it. I'm afraid of liking you."

I had no comeback to that, so we both ate in silence for a bit before Reese asked, "Are you mad at me?"

"No. Why do you keep expecting me to be mad at you? I'm just processing what you said. Please tell me that moron was never abusive to you."

"Not physically, but looking back, I think he was emotionally. I just didn't see it at the time. I was so desperate to please him, to make the relationship work, but I didn't realize he wasn't meant for me. He wasn't the one."

"So you don't regret that your wedding blew up?"

"No. I would have been unhappy with him. I have no regrets about not being married to him."

Once I finished my food, I cleaned my hands off on a napkin, tossed our garbage in one of the cans, and drove out of the parking lot.

"Want me to drop you off at home?" I asked.

"Yes. Thank you."

"No problem. I told you that we'll do whatever you want."

She laughed, but it sounded nervous. "I bet this isn't what you thought I'd say."

"Regardless, Reese, this evening was great."

"It was?"

"Yeah. I kissed a gorgeous woman. It was the best kiss of my life. And then I had Taco Bell."

She jerked her head toward me. "Wait, what? Rewind. What was that about the best kiss of your life?"

I turned onto the main street. "It's true. I don't see why I should keep it a secret."

"Hmm."

"What?" I asked.

"Nothing. Then I can admit that it was the best ever for me too."

"I'm glad we're on the same page about that."

We arrived at her building far too quickly. I pulled the car right in front of the entrance. "Is there anywhere I can park so I can walk you up?"

"No." Her voice sounded like a squeak.

"Reese?"

She cleared her throat. "I mean, it's best if you don't."

"Why not?"

"Because unless I'm way off, you might kiss me again."

"There's a high probability," I admitted.

"And then I'll fall prey to your charms and invite you inside."

"I see."

"Do you?"

"Yeah. I can barely keep myself from kissing you senseless and tearing off your clothes right here, let alone if we were at your place."

She gasped.

"Too direct?" I suggested.

"Um... I... wow, this... I wasn't expecting... never mind. I'm too lost for words, but when I recover, I'll text you."

I laughed.

"Oh, stop it. I know I'm being weird, I'm just... God, this night didn't go at all the way I thought it would."

"Same goes for me," I said, managing to finally stifle my laughter. It was so easy to be happy when I was around Reese.

"Good night, Dom."

"Good night. Text me when you're upstairs."

"You think I might get lost on the way?"

"Just text me, Reese."

"Okay." Then she leaned over closer to me. For a brief second, I thought she wanted me to kiss her, but then she put her lips on my cheek before quickly pulling back. "Thank you for tonight."

I watched her walk inside and waited for a few minutes until I finally got a text.

Reese: I'm up in my apartment still pinching myself, wondering if this evening was real or not. I'm tempted to ask you to come up and prove it was.

I groaned.

Dom: I'm of two minds to come bang on your door anyway.

Reese: You're still here?

Dom: Told you I was waiting for your message. I'm leaving now.

Then I turned on the engine and drove off right away. I needed to put some distance between us, or I was going to do something reckless.

Chapter Twelve
Reese

One of the things I loved most about having such a huge family was that there were plenty of kids to buy presents for. It was truly one of my biggest joys in life. I had a system too: I looked at various blogs and influencers for age-appropriate toys, and then I made lists upon lists on Amazon so I wouldn't forget them. I tried to buy from local sellers, but sometimes I had to order direct from Amazon itself. I had all the packages delivered to my office.

There was always someone either on the floor or downstairs in the reception area, and they didn't mind bringing my packages to me. In the beginning, I'd shipped them to my house, but then the delivery guy would start asking other people in the building to take the packages. He wouldn't leave them with the doorman. I didn't want to annoy my neighbors with all the stuff I'd order. But now my office looked like Santa's workshop, and I had at least eleven or so more gifts on the way. Someone with a sense humor—probably my favorite assistant, Larissa—had put the boxes in the shape of a Christmas tree.

I glanced out of my office. "Larissa, can you come in here quickly?"

When she appeared in my doorway, she gave me a shit-eating grin. Yeah, I was right on the money.

"Is this your work of art?" I asked.

"Of course. Who else would do it?"

"No one." She and I were two peas in a pod. "Did I really order that much?"

"Yes, boss, you did. Might I remind you that Travis said they really don't need so many gifts? I believe your cousin Tate said the same thing."

"Shush, you. Don't ruin my mojo."

I might have a little shopping addiction, but my cousins and I had worked out a system—I wouldn't give the kids all the presents at once. However, that didn't mean I couldn't order them at the same time. Besides, I'd also purchased gifts for the adults. I paid attention whenever someone said they wanted something. We could all buy everything we needed, of course, but it was nice to receive a gift you really wanted.

"Are you going to open the boxes and wrap up the gifts?" Larissa asked.

"No, not right now," I said. "I have a lot of things to do. Thanks for brightening up my day, Larissa."

She smiled warmly. "You're welcome, boss. I knew you'd appreciate it."

"I do."

I was grinning from ear to ear as I sat behind my desk. I had plenty of time to wrap everything nicely before Christmas.

Based on my to-do list, I had my work cut out for me today. I always liked to prepare a list the day before so I was ready to hit the ground running in the morning. I glanced through my inbox, just to make sure there wasn't anything pressing that should take precedence. Then I opened my email. I also checked my phone and saw a new message from an unknown number. If my shopping habits were any indication, it was probably a reminder from one of my million favorite stores advising me that they were having a sale.

I sank farther into my chair as I read the text. It wasn't about a sale. The message was from Malcolm.

I spoke to a bunch of lawyers. They insist I have a case against you and your family. You stopped the spa from moving forward because you had your own plans for a hotel. You premeditated this.

I gasped, pressing my lips together. I inhaled deeply, hoping to calm myself. My door was open, and anyone could pass by and see that I was upset.

I got up and closed the door, then came back to my seat and read the rest of the message.

You'll be hearing from my team. But don't think you'll get away with this. Travis either. I don't care how much Declan tries to intimidate me. I'm coming for what's mine.

For what's his? How dare he?

I pressed my eyelids together, wiping away the tears.

No! I've shed enough tears for Malcolm. Not this time. He isn't worth it.

He'd pulled shit like this before, and I always came out the other side. I drew in a deep breath, pushing my phone away from me.

My to-do list was staring at me, but I couldn't focus for shit right now. I put my head in my palms, drawing in another few breaths.

I knew it. I never should have agreed to work with Travis at the hotel. It took my cousin months to convince me to join before I gave in. He thought I was playing hard to get or that I just needed more time off. Neither was true. I'd been afraid of exactly this—that if Malcolm knew I was involved, he'd strike one way or another.

I thought if he found out that Travis was operating the hotel alone, he'd stay away. But now he could take my involvement as a provocation. After all, Malcolm and I *had* wanted to open our spa in this very same building back then.

But that was bullshit. I had the right to do whatever the hell I wanted with my grandmother's building. I thought we were rid of Malcolm, but the man was never going to leave me alone. Over my dead body would he get any money from the hotel. It was a Maxwell legacy, and he wasn't a Maxwell. Never would be.

My first instinct was to reach out to Declan, but I didn't. I wanted to let this marinate in my mind for a while.

Doubt started creeping in. The months after I canceled the wedding were a blur. I was so heartbroken that I took a step back from dealing with Malcolm. We mainly communicated through Declan, who'd been cutthroat, as usual. For the first time, I asked myself... maybe *too* cutthroat? We'd left him with absolutely nothing. But maybe if we'd given him *something*, he would have gone away for good.

I rose from my desk and paced the room, happy that no one else could see me as I tugged at my lower lip with my thumb and forefinger. I mentally slapped myself, knowing I needed to stop it or I was going to draw blood. I had to tell Travis at some point. The rest of the family too. But that wouldn't be today.

Why would Malcolm do this now? Why not before?

With a pang in my chest, I realized why. Last week we sent out a press release that we were expanding beyond Aspen and Chicago. We'd found another new location in LA. Malcolm knew he had a lot of money to sink his teeth into. My *family*'s money.

He couldn't get away with this.

I had to pull myself together. I wasn't going to solve this right now.

Taking another breath, I decided to open the door. That way, I would have to keep my composure; otherwise, I'd spend the whole day in a meltdown. I hated that Malcolm still had so much power over me; that one single message sent me into a tailspin. I was a strong woman, but this had completely unsettled me.

Sitting behind my desk again, I adjusted my list so I saw it properly and put my phone far out of reach. I didn't think Malcolm would text again, and I knew better than to reply to him. That would just provoke him more.

I did well for a while after that—at least until lunch, when I made the mistake of looking at my phone again. He hadn't written anything new, but the problem came back front and center to my mind. What had he been up to these past years, anyway?

I looked him up on LinkedIn. Nothing came up when I searched his name. Then I searched Francesca. Also nothing.

Hmmmm.

What were they doing back in Chicago? Why had they even attended the De Monet charity event? I was desperate for information, and I didn't want to talk to him to find out. If one message put me in this state, I didn't even want to think about what talking to him might do to me.

At lunch, Kimberly knocked at my door. "Hey, want to join me, Drake, and Travis in the meeting room? We're having lunch. We might fight over pizza again."

I forced the corners of my mouth upward, not wanting my sister to sense I wasn't happy. "No, I'm good. I have a lot to do today, so I'll stay in my office."

"You won't have lunch?"

"Nope," I said.

"You're passing on pizza?" Kimberly asked, as if she couldn't possibly believe it.

Pizza was my kryptonite, which my sister knew.

"Yeah, I had a big breakfast."

"Okay. And I see you're giving me a run for my money in the gifts department." She shook her head, glancing at the pile of presents. "Send me your list, okay? So I don't accidentally buy the same thing."

"Sure," I said, already a bit absentminded.

"Reese, are you sure you're okay?" Kimberly asked.

Damn it. My fake smile was still wide on my face. "Yeah, just... I had a bit of a late start, and now I'm in a manic phase."

"Fine. I won't disturb you. Want me to close the door?"

"No, no. Leave it open." I was likely to spiral out again if I had privacy.

After she left, I got back to my to-do list, but because of my flat-out lie, I got hangry at around three o'clock. I debated going to the sandwich shop my sister loved across the street, but I didn't want to waste any time.

Despite trying my best to focus on work, I'd fallen behind today, and I didn't want to slack off. I prided myself on my work ethic.

A knock at the door startled me an hour later.

"Reese?" My assistant stood there with what I was certain was a club sandwich.

"Oh my God, is that food? You're a lifesaver," I exclaimed.

"Yeah, it is. Kimberly said you weren't joining them for lunch because you had a big breakfast, which I thought was odd. You told me you skipped it."

I cleared my throat. She and I had a mutual understanding about secrets.

"Anyway, I went to buy something at the pharmacy and thought you might like this."

I smiled gratefully. "Thanks. And not a word to Kimberly, okay?"

"You didn't even have to mention that, boss."

"Better safe than sorry."

After she left, I ate the sandwich quickly, then got back to work.

I ended up staying overtime at the office. I'd finished my last to-do item at five thirty, but once everyone filtered out, I basked in the calmness of the empty office. My adrenaline subsided. I still hadn't made any headway as to why Malcolm thought he had a claim on anything, but I wasn't as apprehensive as this morning. Still, an uneasy feeling lingered in my chest.

The phone rang, startling me. I didn't look at it, fearing it might be Malcolm demanding a response. Then I shook myself. I wasn't a chicken. I was acting completely out of character today. I didn't cower, I didn't hide away in fear, and I didn't keep things from my family.

When I finally glanced at the screen, I relaxed.

Dom was calling. My stomach somersaulted, but for entirely different reasons than before. My lips burned with the memory of the kiss. I answered right away.

"Good evening, Reese."

"Dom, hi," I said.

"Am I interrupting anything?"

"No, just me at the office."

"At this hour?"

"It's been an interesting day." *Why do I have the propensity to spill my guts around this man?*

"What's wrong?" he asked.

How did he even pick that from my voice?

"Just got some bad news today."

"What happened?"

"The details don't matter."

"I see."

"It's not like you can do anything about it," I added.

And wasn't that the truth? I wasn't sure who *could* do something about it. Declan, probably, but he and Liz had a lot going on.

"I have a proposition for you."

"Oh, I've come to love sentences that start like that," I said, swinging back and forth in my chair.

"That's great to hear. Let's go somewhere and *not talk*," he suggested.

I laughed, biting my lower lip. "So what exactly would we be doing?"

"You shared a guilty pleasure of yours with me. I want to do the same."

"Meaning?" I asked. "I feel like I should get a few more details."

"Why? Are you afraid?"

"A bit."

"Hmm. Well, you're not getting any. You have to trust me on this one."

My pulse was crazy; I felt it in my ears and my neck and over my whole chest, like my heart had somehow increased in size. "All right," I said. "Let's go wherever you want to. I'm wearing jeans and a sweater. Is that okay?"

I usually wore more formal clothes at work, but today I'd been in the mood for something casual.

"You could wear nothing at all, and it'd still fit." He groaned. "That didn't come out the way it should have."

Holy shit. I was so hot all of a sudden that I felt the need to discard every item of clothing I had on.

"Right, maybe I should insist on you telling me where we're going. Is it someplace where we need clothes?"

"You want to go somewhere with me where we have to be naked?"

I burst out laughing, replaying my previous sentence in my mind.

"Of course we're going somewhere where clothes are necessary, Reese. I would give you a proper heads-up if I had other plans," he murmured.

"Good, I would appreciate that. And before, I meant if we're going somewhere with a dress code."

"No, don't worry about it."

"Want me to pick you up at the office?"

"Yeah, sure. Why not?"

I'd drive my own car, but I planned to drink a glass or two or ten of something yummy, and I didn't want to have to bother with driving. I'd just grab an Uber to the office tomorrow morning.

"See you in a bit, Reese."

"Are you coming from the store?"

"Yes."

"Okay. I'll make sure to be ready in a few minutes." He wasn't far, so he'd be here in ten, maybe fifteen if there was a lot of traffic.

The second he hung up, I opened my laptop, turning on the camera and applying makeup. It was my trick for getting myself ready without going to the restroom. The camera served as a decent mirror, though the lighting in the office wasn't the best for makeup, but I was a pro. I applied blush as well as lipstick. I never bothered with mascara; even with the waterproof ones, I often ended up looking like a panda midway through dinner.

I was a bit jittery, which didn't help with putting on the lipstick. It took me two tries to finally get it right. Once I was done, I took the stairs down to the lobby, happy to get rid of some of the excess energy—I'd skipped my workout today, so I had even more adrenaline than usual.

I waved to the team behind the reception on my way out.

"Bye, Reese," they said in stunned voices. They probably thought I'd left an hour ago.

Once outside, I paced back and forth in front of the hotel. My entire body vibrated when I spotted Dom's Range Rover.

Chapter Thirteen
Dom

She looked like a damn vision. I immediately got out of the car, walking over to her. I liked her in jeans and a sweater. Casual clothing suited her. Her coat was open, so I could look all I wanted.

"You didn't have to get out," she protested.

"Yes, I did," I said, opening the door for her. How was she so beautiful? I didn't think I'd ever get used to it.

"Thanks for picking me up."

"You can call me whenever you need to get away."

"Really?"

"Why do you sound so incredulous?"

"I don't know. this..." She sighed. "God, everything you do just seems out of this world."

I tilted closer. "I always like going the extra mile."

She gave me a sheepish smile. "Clearly."

She got inside the car. I climbed in seconds later, then gunned the engine. Reese started to take off her coat, and I could barely keep my eyes on the road.

"How is it so warm?" she asked.

"I started the seat heater on the way."

She stopped with one arm still in her coat and glanced at me. "You started it for me?"

I nodded. "I know you like being warm."

Finally removing her coat, she placed it in her lap, looking down at her hands and then back up at me. "Thanks."

"Want to talk about what's on your mind?"

"I thought our understanding was no talking."

"Forget I asked. You'll love the place where we're going. There's no need to talk."

"I'm intrigued."

"I'm taking you to a jazz club."

"But you aren't a fan of jazz."

"But *you* are, and tonight is about making you forget whatever is going on. Besides, I like trying out new things, and I do trust your taste."

"But you said we're sharing one of *your* guilty pleasures."

"Lately... my guilty pleasure is pleasing you."

She stilled. "Where is it?"

"Michigan Avenue."

Her eyes glinted. "Ah, I know exactly where we're going. One of my favorite spots."

We arrived a few minutes later, and I parked in a shaded spot at the side of the lot. I went around to Reese's door as she was putting her coat back on, then helped her out of the car. Not that she needed it—I just wanted another excuse to touch her.

The jazz club was dimly lit with a lot of wood paneling, giving it a speakeasy feel. At first glance, it seemed claustrophobic, but as we went deeper into the room, it grew on me. It was extremely intimate. This was even better than I'd hoped.

One of the waiters led us to a nook wedged between two others that were already occupied. I would have preferred for ours to be in a corner, but this would do as well.

As soon as we sat down, the waiter started pulling at some sheer curtains I hadn't seen bunched to the side, and I realized that was why this nook seem different to the ones that were occupied. The curtains hadn't been drawn.

"I love this," Reese said.

"It almost feels like we're alone."

She laughed nervously. "It does. Did you plan it this way?"

"No, but it's a welcome surprise." I looked at her intently. "Does this make you uncomfortable?"

"No, not at all. It's just very unexpected."

She grabbed the menu that was on the table in front of us. "What to drink, what to drink? Well, since this is a twenties-themed bar and the music fits, I'll have the signature twenties cocktail. It's new. I've never seen it before." She raised a brow. "My, my, they mix a lot of alcohol, but it's just what I need tonight. Want to look at the menu?"

She handed it to me just as I reached for it. Our fingers touched.

She startled slightly, looking away. I could swear she was biting her lower lip. On instinct, I glanced down, noticing her legs were held tightly together. She took a deep breath.

Oh yeah, I loved that she reacted like this to me.

One of the waiters approached us. "Did you have time to look over our drink menu?"

"Yes. We'll have your signature cocktail," I replied, finding it easier to order the same thing rather than bothering to look at the drinks list.

"Right away. And here's the menu for food." He handed us two of them.

Reese immediately opened hers, clinging to it as if she wanted to hide. I opened mine too.

I never needed much time to decide, so I lowered the menu only a few minutes later.

Reese also seemed to have found what she wanted, because she snapped her head up and said to the waiter, "I think we're ready order food, too." Turning to me, she added, "Dom, do you need more time?"

"No, I'm good."

She looked back at the waiter. "I'll have the salmon with grilled veggies please."

"And I'll have the steak. With two sides of fries," I added.

"Right away." He took the menus before disappearing.

"Why did you order two fries?" Her voice was laced with suspicion.

"Because a certain sexy woman might start stealing mine otherwise."

She giggled and then covered her mouth with her hand. "I'm sorry, I don't know where that came from. You're right. When you said fries, I was like 'Oh snap. How am I going to resist them?' I mean, I already have trouble resisting you."

Her comment went straight to my cock. "Reese!"

She lowered her hand. "Hmmm, wasn't my best idea to say that out loud, huh? Some things I should just keep to myself."

I tilted my head, wondering how much to push. "What else are you keeping to yourself, Reese?"

"That I think you're the most considerate man I've ever met. I still can't believe you turned on the seat heater for me."

I blinked, jerking my head back a bit. "Right. And that was a big thing because...?"

"You don't even know, do you?"

"No," I said honestly.

"It just shows that you thought about my needs. That you thought about *me*."

Why was this so surprising to her?

"And you wanted to come to a jazz bar even though you don't like the music," she continued.

I moved a bit closer to her, speaking right into her ear. "I'll tell you a secret. It's growing on me, and I think it's 100 percent your doing."

"And now you've ordered fries," she said.

I wiggled my eyebrows again. "If you want, I can order dessert too."

"Now you're just being completely shameless."

The server brought our cocktails, putting them in front of us. We clinked our glasses and tipped them up. I choked several times while I tried to take a sip. This was so damn pink, and it tasted even worse.

Reese glanced at me, but I couldn't read her expression. Then she put her glass down on the table and burst out laughing.

"Oh my God. This is going to make you swear off jazz bars, isn't it? I promise, not all twenties cocktails are as shitty as this one."

I laughed with her, setting my own glass down. I didn't want to risk it spilling over—that's how hard we were laughing.

"Don't worry, I don't mind jazz bars at all. In fact, if you come with me, I'm willing to explore a few more."

"Is that your way of asking to spend more time with me?"

"Hell yes. I wasn't being subtle, Reese."

"I do have a list of my favorite spots. I think you'd like one or two of them."

I swallowed hard. "I wasn't expecting you to offer so easily, but I'm glad you did."

She shrugged, then grabbed her glass again. "Oh, what the hell?" She took another sip. "I need liquid courage."

"You need alcohol to relax around me?"

"No, just my inhibitions. They're up here." She put her left hand about twenty inches above her head. "But I need them down here." She moved her hand down to her knees. "Anyway, you turned on the heat and ordered extra fries. There's no way I can say no to you, at least not tonight."

I growled. She turned abruptly, looking straight at my mouth and then at my eyes.

I sucked in a deep breath, wanting to kiss this woman so damn badly. I was almost certain that she wanted that, too, but I wouldn't do it. Not until she asked me for it. I didn't want to push or make her uncomfortable in any way even though I needed her so badly that I had to grasp the edges of the chair to stop myself from leaning even closer to her.

I didn't get the chance to say anything more because the damn waiter returned. He was starting to be a cockblocker.

"How are your drinks?" he asked.

Reese looked straight at him. "I'm sorry to say this, but they're awful."

The guy actually took a step back.

Reese glanced at me. "I think this gave me a bit too much courage."

I looked at the waiter. "They're not to our taste, not at all."

He dipped his head in apology. "We'll bring you new drinks on the house. What would you like?"

"A martini, please," Reese said.

"And I'll take a bourbon." I didn't care what I was drinking or what I was eating. All I cared about was that I was here with Reese and we were having a damn good time.

I hadn't been lying to her. I was starting to like jazz music. I enjoyed the easy flow. Most of all, I liked the way Reese swayed to it. It fit her—classic elegance and subtle seduction.

"Oh my God," she said after he left. "I was so mean to the waiter. I'm never like that."

"It's fine, Reese. Maybe they'll drop that crap from the cocktail list. Not many customers would have the guts to give them such honest feedback."

"Oh well, what's done is done. No point fretting over it." She started humming the song that was playing to herself.

"You know this tune?"

"Yes. I have a jazz playlist, and this is one of my favorites."

"You're so fucking beautiful," I said.

Her eyes widened. She straightened up, pushing strands of hair behind her ear, then frowned. "Something is vibrating. My phone."

She quickly took it out of her purse and started to laugh.

"What?" I asked.

"My sister says she'll buy a couple more gifts to make sure she's got more than me."

"I'm not following," I said.

"I might have gone a bit overboard while shopping for Christmas. My assistant made a small Christmas tree of the packages in my office. I think Kimberly got a bit jealous seeing I had such a head start on her."

"Who are all the presents for?" I was still confused.

"My cousins and their kids. I've curated lists of stuff they like, and I keep updating wish lists on retailers' sites. Sometimes that works against me. I'm supposed to just choose a few items from the list. But they all look so good that I end up ordering far too much. But I like making people happy, and seeing the way their eyes light up when they get their gifts is priceless."

"You like kids?"

"Oh yeah. I've always wanted to have a lot."

"Define that," I said, because it sounded suspicious.

"Six."

"What? No, that's not possible."

She laughed. "I know. It was my ideal number eight years ago, probably because I have six cousins and always thought it was amazing to have so many people in the house." She sighed. "But, I mean, that ship has sailed. I'm not twenty anymore." She paused for a moment, her eyes a bit sad, then asked, "How about you? You like kids?"

"Yeah. Though I always thought about one or two. Six never even crossed my mind."

I wanted to ask her more about how she saw her own future, but I didn't get the chance because the waiter came with our food. I needed to have Reese all for me—away from any bars, restaurants, hotels, or events.

"Here are your drinks. On the house. And your food. Please let us know if anything isn't to your liking, and we'll change it."

The waiter stood next to the table after setting everything down. I suspected he was waiting for us to taste our food and drinks before leaving.

Reese looked up at him sweetly. "I'm sorry for being so blunt before. And thank you for giving us drinks on the house."

The waiter fidgeted. "Is there any way you won't leave us a bad review?"

She jerked her head back. "That didn't even cross my mind. You have nothing to worry about. We'll let you know if we need anything else."

I detected eagerness in her voice. She wanted him gone just as much as I did.

After he left, we finally turned to our food. It was a great steak, but honestly, I only had Reese on my mind. Nothing else mattered.

She took a sip of her martini. "Mm, now *that's* what I call a drink. Serves me right, experimenting with strange cocktails."

Right now, I just wanted us to get the food out of the way. Despite saying we weren't going to talk tonight, I was finding out more and more about her, and I couldn't wait to ask even more questions—or even better, for her to open up.

I ate quickly, but Reese took her time, enjoying the fires. Just as I swallowed my last bite, the volume of the music exploded.

"Oh God. What is this?" she exclaimed.

Through the curtain, we saw a lot of movement at the front of the room.

"It's a live band," Reese said. "Those are always a bit louder."

"What? I can't hear you."

She brought her mouth to my ear. "Live bands are usually louder. I don't think we'll be able to talk at all."

Feeling her hot breath on my skin made me semihard. On instinct, I put a hand on her back. She straightened, sighing. Involuntarily, I flexed my fingers, digging them slowly into her back.

"You want us to go?" she murmured. Her voice had changed. It sounded almost shy, but the intent behind it was clear.

I turned my head, speaking into her ear now. "Yes. Fuck yes, I want us to go."

"Is your place closer than mine?"

Fuck me. "Yes, it is," I said, then motioned for the waiter to get the bill.

He came so fast, I half expected him to break his neck. "Is everything okay?"

"Yes. We'd like to pay."

His eyes widened a bit. "But you haven't even finished your drinks."

"We've had a very long day," Reese said. It was a good thing she'd stepped in, because I found him too intrusive to remain polite.

"I'll bring the check right away," he replied, then headed toward the register area.

The music became even louder in the meantime, and I couldn't wait to get out of here.

Thankfully, he returned quickly. After paying, and leaving the waiter a generous tip, Reese and I left.

"Where do you live exactly?" she asked when I opened the car door for her.

"In the South Loop neighborhood," I said.

She nodded once but didn't say anything.

"You sure you don't want us to go anywhere else?" My question was loaded, and I hoped she didn't pick up on my eagerness.

"I'm sure," she said.

This evening had taken an unexpected turn, and I couldn't have been happier about it.

When we arrived at my condo a short while later, I ushered her inside with my hand on the small of her back.

"Wow. This place is amazing." She walked straight to the window wall. I called it that because it was made exclusively out of windows overlooking the skyline of Chicago. "I bet this is gorgeous when there's still light outside. I mean, it's breathtaking like this too, of course."

I turned on the light of the reading lamp that hung above an armchair.

"I like the color palette," she said, turning around. "Very masculine."

I tried to view it from her perspective—a black carpet with gray stripes, a round black coffee table, and a dark blue couch.

"Are you going to decorate it for Christmas?" she inquired.

"I haven't thought about that. Maybe. There is still time."

She grinned. "You can never start too early. I've already put a few things up in my condo."

"Damn. You like starting really early. Do you want anything to drink?" I asked her.

"Can you make a martini?"

"I can, actually. The bar is fully stocked."

She sat down on the couch, looking even more beautiful right now than any other time I'd seen her. There was something about seeing her on my couch that tapped into my primal instinct.

I mixed her martini and poured my bourbon. "I don't have any olives," I said as I brought both our glasses to where she was seated.

She laughed. "Honestly, the alcohol is all that matters. I never eat the olive or cherry or whatever they put in it anyway." She glanced around the room, then looked back at me. "So, did you live here with your ex-wife?"

"No, I bought this place after the separation. I wanted something fresh, something that represented me."

"Hence the masculine vibe. Got it. It's very elegant."

I sat next to her on the couch, handing her the drink. Our fingers brushed, and just like back at the restaurant, a spark flew between us. This time, I couldn't hold back a groan.

She looked from the glass up to my lips before finally gathering the courage to make eye contact.

"Dom," she murmured.

I needed to taste her. Right now.

Chapter Fourteen
Dom

I set my glass down, and she did the same. Her hand shook lightly as I gently grasped her wrist, then moved my hand up her palm, interlacing our fingers.

I leaned in and kissed her. She tasted amazing, like martini. She sighed against my mouth, and I couldn't even think past how much I needed her tonight. This was the first time we'd kissed with no one around us. No one to watch. No one to pretend for. This moment right here was real. She was mine. She wanted this kiss as much as I did. Perhaps needed it, even.

But one kiss would never satisfy me.

I pulled her toward me until she was in my lap. She placed her thighs on either side of my body and her hands on my shoulders. I deepened the kiss, pushing my fingers into her hair and tugging gently. I wanted more. I wanted to fist her hair and guide her mouth while she wrapped it around my cock.

Reese moved her pelvis even closer as she straddled me, her pussy right over my crotch.

"Reese," I groaned. Her breath came out in a rush. "I want you so damn bad."

"I want you too," she whispered against my mouth.

"Are you sure about… everything?" I needed her to be absolutely certain before we went any further.

She shook her head. "No."

My stomach twisted.

"But it doesn't matter," she went on.

"Yes, it does," I countered. "I don't want you to do something you'll regret."

She grinned. "Oh, I wouldn't regret it. Not even one bit. I'm not certain of anything tonight except that I want you. I want this. It's everything else I'm not yet sure about. But not this. I'm completely sure about this."

I closed my eyes, trying to gather my wits and failing for the first time in living memory. I couldn't focus. Her words sounded contradictory to what she'd said only a few minutes ago.

Then she pressed her lips to mine, and all thoughts flew from my mind except one: this woman was going to be mine tonight.

Needing to touch more of her, wanting skin-on-skin contact, I pulled her sweater over her head. She was wearing a fucking sexy bra.

"I love this," I murmured. Her breasts were far more gorgeous than I'd imagined, spilling out of the black lace. I needed to worship them.

I lifted her off my lap, placing her on her back on the couch, then hovered above her. I kissed down from her collarbone to her breasts, moving my mouth just over the line where fabric met skin. She arched her back and reached both hands over her head, grasping the armrest. Her hair was wild around her head, splayed out in all directions.

I pulled back, glancing at her up and down.

"What?" she asked.

"Reese Maxwell, you're the most beautiful woman I've ever seen."

She avoided my gaze and even blushed a little. "That can't be true."

"Yes, it is."

I resumed kissing her breasts, then stopped when she made to open the clasp at her back.

"Not yet," I said. "Not yet, beautiful."

I kissed down her belly, and she sucked in her muscles when I reached her navel before going even farther down. I undid the button of her jeans, quickly pulling down the zipper and pushing her pants past her ass. Her black panties matched the bra. I drew my nose down her slit, over the panties.

"Dom!" she gasped.

I moved to her right thigh, kissing a trail and touching it with the tip of my nose, too. At the same time, I lowered her jeans, taking them off completely, along with her socks.

She pressed her thighs together.

"You're incredible," I murmured.

Then I veered to the leg that I'd completely ignored before, repeating my kissing actions until I reached the apex of her thighs. She rolled her hips at the contact, and I pressed my thumb against her opening, over the panties, splaying my fingers on her left thigh while I moved the tip of my nose up her belly.

"Now you can take it off," I said.

Without even opening her eyes, she reached behind her back, unhooked the bra, and discarded it next to the couch. I swallowed hard at the sight, then started worshipping her right breast, drawing large circles with my mouth before closing in on that nipple. I mirrored the movement with my hands on her left breast. She was squirming already, shifting her hips back and forth. Every time she brushed against the fly of my jeans, I grew harder. It was making me even more insatiable for her.

I got down from the couch, nearly tearing off the buttons of my shirt in my haste to get it off. Reese pushed herself up on her elbows, watching me. I took off my pants and boxers next and touched my cock, pressing my thumb on the crown.

"Come closer," she purred. "I want to do that."

I stepped right in front of her. She smiled, licking her lips. In a fraction of a second, she was sitting up and wrapped her mouth around the tip.

"Reese!" I grabbed a fistful of her hair.

She looked up at me, and the vision was so damn sexy that I nearly exploded right here, right now.

"Take it all in, beautiful, as much as you can."

She lowered her mouth slowly. The deeper I went, the closer I was to completely losing my control.

She didn't manage to go all the way to the base. When she pulled back, wrapping her lips even tighter around me, I felt like I was floating outside of my body. She groaned, fidgeting on the couch. I pulled my cock out and lowered my mouth to her, tangling our tongues. At the same time, I reached between her thighs, pressing two fingers over her panties. She'd soaked them completely.

She shuddered, then rolled her hips back and forth. She needed friction. I would give her more than that.

I slipped two fingers beneath her panties, and she groaned hard against my mouth when I pushed them inside her. The angle was perfect, as I could rub her clit, too, and I knew she wasn't going to last long. She needed her release. It was close, and it was going to be quick. It wouldn't be very powerful, but that was all right; I had time to work her up after, and the second one would rock her world.

But for now, I was going to give her what she needed.

I kissed down her neck before putting my ear near her mouth. I wanted to feel every breath, to hear every moan, no matter how loud or how quiet.

"Dom, Dom, I don't even... I'm going to..."

"I know, babe. You're going to come, and then you're going to come again."

She squeezed tight around my fingers and exploded. Her body bowed off the couch, but I kept her steady.

She gasped and took in a deep breath. "Dom, I can't believe this. That was so fast."

"I know. Now I'm going to take my time with you, working up to your second orgasm."

She blinked as if she didn't quite follow. But she didn't need to understand it. She was going to feel it.

I peeled off her panties, which were so soaked that my cock was painfully hard. After pushing her legs as far apart as possible, I kissed up and down her thighs, alternating between the right and the left side of her entrance. Then I blew a cold breath over her sensitive skin.

"Oh, Dom, ah," she exclaimed when I pressed the flat of my tongue right across her entrance. Then I pushed it inside her.

Goose bumps covered her soft skin in a fraction of a second. I pushed my tongue in and out and brushed her clit with my thumb, first up and down and then in a circle. I watched her body for signs of what she liked. I wanted to overwhelm her with pleasure.

Reese was spiraling out right in front of me. She pressed her heels on the cushions and gripped the edges of the couch, then raised her shoulders to her ears and closed her eyes, bracing herself.

I lifted her ass off the couch and licked her exactly how I wanted. Moving my mouth to her clit, I pressed my thumb inside her and then replaced it with two fingers, curling them toward me at the same time as I sucked her clit between my lips.

She exploded again, even louder than the first time and infinitely wilder, thrashing and gripping the pillows on the couch.

"Dom, I can't feel my body anymore," she whispered as I gently set her ass down on the couch.

"I'm not nearly done with you tonight, beautiful."

"You're not? You mean two orgasms weren't enough?"

"They were good, but not perfect. The perfect one will be with my cock buried inside you."

She bit her lower lip, looking between us. Then she wrapped her hand around my cock, squeezing it. "Are you clean?" she whispered. "I am, and I'm on birth control."

"Yes, I'm clean," I said.

I was going to be buried inside this woman with nothing between us. How the hell did I get so lucky?

I'm the most fortunate man on the planet.

I put my knees on the couch and lifted her legs. Placing my elbows under her knees, I positioned her so her pussy was level with my cock, then teased her by pressing the length of my erection along her entrance.

She dropped her head back, moaning softly. I rubbed back and forth, knowing I wasn't teasing her anymore. I was hitting her clit with my crown every time, and it was unbearable for me. The skin-on-skin contact, far from satisfying me, only spurred me more. I needed to be completely wrapped up in her.

I slid in without any warning, pushing in all the way until I was completely buried in her. A jolt of pleasure shot through me so strongly that I buckled forward, my muscles weak.

"Fuck, Reese," I groaned as tension gathered between my shoulder blades and the muscles in my stomach and ass contracted. I was going to go so hard that we'd both lose our minds.

I pulled back and pushed in again and again. Pleasure spiraled through me; I felt it tugging at every cell in my body. My vision blurred, but I could still see Reese trying to scratch everything in sight: the armrest, the pillows, her own body. She touched her breasts, pressing them together. Her senses were heightened, just like mine. When she tightened around me, I could barely breathe through the sensation, let alone fuck.

But I was sure of one thing: she was going to come again before me.

I touched her with my left hand, first her belly and then her thighs. Then I placed my hand back on her belly, lowering it until it covered a bit of her pelvis too. That way, I was going to feel when she was close to the edge.

When her breath shook, I knew she was right there. I brushed her clit with the heel of my palm, and she squeezed so tight around me that I lost sense of myself for a few seconds. Then I exploded inside her, but I wasn't done yet.

I lowered her leg to the couch, and leaned over her, needing a change of angle. I brought my ear to her mouth and pushed my hips in long, hard strokes, riding out the wave.

Her moans turned softer. She was coming down from the cusp.

I followed her soon after, thrusting inside her until every cell in my body had surrendered completely to her.

Chapter Fifteen
Reese

"Your shower gel smells amazing," I said, sniffing my skin after stepping out into the bathroom. "I'd love to know the brand." He had one of those cool dispensers, so I couldn't tell what it was.

He opened a drawer under the sink, taking out a bottle. "You can take it with you if you want."

"Really? Thanks."

He held out a robe for me. I immediately dropped the towel that I'd used to pat myself dry and slid on the robe.

"This is so fluffy and smells like you. Will you put one on too?"

"No, I only have this one."

"You don't have to give it to me," I protested, about to take it off, but he pushed it right back into place, tying the belt too.

"No," he said. "You'll get cold with just a towel. I want you to be comfortable."

How was this sex god such a decent human being? The whole evening had been amazing. I kept wanting to pinch myself.

I yawned as I put the shower gel on one of the open shelves next to the mirror. "Let's hope I don't forget to take this when I leave."

He leaned into me, bringing his mouth to my ear. "If you do, you're more than welcome to come back and grab it. In fact, I don't mind if you forget it on purpose. It would give you a reason to come back."

He wants me to come back! Hell yes!

I turned to him, trying to smile, but ended up yawning again.

"Come on, let's go to bed," he urged. "You're tired."

"Actually... I'm a bit hungry."

"You didn't eat much. Didn't you like the dinner?"

"I did. But I was a bit nervous, and I didn't have an appetite."

"Because of me?" he asked with a wry smile.

I tapped my lips, trying not to grin. "Let me think. Maybe it was because of the hot waiter who kept bringing us weird drinks." His eyes turned cold at that. "Of course it was because of you."

But he didn't relax right away. He kept scrutinizing my face as if searching for signs that I was telling him the truth.

"Come on, I'll feed you," he said finally.

"What's your favorite delivery around here?"

"I'll find something for you in the fridge."

My eyes widened. "What? You have food?"

"Why the surprise?"

"I don't know. You just don't strike me as the type who has any food at home."

He laughed. "Believe it or not, I actually cook. Learned it from Dad. He said that early in his relationship with my mom, he realized that if he didn't want to eat burned or uncooked food for the rest of his life, he'd better take over."

"Oh, that's so cute," I said. My heart was happy hearing him talk about his parents. "Your parents sound wonderful."

"They are. Dad said he never truly had the heart to tell her that she was a terrible cook, so instead he simply took the reins in the kitchen."

"How long ago did she pass away?" I asked.

"Four years."

"I'm sorry for your loss."

He took my hand, walking slightly in front of me as we went to the kitchen. This felt heavenly. I was wearing his robe, he just had boxers on, and now he was leisurely taking me to the kitchen to give me food.

I almost felt uncomfortable with how easy it was. I wasn't used to this. Things with Malcolm had never been easy. Everything had always been a negotiation or a fight. If I wanted something, I was being unreasonable every single time. Eventually, I stopped wanting things or asking for romantic dates or getaways.

Some days I was still mad at myself for staying with him for as long as I did. My dating experience afterward wasn't anything to brag about either.

He opened the fridge and asked, "How hungry are you?"

"I don't know. I think I could wait for a bit. Why? What do you have in mind? Should we order after all?"

"No, I was thinking about making a quiche if you like that."

My eyes bulged, and I couldn't form words.

He looked at me over his shoulder. "Reese?"

"Sorry. I was too stunned to answer. You want to make a quiche *now*?"

"Yeah, I've got all the stuff I need."

"You know how to make one?" I double-checked.

"You don't?"

I shook my head. "Baking isn't my thing. The most cooking I do is when the whole family gathers at my aunt and uncle's."

"Why, you bring your own food?"

"No, but there are so many of us that she assigns us specific tasks. It's smart; otherwise, she'd have to cook for hours."

He took out eggs and cheese and a lot of other ingredients.

"What do you need me to do?" I asked.

"I've got this. I'm not used to delegating like your aunt, so it's easier if I do everything myself."

"Suits me," I said. That meant I had all the time in the world to just watch him move around. *Yum.* Those muscles were a feast for my eyes.

"What do your tattoos mean?" I asked, drinking in the ink on his body. The "private" tattoo he'd teased me with during the drive to the weekend event was on his lower back. It looked like a hawk in flight. It was amazing. The ink on his arms was more subtle—they looked like vines.

"That I had a rebellious streak in my twenties."

"So you have a hawk on your back, but what's that on your arms?"

"I intended for them to be guitar strings. I used to play in a band."

"That's sexy. Why did you stop?"

"Because I started Waldorf Fashion. And it took up all my time. I still enjoy music, but don't play anymore."

"Fair enough. By the way, I'd argue that you still have a rebellious streak. You just hide it really well with those sexy suits."

He winked at me. "Damn right I do."

Forty minutes later, he took the quiche out of the oven. The top looked brown and crispy, and he immediately cut it into slices.

"Do we have to wait for it to cool?" I asked.

"No, you can dig in."

I immediately snagged a spoonful, blew on it a bit, then shoved it in my mouth. I closed my eyes, sighing. "This is good. I have to hide you from my sister. If she finds out about your cooking skills, there will be no escaping her. She loves quiche."

"You already want to introduce me to your sister?"

I opened my eyes, straightening up. "It was a figure of speech. I didn't... I mean..." I bit the inside of my cheek, glancing down at the plate.

"Reese, relax." He took my hand, caressing the back of it with his thumb. "I'd love to meet your sister anytime."

My face exploded in a grin. "Really?"

"Yeah."

"Okay." My stomach somersaulted.

"Why does she love quiche so much?"

"She lived in Paris for a few years and kept saying that she can't find good quiche here, but I think she'd love yours." I was rambling now. I didn't understand why I was so nervous. "You're not going to eat?" I asked when he made no move to grab a bite.

"No, I'm not hungry. I'll just have it for breakfast."

I stared at him. "You cooked all this for me?"

"Reese, why do you keep acting so surprised that I like to do things for you?"

"I don't know. I didn't think... never mind."

The silence stretched between us for a few seconds before he said, "When you're ready to talk about it, just know you can. I'm here for you."

"Thanks."

For some reason, I kept expecting this night to take a turn for the worse, for him to make a sly comment about me leaving or to only consider this night a onetime thing. I'd always been a worrier and overthinker, but even for my standards, I was extra anxious tonight.

I was gun-shy after my past relationship, always waiting for the other shoe to drop. But Dom hadn't done anything to deserve this, and I needed to stop anticipating the worst.

"So, you mentioned that you gather at your aunt and uncle's. How often do you do that?" he asked.

"It depends. Since all my cousins and my sister have a better half, and even have kids, we don't get together regularly. But I'm very close to everyone. My aunt and uncle are like my parents in a way."

"How come?"

Instead of simply saying, "Because we're close," other words poured out of me, ones I didn't usually share with anyone outside my family.

"After Mom passed away, Dad couldn't really deal, to be honest. He used work as an escape, putting all his effort into expanding the chain of bookstores. My grandmother and aunt and uncle practically raised Kimberly and me."

"But things are okay between you now?"

"Oh yes, of course. As I said, he lives in London, so we aren't as close as I'd hoped we'd be, but we do talk a lot, and visit. I've asked him to send me pics of my half sister once a week so even though I'm not there, I can at least see her grow up."

Dom was suspiciously silent. I eyed him carefully. "What?"

"Nothing. I don't think I've ever met someone who's been through a tough spot with their parents and doesn't hold one bit of resentment."

I shrugged. "He did the best with what he had. It's not like he woke up every morning and thought, 'Let's find a way to screw up my girls.' And I think older generations weren't as open to therapy. After my spectacular failure with the marriage, I knew I couldn't cope on my own."

Dom moved around the counter until he was right in front of me. "Let's get one thing straight, Reese. The fact that your ex slept with your best friend is not your failure."

"Mm," I said noncommittally, putting a hand to my stomach. Talking about this was never easy.

"There's something to be said for decency. When you don't want to be in a relationship anymore, you can be honest about it and break up, not cheat. There are better ways of getting out of a relationship, ones that don't include destroying the other person."

I wasn't sure if he was talking about me or him. I put a hand on his chest, drawing my fingers in small circles over his torso. He was tense, but I could practically feel his muscles relax under my touch.

"You're right," I said softly.

He pressed his thumb against my cheek. "Don't think that something you did led to that bastard cheating on you or your best friend betraying you. I've only known you for a hot minute, but I already know you're a wonderful person, Reese. That guy was an idiot. That's all on him."

I dipped my head, smiling slightly. "Thank you for saying that."

"You're welcome. Are you done eating?"

"Yeah. It was delicious."

He laughed and then, without warning, lifted me in his arms, one under my knees and the other around my back. I instinctively put both arms around his neck, snuggling close.

Holy shit. I feel like I'm in a movie.

"Good. Now, we're going to bed," he said.

"We are? I'm not tired anymore."

"Are you sure? You were yawning before."

"Hmm. I could be talked into sleeping," I teased him, "though we might get other ideas once we're in bed."

When we reached the bedroom, the light was off. He set me right in the center of the bed before pulling back the covers.

"Come on. Let's get in so you don't get cold," he said as I discarded the robe. I was buck naked, since I didn't have any pajamas.

He slipped right next to me under the covers. This all felt so sinful with the lamps off, though there were plenty of sources of light outside. Chicago wasn't sleeping yet.

I moved closer to him so our legs were intertwined, then put my hands on his torso, moving them up and down playfully.

"You're going to tempt me the whole night, aren't you?" he asked.

I grinned. "You can be sure of that."

Chapter Sixteen
Reese

I was a bit of a mess over the next few days to the point that I didn't even participate in the Halloween celebrations at the hotel. I just kept thinking about Malcolm's message. He hadn't sent me a follow-up, but I wasn't kidding myself. If he'd taken the trouble to write to me in the first place, he wasn't going to give up just because I didn't answer.

No matter how much I wanted to protect my family, I couldn't keep them in the dark. This affected them just as much as it did me. I considered telling just Travis and Kimberly at first. As the owner of the hotel, Travis would be the one most directly impacted, although Kimberly and I were also co-owners of the Aspen Hotel. But I felt as if this affected the whole Maxwell legacy. I couldn't imagine telling everyone at once. But if I told them separately, I'd have to relay the story several times, and I didn't have it in me.

"Knock, knock. You here?" Kimberly asked.

"Hey, how long have you been standing there, staring at me like a creep?"

"Just a few minutes. Everything okay?"

Everything was decidedly not okay. I leaned back in my chair.

Her eyes widened. "Oh shit. What happened?"

"Think we can get the family together for a dinner?"

Kimberly stilled. "Reese, you're scaring me. What's wrong?"

"I have some things to share with everyone."

She practically ran across the office and sat in front of me. "I need to know now."

"Look, don't worry. It's just not something I want to keep repeating over and over again. That's why it's best if I rip off the Band-Aid when I tell everyone at the same time."

"It's about Malcolm, isn't it?"

I winced. "How did you know?"

"Because it's the only time you get all cagey, and I can practically see you shrinking in front of me."

I sighed. "Every time I think I've gotten rid of him, I'm wrong."

She stood up abruptly, nodding. "I'll get the family together, but not at your place. There's no space for everyone to sit down. I'll call Aunt Lena. I'm sure she'd love to have everyone for dinner."

"Thanks, Kimberly," I said.

"And I heard through the grapevine that a hunk picked you up from the office the other day."

My face lit up. I could practically feel my features going from stressed to relaxed and then to happy. "Yes, he did. And you're going to get the details about that, just not right now."

She scoffed. "What's the point of working together if we can't gossip whenever we want to? I have some time now."

"Me too. My next meeting isn't until ten."

"Perfect. I'll bring coffee."

I stood from my desk chair. "I'll come with you to the kitchen, see if we have any sweets."

"We don't. Trust me. I already checked." She paused for a moment, obviously thinking about something. "Maybe we could make a contract with Liz or something that she could supply us with goodies twice a week."

"Hey, that would be cool," I said. "We love sweet treats, and it would mean more business for her."

We went to the break area, making two coffees. As Kimberly said, there were no treats—I checked all cupboards to make sure—but that was more than fine. We had an excellent machine, so the coffee itself was a treat. We sat with our drinks, and I kept my voice low as I told her about my night with Dom.

"Holy shit. I haven't even met the guy and I like him. I never thought I'd say that."

"What? That you like someone I'm going out with?"

"Well, a guy I haven't, you know, scrutinized first, and someone I didn't make jump through hoops or something. Are you going to see him again soon?"

"I hope so. I mean, we haven't made plans. But the evening was so amazing that I refuse to believe it was a onetime thing."

She grinned. "Attagirl. I like seeing you optimistic for once."

"Yeah. I can barely believe that I am, to be honest."

The office became crowded as more people arrived. Gossip hour was over almost before it had started. I didn't want to broadcast my personal life to everyone.

I'd almost forgotten that Kimberly said she'd take care of the family meeting until I saw a message in our WhatsApp group.

Aunt Lena: Hey, everyone. How about a get-together? I want to cook beef bourguignon.

She also sent us several dates to choose from, including tonight.

Ten minutes later, we'd all agreed on Friday at lunch. I loved that we were all so close and could meet up in a heartbeat. I had no idea how Kimberly and Sam had lived away for so many years. I could never do it. I'd once vacationed in London for a few weeks, and while I was happy to be with Dad and his new family, I'd missed everyone this side of the ocean terribly and couldn't wait to be back.

My phone vibrated again. I wondered who else had messaged, but then noticed it was a notification from a conversation with Dom.

Dom: Our night together is on repeat in my mind.

My heart rate picked up, and my stomach was doing cartwheels.

Dom: I want to spend another evening with you. I've got meetings until late every day except Friday. Are you free?

Reese: I'm meeting the family on Friday for lunch. I'm free after that.

Dom: Text me when you're ready, and we'll take it from there.

I licked my lips, smiling from ear to ear. I was going to see him again. I couldn't wait.

On Friday, I was at my aunt and uncle's at one o'clock. The house smelled amazing when I stepped inside.

"You've already cooked?" I asked Aunt Lena.

"Yes. It needs three hours in the oven. Besides, I got a lot of help. John, Beatrice, and Paisley spent the day here, as well as Lexi." Lexi, Tate's wife, was taking it easy since she'd had her little one and was spending a lot of time at Lena's home.

She raised a brow at me. "When Kimberly said we should get together, I got the impression that it was more for your sake."

"Yep, it is," I replied.

It was a good idea to meet here. Even though it wasn't the house where my cousins grew up, it was still Lena's house. I always felt safe and happy around her.

"Okay, you tell us when you're ready," she said.

Another thing I loved about her was that she didn't push. She waited for people to open up.

I went into the living room and sat next to Lexi, taking the baby in my arms.

"You and Kimberly are absolutely adorable when you're around kids," she gushed.

"They're too cute for me to resist."

"Should we get started with the drinks?" Uncle Emmett asked, stepping into the living room.

"Yes, please," I said. "I'll have white wine."

"I'm good for now," Lexi replied.

"I'll be right back," he replied before heading out of the room.

The rest of the clan arrived minutes apart from each other.

"Well, this is great," Gran exclaimed once we were all in the living room.

Declan and Liz were sharing one of the armchairs, her sitting in his lap. I was worried about his reaction when I told everyone. I knew he would want to take the lead on this, and it simply wasn't fair because he had enough work. On the other hand, I trusted him implicitly.

Travis and Bonnie were standing by the window with their little one, who seemed fascinated with the windowsill.

Tate was in a deep discussion with Paisley over by the bar. By the frown on my cousin's face, I was pretty sure Paisley had brought up one of the topics that gave him the most headache recently: boys. Tyler and Kendra were next to Luke and Megan, chatting in low voices.

Kimberly was staring at me from where she sat next to Gran and John. Drake stood behind my sister. It was a good thing he was here too; since he worked with us, it would affect him as well. Drake surreptitiously massaged Kimberly's shoulders. That's where she held her stress.

I was so happy that she had found someone. Some days, I still couldn't believe it.

Sam and his fiancée, Avery, were sitting on another armchair. Sam looked exhausted. He'd had a night shift yesterday, which was why we were meeting today.

"So," Declan said, startling everyone, "I'm assuming that this isn't just a normal get-together, since you seemed to want it to happen urgently, Mom. What's wrong?"

Damn, he could read the room.

"It's not Lena who needs this to happen. It's me," I said.

The energy in the room shifted instantly. It was completely silent. Even Paisley and Tate had stopped bickering. I felt like I was under a microscope.

Declan trained his eyes on me. "Is Malcolm up to something again?"

I pushed a strand of hair behind my ear. "Yes," I admitted, a bit relieved that his mind went directly there. At least it wouldn't come as a shock. "First, I'd like to say that this doesn't directly concern everyone, but I don't like secrets. It concerns Travis, Kimberly, and me."

"I thought Malcolm moved out of Chicago," Tyler said. His voice was steely. Considering he'd once been benched because of Malcolm, he had every reason to hold resentment. That had been my fault too.

Damn it, I feared this was never going to end.

"He wants to prove that I acted out of ill will when I got out of the spa business because I already wanted to do the hotel." I explained.

"Forward me whatever info you have," Declan said.

"Are you sure? Because if you recommend a lawyer, I'd be happy to take this off your hands."

"Fucking hell, Reese." He closed his eyes, looking over his shoulder at Paisley, who just waved her hand. Sometimes we forgot she wasn't an innocent little girl anymore. "No one else will take care of this. I will."

"But you've got a lot going on."

"Reese." This was Gran. She spoke in a low, strange voice. "This is not the time for you to be brave, okay? Let us all help."

"We'll get through this," Tyler said. "As a family, okay?"

My eyes became glassy, and I breathed in deeply through my nose and out my mouth, trying to calm down. God, I loved these people fiercely. There was nothing more important than family, and my cousins proved that time and time again.

"I just feel so guilty for dragging all of you into this."

"Again, don't worry about it, okay?" Lena said. "We've all dealt with a lot over the years."

That was true. A weight lifted off me, as if I'd been carrying it with me for the past few days, and now I could finally put it down. I wasn't expecting the family to do the heavy lifting, but knowing they were behind me made all the difference.

"All right, I think we need to know a few more details," Declan said. "Did you talk to him? When did he contact you?"

I told them about running into him at the charity event, carefully retelling the story so I wouldn't mention Dom. I didn't want to keep him a secret, but I just didn't want to talk about him today.

Once I finished, Lena asked us all to move to the dining room. I was surprised when Declan sat next to me. I showed him the message.

"What do you think?" I asked after he read it.

"If he contacts you again, let me know right away."

I felt sick to my stomach. "You think he's got something?"

"I think Malcolm doesn't know when to back off. I've got it, Reese. Now come on, let's eat."

"Yeah. I'm starving."

We stayed at the house until early afternoon. God, it was amazing to run your own business. We could slow down on Fridays if we felt like it. It was four o'clock by the time I left.

Once I was in my car, I texted Dom.

Reese: Hey, lunch lasted a bit longer than I thought.

He didn't reply. I closed my eyes, enjoying the silence in my car. My screen lit up, and then my phone started vibrating. I answered immediately.

"Hey," I said.

"Hi," he replied. I loved that deep, sexy baritone voice. "How was lunch?"

"Absolutely delicious. And it was good catching up with the family."

"Was it a special occasion?"

I hesitated, then decided not to lay all the drama on him. "No, we just like to get together."

"You sound off. Is something wrong?"

I closed my eyes. "I realized something today."

"That sounds like it's going to be bad news."

My voice shook as I spoke. "Not necessarily. I just had a light bulb moment. Dating has been very hard for me since the breakup, and I think it's because I wasn't fully healed." I paused, trying to gather myself.

After a few seconds, he added, "Take your time, Reese."

I sighed. "I still don't know if I'm healed yet. And it's not that I have feelings for him. Nothing could be further from the truth. I just feel so empty inside. I'm not sure what I have left to give."

I tapped my fingers on the steering wheel.

"Reese, you've got a fucking lot to give. The fact that you doubt that is a crime. But I understand what you're saying."

"You do?"

"Yes. In a way, I'm in the same boat."

"Is that why you took pity on me and pretended to be my boyfriend that evening? Because you knew where I was coming from?"

"Yes. But also because I needed a good excuse to touch you, to be next to you."

I suddenly felt so awake, you'd think I'd just had three coffees. "What?"

"You heard me. The second I saw you—"

"You were annoyed as hell."

He chuckled. "That, too, but it was more than that. Something inside me told me I needed to be around you."

I sucked in a breath. "I'm not sure what to say."

"I don't think this will be easy, Reese, but I sure as hell am not going to give up."

And just like that, my heart filled with joy.

"No, that's not what I meant. I don't want to give up either."

"Good. Now, I have a question for you. Want to go away for the weekend?" he asked.

"Where?"

"I have a house near the lake. What do you think?"

"Yes." I didn't even hesitate.

Could this day be even more amazing? First the family rallied around me, and now I was going to spend some quality time with Dom. He didn't seem at all fazed about my revelation. Of course, he could always change his mind and run, but I didn't think he'd do that.

"Good. Then go home and pack. I can't wait to see you, Reese."

"I can't wait either."

I had a feeling the rest of the weekend was going to be epic. I might not be ready to explore what was left of my heart yet, but I was ready for whatever Dom had planned.

Chapter Seventeen

Dom

"Dom, can I have a word?" Charlene, my assistant, asked.

I glanced up from the screen of my computer. "Sure. I thought you'd gone."

Most of the employees left early on Fridays, an unspoken agreement we had since they worked their asses off all week.

"Someone has to work late," she said with humor, "but I'm actually glad I caught you when everyone else is gone."

"Why's that?"

"I wanted to talk to you about a delicate thing." She cleared her throat. "I got an email from Kelly yesterday."

I stilled completely. "What? Why would Kelly contact you?"

I hadn't communicated with my ex since we signed the divorce papers.

"She wants us to release the rights to some of the pictures she had done while she was modeling for us. I could just forward it to legal, but I thought I'd run it by you first."

"Give her whatever she wants. I don't care. I'm surprised she didn't bring it up in the divorce proceedings," I said.

"It's possible she didn't know she could do it, or maybe she forgot about it." She hesitated in the doorway.

"What is it, Charlene?"

"Maybe she just wants to get in touch with you."

"She wouldn't. Trust me."

"Oh, who knows? Maybe once she went out there in the big wild world, she realized what a moron she was for letting you slip away."

I started laughing.

Charlene smiled. "That's good. You're laughing again, boss. For a while there it looked like you forgot how."

"You know I like to keep it professional at the office."

"Yes, but there's a difference between that and looking like you're mourning or something. Although, I guess it would be fair to say you're mourning your marriage." She shrugged. "Anyway, that's all I had to say. I'm going."

"I'm coming too. I'm done with work."

"That's progress. You've got plans?"

"I do actually, yeah."

Her eyes widened. "Good for you. I'm not going to butt in, but I haven't seen this"—she pointed at my face—"in a long time, so whatever it is, I'm happy for you."

We hurried together to the elevator. I went down to the parking garage, stopping first at ground level for Charlene, who always rode in on her bike. I had no idea how some people biked year-round in Chicago—winters were brutal.

Kelly. I never wanted to hear her name again. I'd made that clear after the divorce. But I was determined to push her at the back of my mind. I'd promised Reese fun.

I'd been so focused on her and her ex that I'd never stopped to think about mine—about what would happen if my path ever crossed hers again. But that wasn't going to happen. Kelly and I had said everything there was to say, the parting, though messy, was agreed upon, and we were both relieved to be out of the marriage.

As I climbed inside my car, I was determined not to think of Kelly again. She was part of my past. My future was Kelly free, and I was only going to focus on Reese.

I went home and quickly packed a bag, then made a split-second decision to stop on the way, to buy her flowers.

"Hi. How can I help you?" the sales associate asked me when I stepped up to the counter.

"I want a bouquet. The biggest one you can make."

"Special occasion for you and the missus?"

I tensed. Why would she assume I was married? I didn't have a ring on my finger.

Her smile fell when she noticed my expression.

Damn, Dom. It's just a figure of speech. Get your shit together.

"I just want to make her smile," I said honestly.

"Wow. I don't think I've ever had a customer say that. So, do you know what you want in terms of flowers?"

"Give me something you'd like to receive."

She smiled. "What's the budget?"

"No budget."

"That's my kind of customer. Wait here."

It took her fifteen minutes to come back to the front, but I could instantly say it was worth it. I didn't have the first clue about flowers, but the bouquet looked great. There was a mixture of white and pink and something that looked to be between orange and pink.

"I used salmon-colored roses for accents," she explained.

That was the color. *Salmon*.

After paying and climbing back into my car, I raced through the city, hating that I was already late. But I knew in my gut that it would all be all worth it. I'd planned to surprise Reese by bringing the flowers to her doorstep, but she was already in front of the building with the biggest suitcase I'd ever seen next to her.

I stepped out of the car holding the flowers and watched her intently.

Her face only changed subtly at first—dimples appeared in her cheeks, and her eyes crinkled in the corners—but then she flashed me a huge smile. "Dom, those are amazing."

I handed them to her with a grin. "Surprise. Sorry I'm late."

"You can be late anytime you want if you show up with surprises like this." The bouquet was so big that she had to hold it with both hands. "They smell so good and look so pretty." Her eyes turned sad.

"Reese, what's wrong?"

"Absolutely nothing, you gorgeous, amazing man."

"Come on, let's go." I stared at her suitcase.

"The weather forecast is confusing, since it's supposed to be cold in the morning and evenings and warm throughout the day."

I quirked a brow. "So you packed everything you owned?"

She laughed. "No...I would have needed six suitcases for that."

I waited for the punchline, but there was none. She obviously owned a shit ton of clothes.

As I put the suitcase in the trunk of the car, she opened the back door, carefully setting the flowers on the back seat.

"They're so beautiful," she murmured. "I can't wait to put them in water."

"It's not far away. Just an hour's drive," I informed her when we were both in the car.

"How come you bought a house so close to the city?"

"I wanted something on the water without being crammed next to any neighbors."

"But why don't you live there full-time? It's not such a huge commute."

"I like to relax when I'm there. Back at the condo, I work a lot from home. I don't want any of that when I'm at the lake."

She nodded. "Duly noted. So the lake is just for relaxation?"

"Exactly!"

She glanced out the window, and I could see her reflection from the corner of my eye. She was smiling.

"How was your day?" she asked.

"Good. Productive." I had no idea what made me say it, but I found myself adding, "Until my assistant told me that my ex-wife wants us to give up the rights to some pictures of her."

"Oh." Reese was instantly on alert, her shoulders going up to her ears.

Damn, why did I have to bring it up?

I took her hand in mine, brushing her wrist with my thumb. "Don't worry. Sometimes models do that, wanting to monetize the photos themselves. I shouldn't have brought it up."

"No, I'm glad you're sharing things with me. I mean, I'm dumping all of my ex issues on you, after all."

She looked like she wanted to add something more but then cocked her head to one side, avoiding my gaze.

"So what does that mean? Are you going to see her again?" she asked after a moment.

"No. There's no need for that. Legal and HR can deal with it all. They just wanted to let me know."

"How do you feel about... I don't know... anything related to your ex?"

"Every time I talk about her, it leaves an unpleasant taste in my mouth. I keep waiting for that to fade away."

She laughed nervously. "Spoiler alert: it might never happen. Of course, it depends on how much trouble she causes, but in my experience, it only gets marginally better."

"Then let's talk about something else. Tell me about all the Christmas presents you bought for your family."

"Ha! That's going to take up the whole drive."

She wasn't kidding. By the time she finished telling me about the last gift—a makeup kit for Paisley, we arrived at the house. I entered the property slowly and looked at Reese. Her reaction didn't disappoint.

"Hey, you didn't tell me it would be all decorated." She was grinning ear to ear. Thank God the Christmas lighting looked tasteful and wasn't gawdy.

"I hired a company after you were at my condo. I'd planned to invite you here and figured you'd love it."

"This is incredible."

I was addicted to making her smile and loved to see her happy. It filled me with a sense of accomplishment unlike anything I'd ever felt before.

Part of it was that Reese appreciated things. She didn't expect anyone to do anything for her, so when I gave her something, like the flowers, her reaction was over-the-top, and I loved it.

She jumped out of the car and took a few steps toward the house. Then she turned on her heels and came back to the car, opening the back door and grabbing her flowers.

Chuckling, I went to the trunk, taking out our luggage.

"Come on, let's hurry up!" Clearly she couldn't wait. Her childlike enthusiasm was contagious.

She swung her hips slightly from left to right as we walked toward the house. I tried to look at it objectively and not be a scrooge. I'd always felt like decorations were a waste of effort, but maybe because of Reese's reaction, I now appreciated it. The whole place seemed more welcoming.

The company did a decent job. They'd put strings of white lights everywhere, and it really brightened up the outside.

I unlocked the front door and opened it. Reese gasped, and I followed her gaze immediately, wondering if there was any damage inside, a burst pipe or something.

But no, she was just reacting to the Christmas tree. Again, the company had done a decent job. They went for a mix of red and gold with white lights—classy and tasteful.

"I can't believe you told them to put up a tree. Most people would say it's far too early!"

I tried to suppress my laughter, but I couldn't.

She narrowed her eyes. "What?"

"I *am* one of those people. I didn't actually instruct them to do it. I think it might be part of the package. I must have overlooked that detail."

"This is a masterpiece. Can you give me the contact info for the company?"

"Sure. You want to use it for your place?"

She blinked as if I'd said the most obnoxious thing on the planet. "No! I'm decorating my own place. I've got tons of things that I've accumulated over the years. It's too personal to me, so I have to be the one to set everything up. But I want another option for the hotel. I wasn't thrilled with the company we used last year."

"Sure, I'll forward it to you."

She glanced out the window. "They put lights in the backyard too. Can we go explore them?"

I growled, stepping closer to her. "We will. Later. For now, I want to explore you."

She shifted in my arms, leaning against me. "Yes, sir. I'm at your service." Then she purred, "I'm all yours this weekend. You can do whatever you want with me for however long you want."

I felt a straining in my boxers and groaned. "Woman, don't say things like that to me before I feed you."

"First you brought me flowers, and now you want to feed me. This is shaping up to be one of the best weekends ever."

"I'm glad you think that."

Glancing around, she found a vase in the living room and put the flowers in it. Then she focused on the kitchen. "This is impressive."

"It came with the house. I thought it was too big at first, but now I like it."

"Don't we have to shop or something?"

"No, I had it fully stocked. Look in the fridge and tell me what looks good to you."

"You're cooking for me again, not just feeding me?"

"Why do you sound surprised?"

She shrugged as she went to the fridge.

I wrapped an arm around her, standing right behind her. "I'll do it often enough that you're not surprised anymore."

She sighed, sounding content. "I don't think I'll ever take that for granted." She opened the fridge door and whistled. "Wow, when you said it was stocked, I didn't realize you meant with this much food. I can't decide."

"Want me to surprise you?"

"That sounds great." She turned around to face me. "What's with the wicked smile?"

"You'll see later. You want to change into something more comfortable?" I asked, kissing her neck quickly.

She giggled, pushing her pelvis against me, and I barely held back another groan. This woman was going to be the death of me.

"I could, but I don't want to change because I'm dying to go explore everything outside."

I liked her priorities.

"How do you feel about steak and salad?" I suggested.

"Sounds delicious and fast."

Ten minutes later, I was cooking the steak while Reese was preparing the salad.

"Where are the bowls?" she asked.

"Not sure. I keep forgetting because I don't come here too often."

"I'll manage." She opened two cabinets, found a bowl, and then popped open the package, pouring the salad in.

Even the mundane act of cooking dinner was somehow fascinating with her next to me. She made the dressing out of balsamic vinegar, olive oil, and salt.

"I present to you Reese Maxwell's world-renowned signature dish: prepackaged salad."

I laughed. "I'll take it." Then, leaning into her, I said, "I'll take you."

She pressed the side of her hip lightly against mine.

"You're full of sass tonight," she murmured.

"I'm learning from the best."

We ate at the dining room table, sitting across from each other.

"It's so peaceful here, and I can imagine that the view is gorgeous in the morning. I don't think I'd ever go back to the city if I had this place," Reese admitted.

"Then why didn't you buy a home outside the city?"

She sighed. "I lied. I would go back because I like dropping by my cousins' homes now and again to see the kids."

I smirked. "But not your cousins?"

She smiled sheepishly. "Them, too, though lately I mostly ignore them when I'm at their places. It's just that... well, the little ones want my absolute attention when I'm there, and I'd feel bad not giving it to them. They're always so excited to tell me about whatever they've been up to. I like to know what's going on with them, especially the oldest one, Paisley."

I liked that she seemed genuinely interested in their lives. She didn't act like kids' stories bothered her.

"You're a great cook," she said after the first bite of steak. "Ever consider being a chef?"

"No. Dad always said his cooking skills were for the family, and I quite agree with him. I don't think I'd have half the fun I do when cooking if I had to do it professionally."

"It's like me with Christmas decorations. I like to do it for myself but not for the hotel. Gran actually asked me to help her at her house this year, which is bittersweet."

"How so?" I asked, taking a mouthful of salad.

"I'm always happy to decorate, but it also means she knows she can't do it by herself anymore. She didn't come out and say it, but I can read between the lines." She groaned. "Damn, I was starving, and I didn't even know it. I didn't eat too much at my aunt's for lunch," Reese said, shoving in yet another mouthful of steak.

We were completely silent for a few minutes while we downed our food. Reese kept looking over her shoulder, glancing out the window.

"We can go outside now," I said, barely keeping from bursting out laughing.

"I can wait until you're done, or if you want to have, I don't know, dessert or something?"

I shook my head. "We can have the dessert once we come back."

"What is it?"

"It's frozen tiramisu. I'll get it out of the freezer before we go."

"Sure, take your time."

She put on her coat while I took the box out of the freezer, setting it in the sink, then grabbed my jacket.

Chapter Eighteen
Dom

Reese bounced up and down on her toes by the door. "Do you have a back door, or are we going through the front?"

"Let's go through the back," I said. There was a small trail, paved with stones, running from the back door all the way down to the lake.

"This place is truly beautiful," Reese said once we were outside.

For a few seconds, we were both silent, only the sound of our breaths filling the air. I took her hand, leading her down the trail. The decoration company had wrapped strings of lights around a few trees, and it looked great.

"I bet every time you're here with friends, it's a party."

"I don't really invite friends over here."

"Then why bring me?" she murmured.

"Because I wanted to share this with you." I actually wanted to share more with her than I was comfortable to admit. It posed a conundrum even to me.

Deciding not to dwell on it, I kissed her hard. I was hungry for her. Her cheeks were already cold, and her mouth was warm, soft, and inviting. She moaned, parting her lips and giving me even more access, but it wasn't enough. Nothing ever felt enough with her. No matter how much she gave, I always needed more.

I deepened the kiss, but she pulled back a fraction of an inch, then yelped. I didn't realize what was going on until I noticed that she was leaning back and didn't seem to have her balance.

Immediately, I realized we were both falling. I reached forward out of instinct to the nearest tree and grabbed a branch, but it was more of a twig. Reese and I both went down. The twig cracked, and we fell with a thump.

She burst out laughing. I started laughing, too, but propped myself up on an elbow. Half my body was covering hers.

"Are you hurt? Did you hit your head?" I asked.

"No, I have good reflexes. I didn't realize it was so slick."

"Neither did I." The ground was frozen. We hadn't gotten any snow yet, but the temperatures had dropped to freezing at night.

"Oh, Chicago, why don't you bless us with snow, at least, if you have this god-awful freezing temperature?" She gasped. "What happened to the lights?"

I followed her gaze. The lights in the tree next to us were off.

"I probably pulled something when I tried to steady us," I admitted.

Sure enough, the string was broken where the twig snapped.

Reese pouted. "I'm sorry for hurting your tree."

"Fuck, you're adorable. And freezing," I said in a stronger voice, realizing her teeth were chattering. "Let's go back inside."

"But we're not done exploring."

I helped her up to her feet and cupped her face. "You're cold. I don't want you to get sick. We have plenty of time to look around tomorrow. Come on, I'll warm you up."

"Okay." She covered my hands with hers, which were quite cold.

"You don't have gloves?" I asked.

"No, but I have your sexy warm hands, so what would I need gloves for?" she asked playfully.

We hurried inside the house. She didn't take off her coat immediately, and her cheeks were really red.

"Sure you didn't hurt your head?" I double-checked.

"No, but I'm cold, and I can't believe I'm saying this, but I don't think I can eat that tiramisu."

"True, that's not going to help with the cold. Let's get you out of that coat. Some skin-on-skin contact will help."

I took off her coat and noticed her teeth were still chattering. I kissed her cheek, then down to the lobe of her ear, tugging at it.

Her body language instantly changed, going from tense to relaxed. When I put a hand at the small of her back, she arched slightly. I sealed my mouth over hers, and I wasn't gentle about it. I couldn't be—I'd been waiting for this moment for days. I took both her hands in mine, keeping them in place, just transferring my body heat to hers.

"I'm getting warmer," she whispered.

I kissed her again, then took off my coat, wanting to be even closer to her. She smelled delicious. I had no idea what it was—a mix of some floral scent—but it made me think of her.

I took a step back.

"No, why? Come closer." She tugged at my shirt.

"Let's go to the bedroom before I completely lose my mind and forget where we are."

Fuck, am I panting? I was a complete caveman with her.

"Okay."

Taking her hand, I led her upstairs.

"Let's go to the bathroom first. I think a shower will warm you up," I suggested.

"As I said, I'm yours to do whatever you want," she teased, and my cock twitched. She knew exactly how to get me going, and I loved it.

The bathroom had a huge walk-in shower that had always seemed too big until now. I turned on the hot water even though we were still fully clothed. I wanted the whole bathroom to steam up so she'd get warm in no time. Then I turned to her and grabbed the hem of her sweater, pulling it over her head. She was only wearing a bra underneath. No wonder she was freezing.

She looked so damn sexy here in my bathroom. I needed to explore her. But I had her for the whole weekend, so I could take my time with everything.

I threw her sweater somewhere on the floor, and then she pulled mine over my head. We were desperate for each other. I yanked her jeans down next, and she almost lost her balance before gripping my hair with one hand and placing the other on my shoulder. She was wearing matching panties. On instinct, I turned her around and nearly lost it. She barely had a string of fabric between her ass cheeks. I kissed the right one and then the left.

"Ohhhh," she moaned, her voice shaking.

I undid the button of my jeans, pushing them down with both hands while I drew my mouth in a straight line upward on her left ass cheek, then moved downward on her right one. She gasped at the contact, leaning forward and grabbing the edge of the shower. There was enough steam in the bathroom now that her skin had warmed up.

I flipped her around, looking up at her while my cock bobbed between us. "Take off your bra," I instructed.

She nodded, reaching behind her back to undo the clasp and then tossing the bra to the side. At the same time, I pulled down her panties, letting them fall to her ankles. I parted her legs with one hand, and she leaned back against the shower glass.

"It's still a bit cold," she muttered, then she moaned when I put my mouth straight on her clit without any warning. "Dom!"

I licked around her clit once before moving my tongue down, pushing it inside her. She tilted her hips forward so I could lick her better and rested her head on the glass, dropping it slightly back as I kept pushing my tongue in and out. Feeling a light tremor in her thighs, I ran my hands up and down her legs from under her ass cheeks all the way down to her ankles, then back up again.

I liked watching her body transform. I couldn't stop touching her. I'd be a happy man if I got to spend the rest of my life right here with my mouth between her thighs, pleasing her.

When her tremors intensified, I decided to change tactics. I brought one hand between her thighs and took my mouth off her, kissing upward in a straight line.

"Dom," she protested.

"Don't worry, Reese. I'll make you come with my hand, but I want to watch you up close when you do."

She clenched around my fingers as I moved them with precision, alternating between pressing the heel of my hand on her clit and rubbing her G-spot with my middle and index fingers.

She called out my name. Damn, she was so close, but I wasn't in a hurry.

I kissed up her body, feeling every vibration. I straightened up when I felt her clench tight around me. With my other hand, I sustained her weight so she could simply enjoy the orgasm.

Putting both hands on my chest, she pushed her head against the shower glass with so much force that I took a step back. I wanted to feel the vibrations of her moans against my mouth, but in the end, I was content to simply train my eyes on her face and watch it change. She gave herself to the pleasure with complete abandon before flashing me a sated smile.

"That's the best way to warm me up," she murmured.

"Oh yeah," I agreed.

I removed my clothes in the time it took her to step under the spray and change the water temperature to whatever she preferred.

"Now that's better."

I joined her under the water, and she poured my shower gel into her palms, then gestured for me to move away from the stream. She began spreading the gel on my shoulders and my chest. Her hand glided down until she reached my erection.

"Just a bit more soap," she teased, rubbing me with both hands.

Fuck, this feels good. I grinned, moving back and forth, pushing in and out of her fist. The friction was insane, but it was no match for her pussy.

"Reese, I need you," I said.

"I need you too," she whispered, letting go of me.

I guided us back under the water so it washed away the soap, then pushed her farther until her back was against the tiles. She was far too small for me to be able to fuck her while standing, but I had a solution to that.

Resting her hands on top of my arms, I lifted her into the air and then lowered her onto my erection. She was so damn wet that I didn't even need to take it slow.

She cried out, pressing her knees into my waist. "This feels so good. How can it be so intense?"

"I don't know," I admitted. "It's so damn good."

I couldn't say anything more, couldn't put it into words, but I could show her exactly how she made me feel.

I carefully placed her against the wall so I was at a good distance to allow free movement, then turned off the water—we didn't need it anymore. There was so much steam in the bathroom that I could barely breathe or see her, but I could feel her, and it was exquisite.

She held on to me and tightly pressed her fingers into my chest before running her hands up to my shoulders. She cried out in pleasure and then sighed in frustration.

"I want to move even more," she whispered. "I need it."

"Your wish is my command, babe."

I knew exactly what she meant. She didn't have enough leverage and couldn't hold on properly to anything except me, so I carried her out of the shower.

I grabbed a few towels but didn't stop to pat us dry; I was far too gone for that. I led us to the master bedroom. Still deep in her, I felt her contract around me on every step, which was a new sensation altogether. I threw the towels on the bed so we could lie on them.

"How clever," she murmured. "I wondered what you were going to do with those."

I lowered her to her feet. "Turn around, beautiful, and show me that gorgeous ass."

She swallowed hard before twirling.

"Now bend over."

She gasped but did as I said, climbing onto the bed on all fours.

I positioned myself so my cock was right at her entrance, then slowly pushed in all the way.

"Fuck!"

I groaned.

My whole body burned. She was so damn tight. Her muscles pulsed and then clenched down completely, making her tighter still.

"Reese," I growled.

"I'm so close."

I nearly came when I felt her fingers at the side of my cock. She was touching her clit. I was so lost in her that I hadn't even realized it.

I pushed in harder and harder, thrusting in and out. I wasn't even sure who came first. One second, I felt my body burn and my vision darken, and the next, Reese was crying out, shaking, and her inner muscles tightened around me. She arched her back and then lowered her forehead to the sheets, pressing into them.

I wanted to tell her not to hide, but instead, I came hard. I wanted her to hear me, too, to know what she was doing to me. I was giving her this power. I wanted her to have the key to my body.

"I don't think I can kneel much longer," she whimpered.

"Lie down, beautiful," I said.

She moved as I pulled out of her, her smile was even wider than before. I liked seeing this sated expression on her face.

I sat down next to her, putting a hand on her belly. "You all right?"

"I want to put it all in a sentence, but I'm not sure how everything feels." She made a movement with her hand that was completely incomprehensible to me, but judging by her smile, I'd done well. She blinked her eyes open, dropping her head back. "You know what? I'm so hot right now that I could even eat some of that frozen tiramisu."

I started to laugh. "I think it's thawed some by now, but I like where your mind went."

She smiled sheepishly. "I started thinking about it when we were in the shower."

I growled. "I was buried inside you, and you were thinking about dessert?"

"Just a bit, really. You were occupying most of my brain."

I took my hand off her, then kissed her belly. "Stay right here."

First, I headed to the bathroom to get a wet cloth, wiping myself off, then went to attend to Reese. Afterward, I hurried to the kitchen and grabbed the container and two spoons, bringing everything to bed.

Pride swelled in my chest when I realized Reese had indeed followed my command. She hadn't moved at all and was still splayed out on the towels.

Her eyes zeroed in on the box I was holding. I put it between us on the bed. She immediately took a spoonful. "Mm. This is good. And just so I know, in case I get cold, you'll warm me up again?"

"You can count on that," I assured her.

She frowned. "Aren't you going to eat?"

"I am. But I want you to lie down first."

"Why?"

"I'll eat it off you."

She giggled and lay down on the bed, pressing her lips together.

I smeared the tiramisu around her navel and then licked it up. She rolled her pelvis, and though I knew exactly what she needed, I was going to tease her some more first. I moved to her nipples, smearing the left and then the right one before drawing my tongue around each one slowly, torturing her.

"Dom," she murmured.

"I told you I want to explore you, Reese. And I intend to do it all night long."

Chapter Nineteen

Reese

The next day, I seriously had to fight the urge to pinch myself. I'd thought last night was fantastic, but today was even more so. It was by no means beautiful outside—the fog was thick on the lake—but Dom had started the electric fireplace.

"This is so cozy," I said, making myself comfortable on the love seat. At least that was what I called it, as it was the shorter arm of the L-shaped couch. It could comfortably fit two people lying next to each other.

Dom sat right behind me, placing his legs on the outer sides of mine. I pushed my hair to one side as he kissed the back of my neck.

I could feel my entire body relaxing even though I had so much going on. I hadn't heard from Declan in regard to Malcolm, but I was trying not to think about it.

"What happened?" he asked against my skin.

"What?" I asked.

"You tensed up all of a sudden."

"I just have a lot of tension gathered right here." I pointed to a spot just below where he'd kissed me before.

I didn't want to tell him what was going on with Malcolm. This weekend was too beautiful to ruin it with any talk of him. Besides, Dom couldn't do anything about it.

"Is that just a trick to make me touch you here?"

I giggled. "I didn't know I needed any tricks."

"You don't." He tugged my pajama top down until it reached the middle of my back, then kissed a straight line from the base of my neck down to where the fabric covered skin. My center pulsed on each kiss.

"I love this. I can practically feel every muscle relaxing. Why am I wasting my time with professional massages when I can just get you to kiss me?"

"That's right. Every time you need it, just let me know."

I grinned. "Really? What will you do? Pop up at the office?"

"Don't put it past me. I'm at your beck and call."

He doesn't mind possibly running into my family?

"You're doing that thing again," he said, putting a hand on my belly and kissing back up my neck. "You're thinking about something that makes you tense."

I turned around, narrowing my eyes. "Can you read minds or something?"

"No, but I can read your body."

"And what is it telling you?"

He lowered his gaze. "Right now? That you already want me."

I looked down, curious as to what he was seeing. My top had shifted a bit, and my nipples were visible and peeking out.

"You're touching me and kissing me. Nothing I can do about that."

He put two fingers under my chin, pressing his lips to mine. "No, but *I* can."

"I bet," I replied. "And it is the perfect day for this, isn't it? What terrible weather. Thank goodness we went exploring last night."

"I could still show you the house."

I frowned. "I already saw it."

"You didn't see the basement. I think you're going to enjoy it."

I scrunched my nose. "Basements aren't my favorite places. They're dark and creepy."

He kissed my temple. "Not this one. Tell me when you want to explore."

"You've made me curious, so I want to see it now."

He took my hand and led me to the door that led to the basement. I couldn't imagine I'd like it more than the living room.

But I was wrong. It wasn't really a basement because it had a window overlooking the garden. It was much smaller than the one in the living room, of course, but it wasn't at all cave-like. It had a spa and sauna, a whirlpool, and even a gym.

I sighed as I took it all in. "I don't think I'll go back. You can just leave me here to be the house sitter or something."

He grinned, taking me in his arms from behind. I loved when he randomly hugged me—it made me feel safe, and that wasn't a sensation I was familiar with.

"We can come back here next weekend if you want to, Reese."

Not only did he make me feel safe but also happy.

I turned around, moving my hands up his arms to his shoulders. "I want to test out everything: the gym, the sauna, and the whirlpool. Although, I didn't bring a bathing suit."

"That's not a problem."

I raised a brow. "Are you trying to talk me into skinny-dipping?"

"You're the one who brought it up."

"True. Hmm. What to start with first? Maybe the gym."

"You have workout clothes with you?" he asked.

I rolled my eyes. "Duh. Have you seen my luggage? I packed everything I thought could come in handy—except a bathing suit, since I figured it would be too cold to swim. How about you?"

"I run in the morning, so I brought my sneakers."

"I like working out, but watching you while I do it would be extra motivation," I said.

The gym was small—a few weight stations, a cross-trainer, a treadmill, and a rowing machine—but it was more than enough.

"Come on, let's go upstairs and grab our things."

Half an hour later, he was running on the treadmill, and I went on the cross-trainer. It was perfectly positioned so I had a good view of him and the outdoors.

This was the happiest day I'd had in a long time. I loved watching Dom sweat on the treadmill, and it was motivating me to do the same.

After finishing my cardio, I went to the mat and did my Pilates sequence while he moved to the ab bench and then to the weights. The latter was definitely my favorite—those delicious muscles practically pumped up from the effort. After finishing my routine, I lay down and propped up on my elbows, watching him.

"Enjoying the show?" he asked with a grin as he sat up straight on the weight bench.

"Yep, and I'm not even sorry."

"Are you done?" he asked.

"Yes, but I don't even have the energy to get up."

He walked toward me at a lazy pace. Yum. I never found sweaty men appealing, but Dom definitely was. He extended both hands to me. I first gave him the left one and then the right, and he pulled me to my feet.

We showered in the bathroom he had downstairs. It was small, so we had to take turns, and there was no room for any sexy activity.

While Dom washed up, I stood in the shower door. Every time he turned around, I squeezed his ass. I heard him laugh in between the sound of water spilling all over the place.

After he turned off the faucet and faced me, he made to move forward, but I stepped back quickly.

"So this isn't a two-way street, huh?" he asked.

"No, not at all. It's an all-you-can-eat buffet for me, but not for you."

"And why is that?"

"Because if you fondle me, we might end up back in bed."

"I'm good with that."

I looked around. "I want to test the rest of the stuff first."

"Then let's get in the sauna," he said.

He'd turned it on before we'd started working out, so it was smoking hot when we stepped inside. I wrapped my towel around myself so my skin wasn't in contact with the wood.

"Can I put some of this water on the coals?" I asked. There was a bucket of water next to the fake coals. Spraying them would get some humidity in the air.

"Sure. You can even put some essential oils in the water, too, if you want to. They're on the shelf right outside."

"Do you have any preference?" I asked him.

"No. Choose whatever you want, Reese."

I picked the one labeled Pine and put a few drops in the basket before setting the little bottle back outside.

"I'll pour the water," he insisted. "It's hot, and I don't want you to burn yourself."

"Okay." Honestly, I didn't think I would burn myself, but I liked that he was so protective of me.

The second the water fell on the coals, heat filled the room, and the smell was absolutely amazing.

I inhaled deeply, then sighed. "I love this. The scent of pine is relaxing."

He sat down next to me, smiling brilliantly. "I'm glad you're having a good time."

"I am. How long do you think we'll be able to take the heat?" I asked.

"Probably five minutes."

"Okay."

Three minutes later, I practically burst out the door, as did Dom.

"That was intense," I exclaimed.

We were both red and sweating.

"You know, in Northern Europe, they go outside and take a swim in cold water after going in the sauna," he said.

"Um, no thanks. I hate the cold."

"I thought you might say that."

"Let's take another shower, shall we? Just to wash off the sweat. I promise I'll keep my hands off you." I winked at him.

"Mm, we'll see."

I moved my hips in an exaggerated manner right before a ripping sound filled the air. A second later, I realized he'd yanked off my towel.

I gasped, looking at him over my shoulder. "Give a girl some warning."

I hurried to the shower, turning it on. Even though the stall was tiny, he stepped inside with me and kissed me deeply. He immediately moved his hands toward my ass, fondling it, and this time I didn't stop him. This weekend was amazing, and I didn't want it to end.

Chapter Twenty

Reese

On Sunday afternoon, I was a bit melancholic as we drove back to Chicago.

"Can you drop me off at The Happy Place?" I asked.

"You go by there every Sunday?"

I blinked, trying to understand the question. "You mean because I went there after the charity weekend? No. My grandma was there that day, and today, too, along with my sister. I don't want to miss all the fun. Gran is trying out a new thing this year. She wants to sell cocoa and treats, starting from now until the end of February."

"That's not a bad idea."

"I think it's good for her to keep busy. I bet this was Kimberly's idea. Gran is also baking cookies. She loves doing that. My sister and I will probably take turns keeping an eye on her so she doesn't overwork herself. Though John is very good at it. And Travis is already on it as well."

He laughed. "Is everything a group effort?"

"Mostly, yes."

He put the address in the navigation system as we entered the city, since we were coming from a different direction than last time. I wasn't ready to say goodbye to him, though. These two days had been incredible. I'd never experienced this ease and fun with anyone before.

When we arrived, I instructed him to pull the car onto a side street from the hotel where it was less busy.

"I'll get your bag," he said once he'd turned off the engine.

With a sigh, I got out of the car. By the time I reached the trunk, he'd already unloaded the luggage.

"Which way is the entrance to The Happy Place?" he asked.

"You don't have to roll it over there for me. I can do it."

He stared at me. "I'd like to say hello to your grandmother and your sister."

Is that a grin on my face? Yes, it is.

"Okay, just let me grab the flowers from the back seat."

"Why did you want to take them with you?"

"Because the bouquet is amazing, and it would have just gone to waste at the house. Besides, I have plans for it." I wanted to let the flowers dry properly so I could save them. I'd already started watching a YouTube tutorial for it. It was more complicated than it seemed. I kept them in my arms while Dom wheeled my luggage.

We'd moved the entrance of The Happy Place to the side of the building once we opened the hotel. There was a long line in front of the door.

"Wow," I exclaimed. "I think Gran's on to something with her cocoa."

Several of the potential customers were giving us the side-eye.

"We're staff," I said as we unceremoniously cut the line, pushing the door open and walking inside.

The line continued to the counter where Kimberly was serving hot cocoa. Next to her, Gran was manning the cash register. John was in the background as well, unpacking some plastic cups. I loved that he supported Gran in all things.

"What's going on?" I asked.

"The two sales associates came down with the flu," Gran explained.

"'Tis the season," Kimberly said, and then she froze. "Dominic! I was wondering when I would get to meet you." She pressed her lips together, looking sideways at Gran, who waved at Dom.

"Hey, we'll be with you in a minute. Or an hour, depending how long it takes for this line to end."

"Gran, I already asked for reinforcements," Kimberly told her.

"Who's coming?" I asked quickly. I didn't want Dom to feel overwhelmed.

"Travis. He's already at the hotel to catch up on some work. And Declan said he'd drop by."

I turned around to Dom. "You don't have to wait around for my cousins. We're going to have our hands full here trying to sort this out."

"Trying to keep me a secret from the rest of them?" he asked playfully.

I cleared my throat. "No, but they can be a bit much."

"Not for me. I promise they're not. Besides, since I'm here, I think you can use my muscle too."

"Excellent!" Gran exclaimed. "John, stop working for a minute and meet Dominic."

John turned around, extending his hand. Dom shook it. "Nice to meet you, Dom. Beatrice, I'm going in the back to sort out more of the supplies."

"Oh, you don't need to do that on your own."

He kissed her forehead. "Yes, I do. Enjoy the family."

Gran didn't argue, and I sighed as he left. They were adorable.

"So, what can we do?" I asked.

Kimberly surreptitiously reached for her phone, and I instantly moved next to my sister. The customer standing in front of her was already giving me the side-eye. I didn't want to be rude, but if I didn't stop Kimberly, she'd get the whole family here.

"I'll take that," I said, grabbing her phone.

"Why did you do that?"

"Because if I don't, you're liable to tell the whole family that Dom is here."

Kimberly winced, and the customer in front of us started laughing. Obviously, I hadn't been as discreet as I thought.

"I *might* have been about to do that. But now that you've told me not to, can I have my phone back?"

Reluctantly, I handed it to her. "When are Declan and Travis coming?"

"Travis is walking through the door right now."

I lifted my head just in time to see him saunter in—and head straight to Dom. No "Hello" or "How are you doing?" He simply offered his hand and said, "Travis Maxwell. I don't believe we've met."

"No, we haven't. I'm Dominic Waldorf."

Recognition flickered in Travis's eyes. In a fraction of an instant, I joined them.

"Hello, cousin!"

"Hey," he said, still looking at Dominic. "How long has this been going on?"

I groaned. "Travis! A word?"

"Yeah, I'm listening."

"In private," I emphasized.

He finally glanced at me, narrowing his eyes. *What's his deal?* "Sure. It was nice meeting you, Dominic."

"Likewise." I heard the sarcastic undertone in Dom's voice, and I couldn't blame him.

I took Travis to the back.

"What are you doing?" I asked once we were alone.

"I want to know what's going on between the two of you."

"Yeah, I figured that. But can you be more subtle about it? We met the night of the charity event. He did me a favor."

"Christ, I don't need *that* many details."

"Not a sexual favor!" Good God, my cousins could drive me nuts. "Why would you even think that? You know what? Never mind, I don't want to know," I said. "Anyway, I ran into Malcolm there, as I told you. Dom pretended to be my boyfriend."

Travis's eyes bulged. "He what? Why?"

"Because Malcolm was being an ass. One thing led to another, and now we're not faking it anymore."

My cousin's expression changed instantly, going from belligerent to relieved. "Well, that earns him points. Now come on, let's get back before Gran scares him away."

"Yeah, I don't think Gran's the problem here," I said sarcastically.

My jaw dropped when we got back to the front. Kimberly and Dom were both behind the counter now, pouring hot cocoa into cups.

"Travis, Dom, Reese, please serve the hot cocoa to everyone waiting, and Kimberly and I will process payments. It'll be faster this way," Gran said.

That seemed like a good plan to me, so I jumped right into my new role.

"How come there's a line?" Dominic asked. I couldn't believe he was just rolling up his proverbial sleeves along with the rest of us.

"I asked Kimberly to post on the Facebook page that we're serving cocoa," Gran explained. "It's a real draw."

We put the cocoa on trays that Kimberly had prepped already and started going outside to give everyone a cup. Travis, Dom, and I worked side by side until everyone had their drinks, and then we headed back in.

"You're a good sport for doing this, Dominic," Travis said.

"Sure, no problem. I've passed this place many times but haven't been inside the store or the hotel."

"Want to come upstairs and have a drink at the bar once we finish here?"

Dom narrowed his eyes infinitesimally. I'd bet he was wondering why Travis suddenly wanted to bond.

"That's a great idea," Kimberly said, clearly having overheard us. Then again, we were only a few steps away from the register area.

Gran had been right. Now that she and Kimberly didn't have to pour hot cocoa, everything was going smoother.

"But I don't think I'll be able to join you. Someone has to stay down here with Gran," my sister added.

"Nonsense," Gran said. "I can deal with everything. You youngsters go have fun."

"What do I need to do?" Declan's voice came from behind us, startling us. The door had opened and closed so often that I hadn't been paying attention to who was coming in.

He promptly stopped when he noticed Dominic.

Oh, here we go again.

"Declan, this is Dominic Waldorf," I said. "Dom, this is my cousin Declan."

They shook hands. Declan looked straight at me but didn't ask anything.

Surely that can't be right. Declan always jumps to the worst conclusion, yet he isn't even going to ask why Dominic is here?

Then I realized why he was on his best behavior. He nodded toward Kimberly, who gave him a thumbs-up. My sister had obviously warned him. Good for her. I needed to give her more credit.

"All right," Gran said. "I stand by what I said. You all can go upstairs to the bar."

"Yeah, get out," Kimberly ordered. "I'll join you as soon as we close, okay?" The Happy Place was only open another half hour.

"Gran, how are you getting home?" Travis asked.

"John and I came together in the car."

"All right, then. Kimberly, Gran, are you sure you can handle all of this?" Declan asked.

"Yes," Kimberly insisted. "Go ahead and ask Tom to make you a margarita. We have a new recipe that's a big hit with customers."

I turned to Dom. "Can you stay, or do you have other plans?"

"I'll stay."

"Okay then, let's go," Travis said.

Declan was still sizing up Dom as I grabbed the luggage he'd put in a corner, along with the bouquet of flowers. I did that as a strategic move so everyone could see them. Both of my cousins immediately noticed the bouquet, and I knew Dom had earned another point in their books.

"You're taking this upstairs too?" Dom asked, pointing at the bag.

"Yeah. We have connecting elevators, so when I leave, I won't come through the bookstore again. It'll be closed anyway. Ready?"

"Yes. I've been meaning to try the bar for some time."

He put an arm around my shoulders as we all headed toward the elevator in the back.

"Where were you?" Declan asked. His tone wasn't exactly hard, but it had a familiar edge to it.

"Reese and I spent time at my weekend house on the lake," Dom replied.

The fact that he had whisked me away earned him another point, I was sure of that.

Maybe they won't scare him away after all.

Chapter Twenty-One

Reese

"Let's grab a drink," Declan said once we were upstairs.

The guys went to our usual table, but I hurried to the bar to place our order. Tom had his hands full with customers, but as soon as he saw me, he nodded in acknowledgment.

A few seconds later, he came over. "I noticed a gentleman who hasn't been here before."

Tom had been with us since we opened the hotel. Though he was past the retiring age, he insisted he couldn't stay home after his wife passed away and spent an inordinate amount of time at the hotel, even when he wasn't on shift. He knew everything that went on here, including the fact that I'd been single as hell for the past years.

"Yes, he's my date. Can you bring us drinks that will keep my cousins from being a royal pain in the ass? Kimberly said something about a new margarita recipe"

"I'm on it."

"Thanks, Tom. You're a lifesaver," I said before heading back to the table.

"I have no intentions—" Dom was saying, and I almost tripped over my own feet at his words, effectively cutting him off.

I cleared my throat, jumping onto one of the high bar chairs. "Please tell me you didn't ask Dom what his intentions are about me."

Declan stared at me. "No, I asked him if Waldorf Fashion intends to open more stores in Chicago. But I was getting to that too."

Ground, please swallow me whole.

Travis started to laugh, and Dom grabbed my hand under the table. Declan was laughing too.

"Can we forget the last minute happened and move on?" I crossed and uncrossed my legs, trying to release some of my nervous energy.

Dom kissed the side of my head before whispering in my ear. "You're adorable, Reese. Relax, we're just having a drink."

I didn't know how to relax. I hadn't introduced them to anyone I'd dated these past few years, so this was completely uncharted territory for me. I kept waiting for something to go awry.

"So, Dom," Declan said after we got our drinks, "I heard through the grapevine that you offered to be Reese's date the first time you met her."

"News travels fast in your family," Dom replied.

"Now, far from me to be a skeptical person—" Declan began.

"He *is* a very skeptical person," I interjected.

"—but that makes me suspicious. Why would you do that?" he finished.

Dom stood straighter. "Malcolm was being an asshole, and even though I didn't know Reese at all, no one deserves to be talked to like that. And she'd already given me the rundown of what went wrong between them."

"Why?" Declan asked.

"That's between Reese and me," Dom replied.

I swallowed hard. He was a gentleman for not mentioning my meltdown in the coatroom.

"All right, fair enough," Declan said. "Let's cheers again."

"To what are we toasting?" I asked.

"Strange beginnings?" Travis suggested.

"Oh, that does fit."

I kept glancing at the flowers I'd set on one of the empty chairs around the table. This was really happening. I was here with Dom and my cousins, and we were having fun.

Twenty minutes later, Kimberly joined us too. We stayed at the bar for two more hours before I called it a night.

"Guys, I have to unpack, and I want to be at work early tomorrow morning."

"And I told Bonnie I'd be home for dinner," Travis said.

"Do you need a ride?" Declan asked me.

"I'm driving Reese," Dom said, immediately putting a hand on my upper back.

Was I silly for enjoying this so much? I had a man who brought me flowers and was now going to drive me home. My life was good.

Half an hour later, when Dom pulled the car in front of my building, I had to come to terms with the fact that the weekend was officially ending. As he rolled the suitcase into my apartment, my phone vibrated in the pocket of my coat. Just as we stepped inside, I took it out, thinking it was probably from my sister or one of my cousins, maybe even Gran.

I hadn't expected it to be from Malcolm.

I froze, unable to do anything else but read it. I'd deleted his number. Actually, I'd probably blocked it, but he'd obviously gotten a new one.

I wanted to talk to you, not Declan.
Malcolm

He'd signed off with his name, as if I wouldn't possibly know who it was from.

"Reese?" Dom asked, and I immediately put the phone back into my pocket before looking up at him. He was staring at the spot where I'd been holding the phone before. "What was that?"

"Nothing. Just a message."

"From whom?"

"I... It doesn't matter."

"Then why are you nervous?"

I ran my hand through my hair. "I don't know. Because it's... Just forget about it, okay? It's a message."

"It was from Malcolm. I saw the text, Reese."

Shit. "Yes, it was."

"And you still don't want to tell me what it's about?"

I drew in a deep breath. "No. I honestly don't feel like talking about it."

"You didn't tell me you were still in contact with him."

"I'm not. He just messaged me out of the blue."

"Look at me and tell me you haven't heard from him at all until now."

I narrowed my eyes. "Why are you reacting like this?"

"Because I'm starting to feel like a moron. Do you need defending from him, or are you planning on getting back together? Or did you already get back with him, and I'm just your side piece?"

***Dom

I didn't want to believe it, but I also couldn't kid myself. The proof was right in front of me. She'd been so guarded, so careful to hide it from me.

"What the hell?" she exclaimed. "Why would you say that?"

"Because of your reaction."

She crossed her arms. "So even after the weekend we had, this is the conclusion you're jumping to?"

"What do you want me to think, Reese? You're obviously in contact with him, and you don't want me to know."

"So one plus one equals fifty? Well, if that's what you think, then you're welcome to walk out the door."

Just leave, Dom. You can't fall for another woman playing you. Have you learned nothing?

Her eyes turned glassy as she continued to glare at me.

Fuck. This isn't right. This isn't Reese. Why am I being such an asshole?

But she was acting so cagey. In my experience, it was never a good thing.

"Reese, if I'm wrong here—"

"*If?* God, I can't believe you! Just leave, okay?"

"Tell me I'm wrong. God, I want to be wrong."

"Yes, you're fucking wrong! You're so off base, you're not even in the same zip code as what's happening."

I stepped right in front of her. "Then talk to me, Reese. Tell me why he's been messaging you and why you don't want me to know."

She drew in a deep breath. "Because I didn't want to drag you into the drama with Malcolm. Clearly I was right to do so, because if you react like this just because I'm not telling you about the message, then obviously we're not as close as I'd hoped we were."

"Reese, you know that's not true. This weekend was amazing."

She swallowed hard. "Then why are you behaving like this?"

I took another step back. I couldn't find the right words, and they were essential right now. Reese was right on the edge; if I said the wrong thing, I was going to lose her.

"Because the last time a woman kept secrets from me, my life imploded. That's all I've got. Literally. I apologize for reacting like that, but I don't have anything else to say in my defense. I just saw you keeping secrets, and I jumped to the worst conclusion."

Reese was completely still for a few seconds. I knew this was a defining moment for us.

"I want to know what's happening in your life, Reese. Judging by what I've seen and heard about Malcolm up to this point, this can't be good news."

"Yet you thought I was trying to get back with him? It's like you don't know me at all!"

I dipped my head in acknowledgment. "Again, I apologize. I should have known better."

"Yes, you should have." She nodded, and I had the impression that she was having a silent conversation with herself. "Fine, I'll tell you what's going on." She fiddled with her thumbs. "It wasn't how I wanted to end this weekend. I was hoping to go out on a high note, but I think keeping secrets isn't going to work." She still sounded a bit stiff, but I couldn't blame her. I *had* acted like a complete ass, after all.

We took off our coats and shoes as Reese said, "I'm going to make myself a drink. Do you want something?"

"No."

"Actually, I changed my mind. It's better to get it over with." She sat down on her couch, and I sat next to her. "He texted me a while ago. He said he's going to come after me and my family, that we killed the deal he'd organized to open the spa because we wanted to open the hotel. I'm not getting into all the legal stuff right now because I don't understand half of it. I'm good with numbers, not the law. Declan is on top of it."

"Why didn't you tell me about it?"

She straightened up, rolling her shoulders back. "Because it's *my* drama. *My* baggage."

"I'm dating you. I want to know everything that goes on with you, the good things and the drama. And the baggage."

"Why? So you can jump to the worst conclusions?"

I took one of her hands between mine. "I swear to you that it'll never happen again. It was a weak moment. But don't keep things from me, Reese. Even the bad things. We all need support, and I know you have that from your family, but I want the privilege of being right there next to you, no matter what."

"You mean that?" Her eyes searched mine. That fucker obviously hurt her. I had to do a better job showing her how important she was to me.

"Fuck yes."

She nodded once. "Okay. So, this new message said he wants to deal directly with me and not with Declan. He's got another think coming if he believes I'm going to do anything without my cousin's legal counsel." She took a deep breath, letting it out slowly. "Look, I'm sorry I didn't tell you. I realize something like this can rile up your demons. That wasn't my intention. I didn't want you to have a front seat to the drama."

I pulled her onto my lap so swiftly that she gasped, losing her balance for a brief second before I steadied her. "You don't have to protect me from anything, Reese. I want to be right here next to you through all of it. Understood?"

She nodded. "He texted me that night when you took me out to the jazz club."

"That would explain a few things."

"See? In a way, you *were* right there next to me. You just didn't know why."

"I want to know the why and the when. I'm much better at taking care of you if I have all the information."

She laughed and relaxed for the first time since I'd started the goddamn fight. "Really? Because you've been pretty excellent until now."

I pulled her even closer, kissing up her neck. "There's always room for improvement, Reese. And I'm making you another promise. From now on, you're only going to get the very best version of me."

"See, no, I don't like that. This is a two-way street. We have to share all of our moments, the good and the bad, for this to work. Do you promise?" she asked.

I nodded but didn't say anything. For the first time, I realized why she'd tried to keep me out of it. She wasn't used to sharing this with a partner, just like I wasn't. I'd taken vows that included "for better or for worse," but Kelly never showed up during the worst parts. And yet Reese wanted to do just that.

I felt even closer to her than before, as if we'd just created an invisible tie that bound us together. It was a strange feeling, but at the same time, it was exhilarating.

Chapter Twenty-Two

Dom

"Dad, your game is off," I teased. Our regular chess match was being interrupted by the Bears game.

"And yours is even worse. Anyway, multitasking isn't my strong suit now in my old age, but I think we can turn off the Bears. They're going to lose, and I don't need to see that."

I turned off the TV. That had always been Dad's credo: he supported the Bears but didn't need to waste his time watching when they were losing.

"Now, Dad, about Thanksgiving..."

He looked up, freezing in the act of moving his pawn. "Is this when you tell me you're going to make plans with a woman worth your time and ditch my old ass?"

I frowned. "No, I was going to ask if you want us to start dinner earlier than usual."

He looked at the board. "That woman you went to the lake house a few weeks ago is still around?"

I stared at him. "How do you even know about that?"

"You told Dora. You don't think she keeps secret from me, do you?" He tsked. "Son, you've got a thing or two to learn. She tells me everything."

"Got it."

"So, she's still around?"

"Yes," I said without getting into details. Reese and I had been spending a lot of time together since then.

"Good. I want to meet her."

I hadn't counted on this. I was sure Reese had her own thing going on for Thanksgiving, so it hadn't even crossed my mind to ask her to spend it with us.

"You want to have Reese here for Thanksgiving?" I double-checked.

"Yes, I want to meet the woman who's got my son so wrapped around her little finger that he's losing the game even when half my mind was on the Bears. It's a good omen. When I first met your mother, I forgot when meetings were supposed to start or what they were about. Let me tell you, my work colleagues were up in arms."

I had never, not once, heard my father talk about my mother since she passed away.

"Tell me about her," he insisted.

I spoke about Reese while we finished the game. My mind was racing. I wasn't a genius, but I was 100 percent certain she already had plans with her family. We hadn't been going out for a long time, but instinctively, I knew she would fit in here with us. So I came up with a plan, but I was only going to put it in motion after I left Dad's house.

He beat me, of course, but I was enjoying watching him win. He was in an excellent mood afterward. We had an early dinner with Dora, and I only left after they started on his evening routine.

As soon as I stepped outside, I called Reese, still trying to wrap my mind around the fact that he wanted to meet her. She answered just as I got into the car.

"Hi. How's your dad?"

"Happy. He won."

"Oh. Then that's a good thing, right?"

"Yeah. But he got suspicious and concluded that I'd played like shit because I was thinking about you."

"Oh."

"And he was right."

"Huh. Really? What else did he say?" Her tone turned playful.

"He'd like to meet you, and I was thinking, what are you doing on Thanksgiving?"

"There's a huge dinner at Aunt Lena's house."

As I'd figured. "I have a proposition for you."

"I'm listening."

"Dad and I usually have lunch together on Thanksgiving. I can make it a brunch, even, if that works better for you. And afterward, you're free to go to your family's event."

"I'd love that," she exclaimed.

I'd have given anything to see her right then. I liked the way her eyes lit up when she was happy. In fact, her entire body changed.

"But on one condition," she continued.

"Of course."

"Would you like to join me in the evening? The whole family will be there. Your dad is welcome, too, of course."

"He will flatly refuse. But won't there be too many people if I come?" I asked.

"Trust me, one more is really not going to matter. Everyone will be happy to see you."

"Will it make *you* happy, Reese?"

"Of course."

I smiled. "Then I'll be there."

On Thanksgiving, I was at Dad's house at six thirty in the morning to give the turkey plenty of time to cook until lunchtime.

"Dora, how do I look?" Dad asked after I set the table. He'd dressed up smarter than I'd seen him in a while, wearing a dress shirt and a tie too.

"You look very dashing. If you weren't fifteen years my senior, I'd try my chances." Dora winked at him.

"Fifteen? Try fifty, girl."

She frowned. "You're not that old."

"No, but I feel like it."

I was glad Dad and Dora were getting along. We were lucky to have found a caregiver as good as her.

When the doorbell rang, I went straight to open it. As I passed Dora, she whispered, "He insisted on dressing up for Reese."

I figured something was going on to that effect, and it made me grin.

When I opened the front door, I burst out laughing. I could barely see Reese.

"What's all this you're carrying?" I asked as I took the boxes from her.

"I brought a lot of sweets and a pie from Liz's bakery. Everything she makes is delicious."

I kissed her over the boxes but couldn't deepen it as much as I wanted because Dad was right behind us.

I turned around. "Dad, Dora, this is Reese. Reese, Dad and Dora."

"Hi, I'm so pleased to meet you," Reese said.

Dad shook her hand. "I'm Theodore. Glad to meet you, girl. Very nice of you to stop by today."

"Of course. I couldn't miss it."

"I hope you're hungry, because Dom's cooked up a storm."

"I am. I purposefully didn't have any breakfast, and I'm extremely glad that I managed not to taste any of the goodies in these boxes."

"I like you," Dad said. He was usually terse, but there was a subtle change in him since she'd stepped into the house.

"Come on and give me a tour of the kitchen," Reese said, "and put me to work."

"Nonsense," Dad replied. "You're going to keep me company. Dominic's got everything under control, doesn't he?"

Reese looked at me in surprise, and I laughed. "Dad likes to boss people around."

She winked at me. "I guess I know where you get that from. How about this?" Reese said. "I'll chat with you while I help Dom."

I kissed the side of her head, putting a hand on her waist. "There's no need, Reese. Just relax with Dad. I have everything under control. I've done this a few times."

"All right, then. That means I'm all yours, Theodore."

She sat with Dad in the living room while I went back into the kitchen. The turkey was ready on time, and Reese did help me set the table. "This looks so fancy. I've got to take a few pictures." She started to reach for her phone but stopped. "Actually, never mind."

"What were you about to say?" I asked.

"That I could send them to Aunt Lena, but then she's going to be jealous that I'm eating turkey before I taste hers."

I smiled at her. "Come on, let's all sit down and see if it tastes as good as it looks."

The four of us gathered around the table and chatted away during the meal. It pleased me to see Dad and Reese getting along so well. Dora kept smiling as Dad opened up and became more animated.

Once we finished the food, Dad looked at Dora. "Is there any program on TV that's showing Christmas lights around the city?"

"Not that I know of," she replied.

"I have an idea," Reese said, standing a bit straighter. A wave of her perfume reached me. It was a new one, but it was just as addictive as the last one. Slowly, I was starting to realize it didn't matter what perfume she was wearing—I was addicted to *her*. "Why don't we go out and see some lights? The city is full of them."

Dad frowned. "What's an old bag of bones like me going to do out in the freezing cold?"

"We can always go to Light up the Lake at Navy Pier. That's indoors, and it's gorgeous." Reese sounded so enthusiastic. I hadn't had the time to warn her that my father only used to go on Christmas lights strolls with my mother. "I'm sure we'll have fun."

Dad glanced at me and then at Dora. "You make a good case, Reese. I didn't think about indoor lights. I say let's go."

Dora jerked her head back, her shock mirroring mine. Not in a million years had I expected Dad to actually want to go.

"I can put things away and leave now, give you some family time, if you want," Dora offered.

Dad cut his eyes to her. "Tell the truth, girl. Do you want to have free time, or are you just doing it because you think you'll be in the way?"

"As you know, my family isn't in Chicago, so I don't have any plans at all. But if the three of you want to spend time together..."

"Nonsense," Dad said, waving his hand. "You and I can move around at a distance from these two so we're not a third wheel."

"We'll all have fun together," Reese said, smiling from ear to ear.

Dora stood up. "All right, then, let's get you ready," she told Dad. I was still waiting for him to change his mind abruptly and make up an excuse, but none of that happened as they went into the bedroom.

Reese turned to me once we were alone. "Anything wrong? You're frowning."

"I'm surprised," I admitted. "My father hasn't left the house in a long time."

"You told me that. But you also said he used to like Christmas strolls. That's why I looked up where we could go indoors."

"Wait, you researched this?"

She nodded. "Yeah. I like Christmas markets, but I haven't been to an indoor one for some time."

"You're unbelievable, you know that?"

She smiled sheepishly and dipped her head. I pulled her onto my lap, wanting even more body contact.

"Hey, what are you doing?" she said, looking over her shoulder. "They could come back any second now."

"No, that's going to take a while." I kissed up her neck, and she relaxed in my arms. That was always my favorite moment, when she went from composed to being putty in my hands.

She smirked. "You can't even behave when you're in your dad's house, huh?"

"I can't stop wanting to be closer to you, to touch you."

"I like what I'm hearing," she murmured.

A sound startled us both. Reese jumped out of my lap and grabbed some of the plates for no reason at all. The door opened, and Dora stepped into the room.

"We're almost ready," she began. Then her eyes fell on Reese, who was red in the face, clutching the plates tightly. "You don't have to clean up. I'll do it afterward."

"It's just a few plates," Reese said quickly. "We'll manage."

I got up, too, taking the last plate and the four mugs.

"We'll be ready in a few minutes," Dora said. "We should take two cars, right?"

I'd bought Dora a car that could comfortably seat my dad's wheelchair. Even though he hadn't wanted to leave the house, I always wanted him to have that option.

"Sure," I said, and she headed back into the bedroom with Dad.

Reese and I carried everything to the kitchen. I set the mugs and the plate next to the sink, where she was already rinsing the others.

I pushed my hip into hers and grinned at her.

"No," she said under her breath. "See? I knew something like that would happen and we'd get caught."

That made me laugh. "Reese, we're grown-ups. There is no 'catching' us."

"I always feel I'm doing something wrong when I'm under a parent's roof or my aunt and uncle's."

"Fine," I said, kissing the back of her head, then her temple, and then tugging at the lobe of her ear. I could never stop when it came to Reese. I always needed more. "We'll be on our best behavior."

Dora had Dad ready to go just as we finished the dishes, and we piled into our respective vehicles. We arrived at Navy Pier half an hour later. I parked first, then waited for Dora and Dad. She didn't need much help getting Dad out, as the car did most of the heavy lifting.

Reese went straight to him once he was settled. "They've got a lot of amazing things. You're going to enjoy it, and so am I."

Dad looked up at her with a smile. I hadn't seen him this happy in a long time. But that was the effect Reese had on people. She had an inner warmth and joy and goodness that spread around without her even trying.

I couldn't understand how Malcolm never appreciated her. How could anyone have this woman by their side and not be madly in love?

That was the exact moment that I knew. Here, in the dim parking lot, watching Dad and Reese laugh together, I knew I loved her.

And I'd never ever feel about anyone else the way I felt about Reese.

Chapter Twenty-Three
Reese

Light up the Lake instantly became one of my new favorite Christmas activities to do. Theodore glanced around, curiosity etched on his features. I was so glad I could make him happy.

The pier was packed, which wasn't a surprise. The hall was large enough that it wasn't claustrophobic, and the high ceiling gave the impression of being in the open air. I was grateful to be indoors; I didn't miss the cold at all, or the icy wind.

My eyes needed a few seconds to adjust to the multitude of lights as we went through a tunnel of golden illumination. Dora was pushing Theodore's wheelchair, and they both looked around curiously.

"You're a witch," Dom said in my ear.

"Huh?" I asked, turning to him.

"I'm telling you, you've put a spell on my father."

"Because I convinced him to go out?"

"He likes you. And Dad doesn't like anyone. Trust me."

"He likes Dora."

"She's his fifteenth caretaker in the span of three years."

I winced. "Wow. Okay."

My phone beeped in my pocket. I took it out and pouted. "Oh no."

Dom frowned. "What's wrong?"

"I didn't win the tree."

"I'm going to need more details."

"So, every year, I hunt for a huge-ass Christmas tree for my living room. There aren't many of them, so there's literally a waitlist. They pick someone randomly from the list, and I didn't get it."

"I'm sorry, Reese."

"Doesn't matter. I'll buy one that's huge anyway—just not *that* huge."

"When do you put your tree up?"

"Ah... that's a funny story. I always have two trees: one from the beginning of December until the twenty-third, and then I put up the big one on Christmas Eve."

Dom stared at me but didn't comment as we passed a huge, decorated duck. That made me laugh, especially when Theodore said, "People these days. What's a duck got to do with Christmas?"

"Just enjoy it, Dad," Dom said.

"I am. Just wondering what the purpose of that is."

We were surrounded by white, yellow, and red lights. The crowd chattered happily. The smell of eggnog and mulled wine was thick in the air, even more so than at an outdoor Christmas market. I especially loved the trees made out of lights and the giant reindeer.

"Can you take a picture of me with the reindeer? And with Theodore?" I asked.

"Sure," Dom said.

"Nonsense!" Theodore exclaimed. "Reese, you don't want me ruining your picture."

"You're not. Then maybe we can all take a picture together, a selfie or something. Come on, give me a smile, Theodore," I said as I stood next to him.

"How do you know I'm not smiling?" he asked in a belligerent tone.

"I had a hunch."

He burst out laughing. Actually burst out laughing.

Dom, who was about to take a photo of us, lowered the phone slightly and looked at us incredulously. I winked at him.

God, this is such a great day.

He snapped a picture just then, even though neither Theodore nor I was posing. But that was fine. I always thought candid pictures were the best anyway.

"Come on, let's all take a picture," Dom said before asking another guy who was standing in line to get a picture with his family to take one of us.

As Dom headed back to us, I noticed his smile was a bit different today. I wasn't sure why, but he looked happy, and that was all that mattered. He came next to me, putting an arm around my waist. Dora joined us in the picture, the three of us standing behind Theodore's chair.

The stranger snapped a few and then said, "Okay, that's it. I think you can find something you like among these." From his impatient tone, it was obvious he wanted us to move.

He had a point. We didn't have to monopolize the reindeer, even though it was one of my favorite parts.

"Let's move to the igloos," I said.

"The what?" Theodore asked.

"Well, that's what I call them because they sort of look like it."

"The giant balls there?" he said, and we all started to laugh.

"Yes, Dad, the giant balls," Dom replied with a grin.

We headed toward them, taking in all the lights and decorations as we walked.

"You're right. They do look like igloos," Theodore said once we were right in front of them. They were mostly gold, but some were red as well.

"I've always thought about what it must feel like to sleep in an igloo," I told Dom. "Then I remember that I hate the cold and would probably be freezing."

"I'd warm you up with some skin-on-skin contact," Dom murmured into my ear.

"Now that you mention it, I'm going to think about it some more. But for right now, I'm ready to explore this one where it's warm and cozy."

I darted inside the igloo, and Theodore joined me. I looked around then back to him, and to my astonishment, his eyes were a bit glassy.

"Theodore?" I asked softly.

"My wife would have had a field day here. We mostly went to the outdoor market and the Christmas parade on the Magnificent Mile. She would have liked us being here. And she would have liked you very much."

"Thank you." I put my hands on my chest. I was truly moved. "That's very kind of you to say." I looked over my shoulder to see if Dom was within earshot, but he and Dora were nowhere in sight.

"Where did they disappear to?" I asked. "They were right here seconds ago."

"I think Dora said something about buying mulled wine. She was probably fed up with my sunny personality."

I bumped his arm with my elbow. "I have to say, you're behaving well today."

"I'm doing my best."

"Now, what do you say about taking a few more selfies?" I asked him, taking out my phone.

He laughed, smiling into the camera, and I snapped a few pics. We had an inordinate amount of fun being silly in the igloo. There was plenty of room in here, so we didn't have to hurry at all, and I loved making Theodore laugh.

"Someone's cheerful enough that they don't even need a mulled wine anymore," Dora said.

When I glanced up, I saw she and Dom were each holding two cups. I immediately took mine and sipped it, enjoying the warmth and spices.

I sniffed the air. "I'm smelling roasted almonds or peanuts with honey or something."

Dom looked at Dora. "I told you she'd realize we'd bought some before she even saw them." He took a paper cone from his pocket.

"Oh! Give me that!" In my excitement, I nearly spilled my mulled wine on me.

"Careful, Reese. Don't burn yourself, babe," he said.

I nearly melted. He'd called me "babe" right in front of his dad.

He opened the cone, and I snagged a few treats. They were nuts glazed with honey, cinnamon, and vanilla powder.

"These are good," I said after swallowing my mouthful. "And they go so well with that mulled wine."

"It was worth getting out of the house just for this," Theodore exclaimed.

I took small sips from my cup, alternating with eating a few nuts.

"They do go well together," Dora exclaimed.

"I know, right?" I said, grinning.

Once he finished his drink, Theodore said, "Dora, I think that's our cue. Let's go home and leave these two to enjoy the rest of the day."

"What? No. You can stay with us for as long as you want," I told him sincerely. But I knew there would be no convincing him. The way he held his head high reminded me of the way Dom looked when he'd already made up his mind.

"All right, then. Theodore, let's go," Dora said in her no-nonsense way.

I couldn't help myself and gave Theodore a hug.

He hugged me right back. "Take care of him, will you?" he said.

"I will. I promise," I murmured so only he could hear me. But Dom looked at me with narrowed eyes when I straightened up.

After we bid Theodore and Dora goodbye and they left, he turned me around so I was facing him. "What did he tell you?"

"That's a secret between him and me."

He looked at me intently, then kissed my free hand. I was still holding my cup of mulled wine tightly in the other one.

I opened the bag of treats, taking more nuts. They were covered in powdered sugar, which I got all over my hair. "Oh, damn it. How did that happen?"

"I'll help you clean up. Don't worry."

"We'll never get it out of my hair. There are crumbs everywhere. Oh, I'm truly a mess."

"No, you're not. You're fucking adorable, and I love you."

I sucked in a breath, looking up and blinking rapidly. Had I imagined it? Just because this day had been magic? He couldn't have possibly said that right here in the middle of the Christmas market, when we were inside an igloo.

I swallowed hard, afraid to say anything.

"I love you, Reese."

"Oh my God. I thought I'd imagined that."

He chuckled. "What?"

"You saying it, because today was so, you know, perfect." I glanced down at his cup, peering inside. "You did have a bit of mulled wine."

"I'm not drunk, Reese. I mean it. I love you."

"Are you sure? Because I fell for you a while ago, and I just don't want to get my hopes up too much."

"I wouldn't say it if I wasn't sure. And if I'd waited until the bedroom to tell you, I could also show you just how much I mean it."

"You chose the perfect time. I will forever remember this place, and time, and day when you told me that."

"Yes, but I can't have you the way I want to."

I grinned at him. "Hold on to that thought, and you can put it into practice as soon as we're done with our stroll."

"You mean we're not done yet?"

"Ha. No, of course not. I was only slowing down for your dad's benefit. Did you know there are six hundred thousand lights here?"

"No," he replied in a measured tone.

"Oh yeah. And trust me, we haven't seen even half of them."

"Reese!"

"No. We're not negotiating this," I insisted.

He kissed my forehead. "Fine. If it makes you happy, we'll spend more time here. But we still have to go to your aunt's for dinner."

I melted against him, putting my free arm around his torso. I turned my head, resting my nose in the crook of his neck as I kissed it lightly, careful not to crush the cup between us.

"What are you doing, Reese?"

"Oops." I took a step back. "Sorry, it won't happen again. You just smell too delicious. And you know it's my favorite place to kiss."

"Come on, beautiful. Let's finish this stroll," Dom said, taking a step to the side and grabbing my free hand with his, squeezing my fingers tightly. "Have your fill of the Christmas market. Then we'll go home, and I'll have my fill of you before we go to your aunt's."

My aunt's Thanksgiving dinner was always legendary. Usually, the whole family helped, and I was certain that today it was no different. I felt like a slacker for having been gone the whole day, though I couldn't feel too guilty either because it had been amazing.

I led Dom inside the house, laughing as I heard a tumult of voices and a baby's cry from the kitchen.

"All right," I said, smiling broadly. "Here goes nothing."

He squeezed my hand. "Reese, this will be fun."

Declan, Travis, and Kimberly were closest to us, along with their better halves, but Gran spotted us first. She and John walked toward us.

"Reese, darling, and Dominic. So great of you to join us." Gran hugged each of us in turn.

John gave me a hug as well, then turned to Dom.

"Nice to see you again," Dom said, shaking his hand.

Aunt Lena smiled at us, but she held up her hands. They were full of chopped parsley. "Sorry, I can't really greet you properly right now, Dom. But it's good to have you here."

Uncle Emmett washed quickly at the sink and then proceeded to pat Dom's shoulder and shake his hand. "Hi, I'm Emmett, Reese's uncle."

"And these are my cousins Luke, Tyler, and Tate," I introduced down the line.

"It's good to meet all of you," Dom said. "I've heard a lot about everyone in the family."

"And we heard that you and Reese already had a Thanksgiving meal with your dad," Lena said.

"That's right."

"Well, I hope you still have some space for my treats."

I looked out the corner of my eye at Dom, fighting laugher.

He grinned. "Reese gave me plenty of warning, so I saved some space."

I could *feel* my aunt warming up to him.

"All right, well, the turkey is resting, and we're just putting on the finishing touches," she told us.

"It looks like it," Dom said. "And Reese told me that you have a clever strategy where everyone does bits and pieces, so put me to work."

Oh yeah. He'd completely won her over.

As we worked side by side, I noticed Lexi and Kendra whispering under their breaths. When they realized I was watching them, they both smiled at me. I had a hunch they were going to keep an eye on us the whole evening—but that was par the course with my family.

Dom was the center of attention, and I loved it. I hadn't felt as happy as I was today in years. I was grateful that my family got to experience this joyful side of me after they'd had to put up with the Grinch version for so long.

This Thanksgiving is absolutely perfect.

Chapter Twenty-Four
Reese

As the weather in Chicago got colder, we started organizing fun indoor events at work. At the beginning of December, we set up a punch station right next to the coffee machine—alcohol-free, of course.

This year we were throwing the office Christmas party earlier than usual because so many people were leaving on vacation right after.

The party began at 6:00 p.m., and it was taking place at the bar. We'd closed it off to the public at four o'clock so the team could put up the decorations and rearrange the tables.

I'd invited Dom, too, because I wanted to show off my man to everyone. I'd already gone with him to his company's Christmas party as well as two more that he couldn't get out of. I was loving all the festivities.

Kimberly and I had a few shopping sprees at his store. We'd been there before I'd met him, of course, but it was even more fun now. I kept hoping he'd pop into the store while we were there, but it never happened.

Today was going to be fantastic. Luke and Meg said they'd stop by, as did Tyler and Kendra. We always invited the whole family. Typically not many could make it because they were busy enough during the holiday season, but Dom was a big draw for them. I was honestly surprised that the whole family wasn't attending.

A knock at my door startled me out of my thoughts.

"Come in," I said.

The door opened, and Declan stepped in.

I leaned back in my chair, grinning. "You decided to join the party after all?"

But he wasn't smiling as he took a seat in the chair opposite mine.

I straightened up, realizing he hadn't come here to talk about that.

"No. I actually forgot that the party is today. I just wanted to tell you that I've met with Malcolm's team of lawyers. They have no legal means to go after anything regarding the hotel."

I frowned. "Then why even try?"

Declan grimaced. "I don't know."

"But you have an idea. You have that face where you're not sure if you want to share it with me or not."

He sighed. "I think he's hoping you'll cave and just give him a check."

I jerked my head back. "Why would he even think that? I haven't caved in all these years. I've done nothing wrong. Why does he think I will now?"

"Beats me," Declan said. "Do you have any idea? I mean, he's married now and employed, so I find it hard to believe it's for pure revenge."

"Yeah, that is odd. Maybe he just needs the money?" I groaned, my shoulders sagging. "I'm sorry, Declan. I wish I had an answer."

He nodded. "We'll figure it out. But you have nothing to worry about."

"Thanks for taking care of everything. I'm ashamed that I always need you so much."

"Reese, I don't mind taking care of family business."

"I know, but I have like 500 percent more legal issues than anyone else."

"Don't worry about it, okay?"

"Well, since you're here, do you want us to go upstairs together? Can I tempt you with a drink?" I asked.

He shrugged. "Why the hell not? It's December, and I've got nothing else to do tonight."

"What's Liz doing?"

"Catering an event." His voice turned flat.

"And you don't like that?"

"I don't understand why she's overworking herself so much. I can take care of her."

My heart swelled as we both rose from our seats. "She knows that, but the bakery has been her dream for so long. I don't think this feels like work to her."

"That's what she keeps saying," he grumbled under his breath.

"See? Listen to her. Oh, I love the smell already," I said as we walked up the stairs to the bar.

"But it's smelled like mulled wine for a while," Declan countered.

"True, but this one's spiked with rum."

"How can you tell the difference?"

I tapped my nose. "I just can."

Upstairs, the bar had been completely transformed. The decoration was subtle, just red and gold globes strategically placed around the room in addition to the two Christmas trees. I was glad I'd changed companies. The one last year had tried to be a bit too modern for my taste. I didn't think Christmas needed to be modernized.

"When is the gang arriving?" Declan asked.

"Twenty minutes, give or take. Let's get you something to drink."

We stepped up to the bar, and Tom gave us each a mulled wine. Declan and I clinked glasses, and we alternated between sipping our drinks and catching each other up on our lives.

Dom arrived about ten minutes later. Then Tyler, Kendra, Luke, and Megan all came in at the same time a few minutes afterward.

"Declan, we didn't know you'd be here too," Luke said.

"I thought you guys might need some support questioning Dom here," Declan said with a wink.

Dom laughed. "You all take this very seriously."

"Yeah, we do," Tyler said, eyeing Dom intently.

They started shooting question after question at him, some about the company, some about us. Dom was very smooth with his replies. I was so proud of him.

Slowly, the team started to filter in. Some came directly from the office; some of them went home and changed first. The only one who wasn't able to attend was Sarah, our receptionist, but I'd planned a surprise for her later on. After I gave my speech and worked the room for a bit, I was going to go downstairs and switch with her so she could at least have a glass of mulled wine. The bellhops would take turns coming up to enjoy the festivities.

As more and more people started to arrive, I wondered if I should wait to give my speech; Travis and Kimberly weren't here yet, and I wanted them to be able to say a few words too.

I tensed when one of our bellhops stepped into the bar. He wouldn't come up just yet unless there was a problem. Sure enough, he made a beeline for me.

"What's wrong?" I asked.

"There's a man insisting on seeing you. We don't want to let him up, but he's causing a ruckus in the reception area. The guests are getting uncomfortable."

"Who is it?" I asked, but then it dawned on me. "Malcolm?"

He nodded.

"Fucking hell," Declan exclaimed. "His lawyer must have already informed him of our meeting."

I drew in a deep breath before turning around to face the group. "I want you all to stay here. I'll just go downstairs and talk to him."

"Like hell you'll go alone," Dom said. "I'm coming with you."

"No, you're not. I—"

"Oh my God," Kendra gasped. Her eyes were wide.

I turned and saw Malcolm striding toward us.

"Shit, he must have gotten by the guys downstairs," the bellhop said.

"For fuck's sake, I can't believe the whole clan is here," Malcolm said sarcastically, zeroing in on Declan.

Dom stepped forward. "Get out of here."

Malcolm ignored him and focused on me instead. "Reese, I need to talk to you."

"This is our hotel Christmas party. How dare you show up here?" I seethed.

He smirked. "I knew I'd get your attention this way. Though I have to say, I hadn't counted on everyone being here."

"Get out!" Tyler bellowed.

I had to get Malcolm out of here. He was good at provoking everyone, and the last thing I wanted was for anyone else in the family to have to deal with this. Tyler had already gotten in enough trouble a while back because of Malcolm, and the hockey league benched him. I refused to let him hurt anyone else.

"You think you're untouchable? That you can just cheat me out of my business?" Malcolm snarled, spittle flying everywhere.

"For fuck's sake," Declan said. "I already told your team that you've got absolutely no legal claim."

"Yeah, there's such a thing as—"

"Malcolm, this isn't the time and place. I will contact you, and we will talk," I said as calmly as possible.

"The hell you will. You've been a coward for years. You've never showed up without Declan by your side."

Dom stepped right in front of him and took him by the collar. "If you don't leave this place, I will take you out with my fists."

"And then I'll have a reason to go after *you*." He took a huge step back, and Dom let him go.

I felt chilled to the bone.

No! He couldn't go after Dom. He'd already caused enough damage to the people I loved.

The employees were staring at us with stricken expressions.

"Malcolm, you're not going to get what you want tonight," I told him.

His expression instantly changed. He seemed to back down, realizing this was not the time to discuss this and win. I just needed him to leave the premises before this turned into even more of a shit show.

"Fine. But if you think I won't get what I deserve, which is a piece of this, then you'd better think again."

Declan opened his mouth, but I threw him a warning glance. I just needed Malcolm to think he would get what he wanted so he would leave us alone. I wanted to have a Christmas party with my team. He wouldn't get anything out of me tonight.

"You've always hid behind your family, Reese," Malcolm sneered.

"Get out!" I shouted.

I knew he wanted to corner me alone, and I wasn't going to give him that satisfaction.

Malcolm looked behind him. Our two security guards had come forward from the entrance, flanking him on either side.

"All right, I'll go. But don't think this is the last conversation we'll have on this topic."

"I wouldn't dream of it," I said sarcastically.

I had trouble breathing as I watched him leave, the security guards walking right behind him. I should have given them his photo to make sure he would never be allowed inside, but I hadn't thought of it until now.

Once he was out of the room, I drew in a deep breath. I eventually realized my family were all talking, and Declan was explaining something to them in a stern voice.

"Reese, what do you need?" Dom asked.

"Some privacy, I think."

"Where can we go? I'll come with you."

"Let's go to the supplies room behind the bar."

Dom put an arm around my waist, leading me toward the back room. Once inside, he immediately cupped my face. "Reese, talk to me."

I took another breath. "I need to get out of here. I don't want to let down my family and my team, but I don't think I can keep my composure for the rest of the evening."

"You won't let them down. Come on, I'll get you out of here."

"I just need a few more seconds, okay?"

"Sure," he said. "I'll stay here with you."

He kept me against his chest, and though I felt stronger in his arms, I knew I wouldn't be any fun tonight. I wanted our employees to have a good time, not wonder why the boss was having a mental breakdown.

"We can go now," I said after a few minutes.

He took my hand, and we both stepped out. My family were all in the exact same spot as before. Travis and Kimberly had arrived too. We hurried to them.

"Listen," I said. "I, um, hope you don't mind, all of you, but I need to take off tonight."

"Don't worry about it," Travis said. From his grim expression, I assumed he knew what happened. "Kimberly and I have everything under control. Dom, take care of her."

He nodded. "That's the plan."

I wondered if I should say goodbye to the team, but only half of them were here, and saying anything would just draw even more attention to me.

I glanced at Dom. "Okay, let's go."

He grabbed my hand again, squeezing my fingers lightly.

Chapter Twenty-Five
Reese

"Are you up for something spontaneous?" he asked me.

"Sure."

Honestly, I was in the mood to simply curl up with a cozy blanket, but I couldn't say that out loud.

"All right. Then we're heading to the lake house."

I beamed. "That's such a great idea. But is it ready for us?"

"I'll take care of everything. Don't worry."

He immediately called a number from his phone. The ringing reverberated through the car through the speakers, and a female voice answered. "Mr. Waldorf, good evening."

"Hi, Agnes. Can you please go over to the house and check that everything is ready? I'm heading there."

"Certainly. The fridge isn't stocked, though. Would you like me to buy something for dinner or breakfast?"

"Buy something for tomorrow, yes. We've already had dinner tonight."

"Right away. Everything will be ready by the time you arrive."

As soon as the phone clicked off, I turned to him. "You can't make that poor woman work this late."

"I know how much you like the lake house. You'll be happy there. Besides, she lives five minutes away. Trust me, she doesn't mind. She wants to do this because she bills me by the hour. And she needs the extra money."

"But why? I mean, if she lives nearby... I can't imagine any property there not being expensive."

"It's a complicated story. But now, no more talk about her. Let's talk about you."

"No," I said firmly. "Let's talk about anything else. Please."

"Are you sure? You always say it helps to talk."

I sighed. "I know, but tonight has been a complete shit show, and I don't feel like thinking about it for one second more."

Part of me still feared that Dom might come to his senses and run in the opposite direction. No one needed Malcolm or his drama in their life. I was stuck with him, it seemed, and so was my family. But Dom didn't need to deal with it.

"Fine, if that's what you want. But if you change your mind at any time, you can tell me, okay?"

"Sure." I knew I wasn't going to change my mind tonight at all.

"So what *do* you want to talk about?" he asked.

I turned to him, pulling a bit at the seat belt so it didn't cut into my neck anymore. "I have a few options for presents for your dad."

"What?"

"Yeah. I tried to figure out what he might like, and I'd like your opinion before I order it."

"You've got options?"

"Why do you keep parroting what I'm saying?"

"I'm processing it. I wasn't expecting it."

"I do it often. Sometimes we all think about options for presents, especially for my aunt and uncle, and then we put our heads together and decide what would make them happiest. We have a system."

"A system," he repeated, stunned.

I started to laugh. "Can I tell you the options?"

"Sure."

"All right. I found a special edition chessboard with collectible items, plus an outdoor sitting area where he could move around on his own."

"I think that chessboard is a sure deal."

I grinned. "That was easy."

"You've got a list of options for me too?"

"Yes," I said, a bit suspicious. "But I'm not going to reveal them to you."

"Why not?"

"Because it's a surprise."

"Then how are you going to pick out what's best for me?"

"By talking it out with your dad, obviously."

He jerked his head in my direction. "You're talking to my father?"

"Yes. He said I can contact him anytime."

"You've..." He stopped talking, focusing on the road again. "Reese, you are truly the most amazing person I've ever met. I don't think anyone's ever put any effort into giving me something. Actually, I'm sure of it."

"That can't be true," I said.

He might not be used to anyone thinking about him, but I planned to do it a lot.

"I really like your dad," I added. "He's been telling me some fun stories about you and the family. I think he enjoys remembering those times."

"Oh, there's no doubt in my mind that he likes talking about the past. I bet that gives the caregiver some downtime, too, which I'm sure she appreciates." Dom was so serious when he said this that I just wanted to kiss him. He meant more to me than he knew, and I needed to make sure he understood that. "Thank you for doing that. It means a lot."

"Nonsense, I'm having fun with him." Dom would get used to my ways, and then soon enough he'd call me a busybody like the rest of the Maxwell clan did. "Hey, can we stop by my condo first? I want to change and maybe pack a small overnight bag."

"Sure."

"Do you need to pick something from your place too?"

"No, I have some clothes at the lake house."

Once at the condo, I changed clothes and packed as quickly as I could...but it still took almost an hour. Dom was patiently waiting for me, occasionally chuckling when I kept adding stuff to my carryon.

After we finally got in the car, I brought up the chessboard for his dad again, not wanting to risk the conversation circling back to Malcolm. Besides, I was still considering the sitting area. But in the end, I had to go with what Dom thought was best for his dad. After all, he knew him much better than I did.

When he pulled the car into the driveway, the house looked like it was currently being lived in. I expected the housekeeper to still be inside when Dom opened the door, but it was empty.

"She's already left?" I asked.

"She always makes it a point not to be here when I arrive."

"Okay."

"I told her I don't mind at all. But I have to say, right now, I'm happy it's just the two of us." He smiled. "Want a drink?"

"Sure. Surprise me with something."

We both went to the kitchen. He took out ice from the freezer, then bottles of amaretto, rum, and orange juice. I watched him mix them together, and it looked delicious. We clinked glasses, taking a sip at the same time.

Yum, it tasted delicious too.

I brushed my hair behind my ear, and Dom leaned into it. "I've wanted to be alone with you the whole damn evening," he said.

"I was half expecting you to leave. I wouldn't have blamed you, you know, if you'd bolted earlier."

He stared at me. "And leave you there on your own?"

I shrugged. "It's not your drama."

"Reese, you're mine. Do you understand?" He stepped in front of me, touching my face and the side of my neck. "I don't care how long fighting with Malcolm will take. I'll be there every step of the way, by your side, supporting you. I can't fight for you, though I'd very much like to."

"You would?" I whispered. Suddenly, I was melting. This man wanted to be everything to me. My love for him couldn't get any stronger.

"Yes. I'd do anything to make your life better. You deserve a life where you don't have to worry about one damn thing. That's what I want to give you. Tell me what you need."

"This. You. Really, it's more than enough. I love you so much," I whispered.

"And I love you. Never think I'd bolt, okay? No matter what happens. If you believe one thing, then believe that."

"Okay," I murmured.

"Now, let's get you out of these clothes." He started fiddling with my scarf, trying to remove it, but to no avail. "I can't undo this," he said, frustration thick in his voice.

I chuckled. "I'll do it."

While I took it off, Dom undid the buttons of my coat. He placed a kiss on my collarbone for good measure. I loved that he did that whenever he had the chance.

"Your skin is so damn soft," he murmured, then threw the coat on the couch.

"Now you take yours off," I said, working his buttons.

I still felt off in a way I couldn't explain even to myself. But the way he touched me and kissed me made it all better.

Chapter Twenty-Six
Dom

I kissed her hard. I wanted Reese. No, I *needed* her. We hadn't even finished our drinks, but I had an idea of what to do about that. I was going to please her in every way possible. She tasted like amaretto and rum, and from the way she kissed me back, slowly but determinedly, I knew she was already just a bit drunk.

"Reese, I want you so damn much."

She hummed against my mouth, and I felt the reverberation all the way down my throat. I gripped the hem of her sweater, pulling it over her shoulders. She took out her arms, and then I pulled it over her head, messing up her hair in the process. I liked seeing her like this.

I nearly swallowed my tongue when I realized she wasn't wearing a bra underneath her clothes. I grinned wickedly at the sight.

She flashed me a smile. "Surprised, huh?"

"Fuck yes," I growled, cupping both breasts. She was a bit cold from being outside, but I was going to warm her up in no time.

I slowly massaged her nipples with my palms and kissed her again, swirling my tongue in the same rhythm. She hummed again, but her sounds soon transformed into moans. Moving my hands onto her back, I pressed my fingers deeply into her skin. I wanted to touch her everywhere, to kiss all parts of her, and I wanted to do everything at once.

But first I needed to get the rest of her clothes out of the way.

She was ahead of me, already unbuttoning her pants. When I yanked them down unceremoniously, she gasped, and I only realized why when I saw her torn panties.

"You're a beast," she exclaimed. "How did you even rip those?"

"I don't know," I said with a growl. And I didn't care. I'd buy her fifty more pairs.

I pushed her pants and underwear all the way down her ankles, and she lifted her legs so I could get them off, throwing them away somewhere in the room. I looked at her, just drinking her in for a few moments, then dropped onto my knees in front of her.

She was incredibly beautiful, her dark hair cascading over her shoulders and hiding her left breast. Her chest rose and fell in quick succession as she put her hand just above her navel, sucking in her belly as she tilted forward. I smiled when we made eye contact, then kissed the side of her left knee before moving farther up around her thighs. I wanted access to her pussy.

She spread her legs before I even asked. But instead of doing what she expected, I pressed her thighs together firmly and only licked the top of her pussy, including her clit. She gasped, pushing her hips forward before buckling over me. I smiled against her skin. I liked surprising her.

She tugged at the collar of my shirt as I kept kissing her thigh, and I stopped briefly. She tugged even harder at it. I undid the top buttons, and she pulled it over my head before throwing it in the heap with her clothes.

I stood up slowly, kissing up her torso and her ribs as I went, avoiding her breasts on purpose. Instead, I kissed the side of her body before veering back onto her chest and then farther up. She took her cues from me and bent her head back, exposing her neck.

"I love your neck," I said. "And your breasts, and your ass, and your pussy. I especially love your pussy."

She gasped, desperately tugging at the waistband of my pants.

"Not so fast."

"I need to see you. And feel you. I want you naked."

I stepped back, letting her do what she wanted. She got rid of my pants even faster than I took hers off. Then I kissed her again, walking her backward, away from the counter. I grabbed one of the glasses as I led her to the nearest piece of furniture: an armchair.

She sat down on it, and I set the glass on the coffee table next to the armrest.

"What are you doing with that?" she asked.

I took out an ice cube in response.

"Oh." Her skin broke out in goose bumps, and my cock twitched.

Seeing her reactions unleashed something ferocious and primal inside me—devoid of any reason. I bared my desire and my feelings to Reese without any restraint. In the beginning, I'd questioned it. Now I didn't. It was the best damn thing that had ever happened to me. She'd transformed my existence. And I was going to prove to her just how grateful I was, and how happy she made me.

I put the ice cube under her clavicle, the slid it down in a straight line, stopping briefly at her navel. She sucked in her belly, and the ice slid farther down. I caught it just as it brushed her clit. Reese jackknifed in the armchair.

She was already overwhelmed by the sensations, and we still had a long way to go. I planned to push all her limits.

She'd barely calmed down when I dipped the cube in my mouth right before I brought my lips to her nipple. At the same time, I circled her other nipple with the ice. Reese moaned, sliding farther down the armchair. She parted her thighs as I put the ice cube away on the coffee table, focusing on her.

I kissed along the trail where the ice cube had left a mark, warming her up. Then I pulled her down the chair even more.

"Dom," she murmured. "What are you doing to me?"

"I want to drive you completely crazy."

Looking up at her, I drew a circle with the tip of my tongue around her clit. She squeezed her eyes shut, digging her fingers into the armchair. I watched her, slowly increasing my speed, feeling her body tremble beneath my touch.

When I knew she was about to explode, I pressed the flat of my tongue against her clit, sliding down until I was in a position to push it inside her. She dropped her head back, crying out. She was still on edge and needed just a little bit more to go right over it.

The sight of her naked in this armchair, hair wild around her, was everything I needed. I alternated between pushing my tongue inside her and pressing it against her clit until I felt her ass muscles clench. Then I focused on her clit only, pulling it between my lips as I grabbed her ass until it came off the chair.

I pushed two fingers inside her and gently slapped her clit with my other hand.

She came harder than ever. Her entire body transformed. She opened her mouth and couldn't even cry out as her body convulsed.

It was beautiful to watch her completely come apart. I wanted all the tension to leave her body. I curled my fingers inside her, and she finally cried out so hard that she broke out in a sweat, her hair sticking to her temples.

When I was confident that she was completely spent, I rose to my feet. I bent at the waist, intending to take her in my arms and carry her upstairs, but she pushed me away wordlessly and sat up straighter.

There was a wicked glint in her eyes as she slid out of the armchair onto her knees. She glanced at the glass on the coffee table, taking a sip of it. I figured she was probably thirsty, but then she surprised me by taking my cock into her mouth the very next second. It was cold, and my balls twitched at the sensation.

I hadn't expected this. She was giving me a taste of my own medicine, and I loved it. She moved her head rhythmically, going from the tip to the base and then back to the tip, alternating between licking the length of my cock and taking it all into her mouth. Now she was the one driving me completely crazy.

She pulled her head back, pouting. "It's too big. My jaw is starting to clench."

Before I could reply, she focused on the tip, sucking it.

Fucking hell!

"Reese," I growled, "I love your mouth, but I want your pussy now."

She didn't let go. Her eyes turned playful, and I noticed her shoulder moving and glanced down. Fuck, she was touching herself. She was going to come again.

Energy shot through me, followed by a wave of pleasure. I exhaled sharply, watching her touch herself while she had her mouth on me. I knew she was about to come before I heard her. Her shoulders spasmed, and she moved her hand even faster. She clamped her lips tighter around me, and then she groaned just like that, with my cock in her mouth.

I exploded, giving her my release even as I felt her climax. My body was so tightly strung that I wasn't even sure how I was standing anymore.

When I finally came back to myself, I realized her eyes were glazed, completely unfocused. I pulled back, bending at the waist and picking her up. She was unsteady on her feet, but that was okay.

"I've got you. You're fucking amazing, you know that?"

She smiled, nodding as I pulled her close to me. I kissed her slowly, lazily, tangling our tongues, showing her how much she meant to me.

"Come on," I said, lifting her by her ass. She was so sleepy, she didn't even attempt to wrap her legs around me, but that was fine. I was strong enough to carry her like that.

The master bedroom was completely dark when I walked inside, but there was a faint light coming from all the decorations in the front yard. I set her down on the bed, then lay next to her.

She touched my chest, moving her hand all the way down to my cock. I quickly realized she was checking if I had an erection. She laughed when she felt that I did.

"I'm always turned on when I'm around you," I confessed.

She turned around onto her side, facing me. I moved even closer, gripping myself at the base. I had just climaxed, yet I wanted her again, but this time I needed to be buried inside her.

I aligned my pelvis with hers, but instead of sliding straight in, I slapped her clit with my erection a few times. She gasped right before she groaned.

"How can I be so on edge already?" she panted.

"It's the same for me, Reese," I assured her, but then I couldn't do anything else but slide inside her. I craved her too much. This connection between us was surreal.

I intertwined our legs, keeping the one she had on top at an angle so we could both move. I wasn't slow or gentle.

"Fuck!" I exclaimed.

I was so close to losing myself in this woman.

I touched her breasts, moving my hand over her waist and then down to her ass, squeezing her buttocks before pressing the cheeks together, holding them tight. Then I pushed myself into her even deeper. She came first and pulled me right over with her.

Once we both slowed down, I heard her catch her breath. She was humming lightly. I liked knowing this intimate detail about her. And I was the only one who got to hear it. I also liked seeing her in the dim light with drops of sweat running down her neck and chest.

Out of nowhere, she started to laugh.

"Reese?" I asked, and then she laughed even louder.

I frowned. "Babe, I'm starting to get ideas. Bad ones."

"I was just thinking, thank God your housekeeper wasn't here. But she'll probably put two and two together. I'm not even sure how I'll look her in the eyes the next time I see her, after everything that happened in the kitchen, on the floor, and in the armchair."

"We've got plenty more pieces of furniture to try out."

She grinned. "That's right, we do."

She turned onto her belly, and I put my hands behind my head, looking at her. When I bought this house, it felt like something was missing, but now it didn't anymore. I was a happy man, being here with Reese.

She took one of my hands from under my head, laying it down on the bed. I was about to ask what she had in mind when I felt her lips on my shoulder and then farther down my biceps.

"I like how they feel right after we're together, or after you carry me," she said.

"What do you mean?"

"Your muscles pump up from the effort."

She kissed my abs, moving her mouth in a straight line over the top of my six-pack. It took a lot of effort at the gym to look like this. But if it made her this happy, I was going to put in that damn effort every day.

"Where do you plan to devour me next?" she asked.

I scoffed. "Like I'd tell you. I like surprising you."

"Hmm, I'm conflicted," she said. "On the one hand, I do like your sexy surprises. On the other hand, the anticipation will kill me."

"You know how to make your case," I said, grinning.

She stopped kissing and looked sideways at me. "I know, right? So, which way is it going to go?"

"Babe, I'm not going to tell you one thing. I like rocking your world, and I like taking you by surprise when I do it. The effect it has on you is..."

She sighed. "Amazing. Yeah, I know. In fact, you instinctively know exactly what my body needs."

"I like discovering you." I put a hand on her chest, straight over her heart. "And I like discovering what's inside you as well."

She dipped her head so the lights weren't shining on her anymore, but I still saw the hint of a smile on her face.

"You make my heart happy in ways you don't even understand," she murmured.

"I don't have to. As long as I keep doing it and you reward me with that smile, all is right in the world."

Chapter Twenty-Seven

Reese

"I've never been here!" I exclaimed.

Dom had brought me to Christkindlmarket, Chicago's Irish Christmas market.

"I thought we could both try something new."

I grinned up at him. December was always my favorite month of the year, but so much more this time around because I could share it all with Dom. Usually, I dragged anyone who had time to Christmas markets, but since everyone in the family got hitched, I kind of felt guilty taking them away from their loved ones. Thankfully, Dom liked to indulge me.

The booths reminded me of European Christmas markets. I once went to see Kimberly in Paris in December and visited quite a few.

My phone beeped as I took pictures of the decorations. My stomach clenched when I saw the text.

Malcolm: Maybe now you'll pay attention to me.

I scrolled up and down, but he didn't say anything else.

What the hell is he talking about? After all, I hadn't heard from him since last week when he burst into the hotel.

I put my phone away, determined to enjoy the evening. Declan said Malcolm had no legal means to claim any money. He just wanted to intimidate me, and I wouldn't allow it.

As we walked around the stands, I could barely restrain myself from buying all sort of goodies.

"Come on, Reese. Tell me what you want," Dom said.

I grinned at him. "How can you tell I even want something?"

"You keep leaning in whenever you smell something good."

"I'm in the mood for those honey-glazed peanuts."

We stopped in front of one of the stands, and I bought a cone chock-full of goodies.

"They're delicious," I exclaimed. "And so are you."

He pinned me with his gaze. "Don't talk like that in public. You know I can't control myself."

I chuckled. "Duly noted."

"You want us to look at every booth?"

"That's what I was going to suggest."

We were freezing, so we speed-walked around the Christmas market. I couldn't help myself and stopped at every single booth. They sold everything from candles to hand-painted globes. Some were gorgeous, some downright kitschy, but it was all fun.

Dom stiffened when we reached a booth with drinks.

"Are you cold?" I asked him before realizing he was holding his phone. Whatever he was reading was bad news. I was sure of it. "Dom?"

He cleared his throat, immediately sliding his phone back into his pocket.

"What's wrong?" I asked.

"Nothing." He replied so quickly that I knew it wasn't just bad news—it was something personal. If it were business related, he'd tell me. "Is everything okay? Is your dad fine?"

He looked at me incredulously before kissing my forehead. "Yeah, Reese, Dad's fine." He hesitated and then said, "Fuck it. I don't want to keep anything a secret from you."

My body tensed, and I suddenly didn't feel cold anymore.

He nodded to one of the tables where people stood, drinking mulled wine. One of them was empty. He pulled his phone back out, handing it to me. I stared at the screen, and for a few minutes, my brain didn't understand what I was looking at. Then I realized it was an article about him: "Fashion Mogul and Maxwell Heiress." I speedread it.

I knew how much Dom hated being in the spotlight, but this was all right—or so I thought. Right at the end, they speculated that he might have been cheating on his wife with me because we'd been an item since that charity evening, which was, after all, only a short while after he'd signed the divorce papers.

"A lot of people know about us since we've attended a few high-profile parties together. But I don't understand why they're taking this angle—or how they would even know about the charity evening," Dom said.

My stomach clenched. I had a terrible feeling.

"I think this might be Malcolm's doing," I whispered.

"Why would you say that?"

"I got a message from him a few minutes ago that didn't make any sense, so I completely ignored it. It said that maybe now I'll pay attention to him."

"Reese, it's not your fault. And the article wasn't bad." His voice was tight.

"Will this impact your business?"

"No way to tell. I don't like people speculating that I'm a cheater. But it's not important. It's nothing I can't deal with. Don't waste your time worrying about it, okay?"

"How can I not worry? None of this would have happened if I didn't have so much drama going on in my life."

"Reese, we're in this together, remember? And honestly, this could be a good thing. If I can trace it back to him, then I can sue him for defamation."

"You're grasping at straws," I insisted.

I wanted to disappear. I *knew* he was trying to maintain a calm facade for me. He'd told me when I first met him that he valued his privacy above anything else, and that he wouldn't date someone with a high profile again.

"I feel cold," I said.

"You want a drink?"

"Yes, please."

Nodding, he went to stand in line.

He handed me a cup of hot mulled wine not two minutes later. I took a sip, enjoying feeling warm inside. My hands were frozen from holding the phone for so long.

"What are you thinking about?" Dom asked.

"I don't think Malcolm will stop. I thought he would have by now, but obviously I was wrong."

"So what? We'll fight him."

I looked up at him. "But it's not your fight. And you hate being in the press."

"It's nothing I can't deal with."

"Stop saying that. I don't want you to put up with anything because of me."

"I don't mind." He spoke slowly, as if he wasn't sure I understood him. "We're in this together," he said, kissing my temple. "We both have been through a lot. It's normal for stuff like this to pop up from time to time."

I shook my head. "Yeah, but my stuff tends to hurt the people I love and care about."

I put my hand to my forehead, pressing into it.

"Are you feeling okay?" he asked.

"No, I'm starting to get a headache."

"Where do you want to go?" he asked. "My place or yours?"

"Let's go to my place," I said.

"Okay. Come on."

He brought the peanuts with us, and I took a few more sips of the mulled wine, but I wasn't in the mood for the latter anymore.

Once we were inside the car, he immediately turned up the heat. I wanted to curl into a tight ball and just sink into myself, but I didn't want to be rude to Dom.

We didn't speak at all on the drive home or on the way up to my condo. Once inside, he made me hot tea. I curled up on the couch with the cup he gave me and drank it immediately.

"You don't want a sip?"

He sat next to me, watching me intently. "No, I'm good. I just want to make sure you're okay too. Do you want to talk about it?"

I shook my head. "I don't know what to say."

I wanted to keep him safe, but I didn't think I could. I wanted to be alone, with my thoughts, yet I didn't want to push him away. He'd told me many times that he wanted us to fight through things together, but I wasn't sure I knew how to do that. That's why when we went to bed, I pretended to be asleep when he came out of the shower.

Ever since Dom and I got together, my insomnia seemed to have disappeared. But I was awake for most of that night.

Chapter Twenty-Eight
Reese

The next morning, Dom left early for a meeting. I woke up with renewed energy and a plan.

I kept replaying in my mind the evening Malcolm came to the hotel. He'd called me a coward. And I *had* been a coward for these past few years. Every time he wanted to meet me, there was someone from my family with me. The truth was, I couldn't bear the idea of being alone with him. He was always more vicious if it was just the two of us. Even when only Francesca was around, he didn't dare talk to me the way he did when he thought no one else could hear him.

But today, that was going to change.

I didn't want to call him because I wasn't ready to hear his voice yet, so I shot him a message.

Reese: I want to talk to you and Francesca.
Malcolm: Where?
Reese: Give me your address.

I wouldn't have the meeting in a public place. If there was going to be a scene, no one else would witness it. I was done with these two.

The last time I'd been alone with them in the same room was when I caught them having sex. It had been an awful evening. In the span of fifteen seconds, my life fell apart, and my heart cracked in two. It hadn't healed until I met Dom.

I was astounded when he texted me the address. They were living in a nice neighborhood. Why would he need money then? I called a car and Ubered there—I didn't want to drive myself because once I was done with them, I knew I wouldn't feel like driving.

I looked around when I stepped out of the car. The house they lived in was relatively small, but the rent still had to be enormous based on this location.

I walked up to the front door, knocking twice. It swung open immediately, Malcolm obviously having been waiting for me. Francesca was farther inside the room. I stepped in and felt the tension in the air. No one said anything at all.

"Well, I'm here," I said when it became apparent that neither of them was going to speak. "I thought that after hounding me for so long, you'd have something to say when I finally saw you on my own."

The two of them exchanged a glance. I realized on the spot that they'd hoped to corner me on their terms, like they did at the charity event. Perhaps that was why they signed up for it—not because they planned to donate any money or get any business contacts, but to reach me.

"So, let me get this straight," I started, sounding braver than I felt. "You thought you could move back to Chicago and what? Intimidate me into giving you money?"

They remained silent. I looked from one to the other.

Finally, Malcolm spoke up. "Killing the spa business wasn't fair, and you know that."

"I hope this is not your way of appealing to my conscience," I told Malcolm. "The deal fell apart because I found you fucking her."

Francesca turned red. She glanced to one side, avoiding my gaze.

"You two have spent far too much time thinking you can push me around. You destroyed me after using me as an ATM for years."

"No, we didn't," Malcolm denied.

"Really? All those trips and stuff I bought. I never minded because I always liked sharing my wealth with the people I cared about. But you two are on another level altogether. I just have one question: How long had this been going on before I discovered it?"

I looked straight at Francesca. She'd been my best friend for years before I met Malcolm. We'd been like sisters since college; we'd met on orientation day and had been joined at the hip ever since.

"Almost since you started dating him," she said.

My heart started to crack again. I felt light-headed knowing now this had been going on for years. I'd made up so many scenarios in my mind, wondering when he might have turned to her. But they'd been cheating on me for *years*. My vision faded at the corners, but the knowledge only gave me strength.

"I can't believe you two are so callous. Especially after you had a baby."

I wondered where the baby was. Maybe with Francesca's mother. She'd always hinted she wanted to be a grandmother.

She turned to Malcolm. "Well, he can't make enough money otherwise. His job barely covers the cost, and I want a certain lifestyle," she said, sounding more vicious than I'd ever heard her.

"So he turned to the only source of money he knew: me." The room faded away before slowly taking shape again.

How could I have been so utterly manipulated?

"You don't get to come here and belittle me in front of my wife," Malcolm snapped.

Strangely, I didn't feel anything at his mention of the word *wife*. It didn't hurt that they were together anymore. The betrayal was the only thing that had left deep marks, but I was starting to accept them as part of me. It didn't mean I wasn't whole or that I wasn't worthy of love. It simply meant I had a past, just as Dom said.

"You two aren't going to get a thing from me."

Malcolm turned white. Francesca looked at him in disgust.

"So if that's why you came to Chicago," I continued, "you can move back to wherever you came from. I'm not giving you any money."

Malcolm set his jaw.

Yep, Declan was right.

"I'm not that scared and hurt woman you left behind years ago. I'm strong. I know my worth, and nothing you can do is going to diminish it, so get the fuck out of my city," I sneered.

Francesca threw her hands up in the air. "God! You're an idiot, Malcolm. I told you this would never work. I'm moving back to my parents' with our daughter."

"Babe, you can't do this. I promise I'll get money one way or another," he pleaded.

But she just turned around, disappearing into one of the rooms.

I couldn't even pity him. This was exactly what he deserved. "It feels horrible, doesn't it? To be left like this?"

I walked to the front door with determined steps. He made no move to stop me. The second I was outside, I drew in a deep breath, exhaling slowly.

I couldn't believe what I'd just done. I mentally high-fived myself.

I was free.

Dom

"What do you mean, cancel all meetings?" Charlene asked the second I stepped into the office.

"I need to take care of something this morning."

"Is it related to the article?" she asked as I sat down.

"Do we have any reactions regarding that?"

She winced. "The publication reached out to you for a comment. I declined."

"Thank you," I said sincerely.

"And the press that's covering the next collection launch also reached out."

I set my jaw. "That can't be helped. We'll just placate them."

She raised a brow. "I must say, you're taking this far better than I imagined."

Only a few months ago, this would have bothered me enormously. But right now, all I wanted was to make sure Reese was okay.

"Do you need anything else from me?" she asked.

"No, thanks."

The second she left, I made a plan. I hadn't bothered asking my investigative team to get Malcolm's address when I first looked into him, but I had an idea about how to get it.

I didn't have Declan Maxwell's number, but since he was an attorney, I assumed I'd find his information online. His website had a phone number listed. *What do you know? There's at least one Maxwell listing their number.* I called it immediately.

"Declan Maxwell's office. How may I help you?" a guy answered.

"Hello, I'm looking for Declan Maxwell."

"Are you a client?"

"No."

"What can we help you with?"

"Tell him Dominic Waldorf wants to speak to him about Reese."

The other guy made a sound I didn't comprehend, and then I heard a muffled "He says it's Dominic Waldorf."

"Transfer the call to me," I heard another voice say—probably Declan himself.

"He'll be right with you," the same guy said.

A few seconds later, there was a static sound, and then Declan's voice came on. "Dominic?"

"Yes."

"What's wrong?" he asked.

"I need Malcolm's address. I have a feeling you know it."

"Of course I do."

"I need to talk to him face-to-face."

"I'm coming with you," Declan said.

"I appreciate the offer, but I'm handling this."

"Listen, that guy is a moron. He knows how to push people's buttons."

"He knows how to push Reese's buttons and all of yours because he's known you for years," I said calmly. "He doesn't know me."

"Intimidation doesn't work. I've done that for a few years myself."

"From what I've seen, it hasn't gotten into his thick skull that Reese isn't on her own. I'm going to change that."

"Fair enough. I'm going to message you the address."

I left my office the second Declan texted me the address. I had a lot of adrenaline, so I just hopped into the car and drove straight to his neighborhood. I was seeing red, and I didn't even have the guy in front of me. Seeing Reese like that last evening was excruciating, especially because she didn't allow me to be there for her. She thought I didn't realize she was faking sleeping, but of course I did. I knew her body; I could tell when she was awake and when she wasn't. But I'd taken that as a cue that she needed her space.

Malcolm was in front of the house when I arrived, and so was Francesca.

Just my luck!

A few seconds later, I realized they were fighting. She was loading luggage into her car.

"Come on, Fran. You can't just leave."

"Yes, I can. You've promised me you'd get your shit together and start earning some real money for years. I'm done waiting. I've got a life to live."

"What the hell are you doing here?" Malcolm asked, noticing me.

"Oh, for fuck's sake!" Francesca exclaimed. "First Reese and then this dude? What did you do? Plaster our address in the newspaper?"

She's leaving him? Karma is good.

But then I registered what they'd said.

"Reese was here?" I asked.

"Yes," Malcolm replied. "Came to do her own bidding for once."

He looked beat. What did Reese tell him? Whatever it was, he deserved it.

"So, what, I'm guessing you're here to give me a piece of *your* mind, too? To feel like a macho man because you're protecting her?"

"At least he *is* protecting her," Francesca shot back. "You can't even *provide* for your family."

"Fran, give it a rest." He turned back to me. "What did you even come for?" he asked.

"First, if you ever plant any more stories in rag magazines, you'll be so fucking sorry. The reason I'm not going after you legally right now is to spare Reese. I'm glad she gave you a piece of her mind," I said calmly. "You deserve nothing less. I'm not here to get things off my chest. I couldn't care less what you two do. I have no history with you. But mark my words, Reese is not alone. She doesn't only have the Maxwells at her side now. She's got me, and I'm not going to let you get away with any more of this shit. It's my understanding that you're working for Andamosi Investments."

He took a step back. "No, I'm not."

I rolled my eyes. "I've got contacts in all industries. Don't try to deny it. And from what I've heard here, you're not doing so great financially, right? So here's the deal. Disappear from Reese's life, or you'll find yourself without that job too. Got it?"

"Oh, for fuck's sake. Malcolm, don't screw that up too. You could barely *get* the job," Francesca said. "You'll have to pay alimony, trust me."

Damn, she was a piece of work. He was a scumbag, sure, but he was still her husband, yet she was kicking him when he was down.

Then again, it was exactly what he deserved.

"How do you know that?" he questioned me. "Not even Declan Maxwell found that out."

"You've paid off the wrong people. The Maxwells aren't the only ones who can investigate you." I crossed my arms and glared at him. "So here's what we'll do. You will never attempt to contact Reese or the other Maxwells again. You will not go to the press. And you will never, not once, see Reese again."

I didn't wait to see their reactions, just turned around and got in my car. I had better things to do—like showing Reese that she was my world.

She'd come here without even telling me about it. It was time for my woman to understand that we were in this together.

Chapter Twenty-Nine
Reese

Subject: Order Ready

Dear Ms. Maxwell,

We're pleased to inform you that your custom-ordered dress is ready for pickup. We strongly suggest you come after 9:00 p.m., as the store is very busy before.

I reread the email again as I got out of the Uber in front of the store. I didn't remember ordering anything from Waldorf Fashion recently. I'd browsed their website often, including the section where you could customize dresses, but did I actually go through with it?

Wouldn't be the first time I went overboard once I started a shopping spree.

The store looked empty when I arrived. I glanced at the business hours written on the door. Maybe the sales assistant had made a mistake, and I was supposed to come one hour earlier, because according to the schedule, they'd closed twenty minutes ago. But since I was here anyway, I tried the door, and to my surprise, it was open.

Right, maybe she's waiting for me.

"Hello?" I said, stepping inside. "Are you still open? This is Reese Maxwell. I have an appointment to pick something up."

No one answered. I was about to turn around and leave when I heard footsteps coming from the back.

I went to the counter, already taking out my wallet and putting it on the cash register. "I thought you were closed."

"We are," Dom's booming voice replied.

I expelled a breath, turning around. "Dom, I wasn't expecting you."

He smiled. "Really? You didn't see through my paper-thin email?"

I swallowed hard. "Wait a second. You made this all up, so I'd come here, right?"

"Guilty."

"Why?"

"I figured it was high time we turned the story about our meeting into the actual truth."

"Oh!" I looked around, smiling. "That's right."

"You walked in here after hours, requiring a specific dress. But instead of getting anyone to help you, you got me. I love you, Reese. So much that I would do anything to make you happy, absolutely anything. I won't let anyone come between us."

I felt my legs move of their own accord until we were right in front of each other. "I love you too. I can't believe you remembered the story so vividly."

"Every detail. I have to say, I like our actual story so much more."

I looked down at my toes. "My mental breakdown in the coatroom?"

"You were just being yourself, completely open and unrestrained, and you charmed me."

As I looked up, my heart was starting to beat faster. The lights went off, and I glanced around. "What's happening?"

"It's nine o'clock. The lights automatically go off." The only slivers of light were the Christmas decorations in the window display.

I glanced back at Dom. He looked even sexier than before, more sensual.

"I don't care how the story started. All I know is I want it to continue." He took my hands in his. He was very close to me now. "You saw Malcolm this morning."

I gasped. "How do you know that?"

"Because I went to see him, too, and he told me."

"Oh my God."

"Listen to me, Reese. I meant when I said we're in this together. I know you're strong and you can do everything on your own. But I'm yours. And I want you to be certain of that."

"I am."

"Promise me you won't fake sleep again."

I gasped again. "I promise."

"Good, because I want to make you as happy as you make me."

"You mean that?"

"Yes. God yes. I haven't meant anything more in my life. You showed me what happiness feels like, Reese. Utter and complete happiness. I didn't think it was possible, or that it existed at all. But you didn't leave me a choice."

"Huh. I coerced you into loving me?" I smirked.

"Something like that. You're so damn lovable, I never stood a chance." He tilted his head forward until our foreheads brushed. I felt warm and so *alive*.

"I resisted at first. I was a fool," he whispered. "From now on, I will love you my whole life."

He kissed my cheek, moving his lips exquisitely slowly. I loved his smell. I loved *him*.

He had a five-o'clock shadow, and it lightly scratched me. I shuddered at the sensation. I loved everything this man did to me.

When his mouth was at the corner of my lips, he stilled completely. I turned my head slowly. He kissed me then, and I opened up without restraint. This kiss reminded me so much of our first one.

I'd been so surprised, but all I wanted to do was let him kiss me. The same was true right now. I wanted nothing more than his mouth on mine, his hands all over my body.

He slipped his hands under my coat, undoing a few buttons to gain more space. I felt his fingers dig into my waist. As he moved back, I leaned into him hungrily. As if through a haze, I realized we were moving.

"Where are we going?" I asked when we paused to breathe.

"Out of sight."

"Oh yeah, that's probably a good idea." I trusted him implicitly.

Then I heard the sound of a curtain moving, and I opened my eyes, glancing around. He'd brought us into the changing room. Two neon lights lit up sideways, activated by our movement. He looked so sexy.

"In this light," I murmured, "all I want to do is take off your clothes."

His eyes glinted in the dark, and my entire body tightened, especially the peaks of my breasts. "I was thinking the same."

"I see. So you lured me here with a purpose."

"Yes. This wasn't actually the purpose, but now that you're here, it's all that I can think about. Take off all your clothes," he said in that low baritone voice. He sat on the chair, tilting forward and resting his elbows on his knees, eyes intent on me.

"Where do you want me to start?" I asked.

"You can decide on that."

Well, well, isn't he generous today?

I unbuttoned my blouse slowly, starting from the top and going down to my skirt before pulling it out of the waistband and undoing the rest of them. Then I proceeded to open the buttons of my sleeves and took the blouse off very slowly before moving on to my skirt. I didn't make eye contact, certain I was going to completely forget myself if I looked straight into his eyes. I was hyperaware of him; I could hear his breath, even from a few feet away. I was even more aware of my body as I leisurely lowered the zipper at the back of my skirt.

I smiled to myself as I pushed my skirt, tights, and panties all the way down, stepping out of them and leaving a pile of clothes on the floor. When I straightened up, I heard an audible gasp. I glanced at him again. He'd shifted forward on the seat.

"Come to me."

"Right now?"

"Yes, right fucking now."

I reached between my breasts, undoing my bra and letting it drop behind me. I'd never felt as sexy as now.

He straightened in the seat, looking up at me, and drew three fingers up my right thigh. I gasped as an unexpected shock of pleasure rippled through me. He moved those fingers around to my buttock. The touch went from light to featherlight, yet it still reached deep inside my body. He started caressing my other side, too, moving upward even slower than before. Then his mouth was on the underside of my breasts. I dropped my head back, relishing the feeling.

He touched between my thighs, making me moan in delight. Then he pressed two fingers along the length of my opening. Out of instinct, I rubbed against him. He yanked me down onto his lap, and I clutched his shoulders as he kissed me voraciously. I responded with all the passion I had, all my love, and all my heart. I loved this man so much. Feeling his hands on me was absolutely exquisite. Every time I thought he couldn't surprise me anymore, he proved differently.

"I'm ready as fuck, babe. I need you so damn bad." He spoke against my mouth while I tugged at his shirt, taking it out of his pants. I moved farther back on his thighs, opening his belt and freeing his erection as quickly as possible. I couldn't believe he was already so hard for me.

He shifted my ass back on his lap, and I realized what he was about to do seconds before he did it. He ran his erection along the length of my opening, and I was drenched within seconds. I squeezed my eyes shut, shaking when the first spasm rocked my body. I wasn't ashamed anymore of how fast he turned me on. I was basking in it. My body trusted him, utterly and completely, and it was delicious.

His hand slid from the back of my neck up to my scalp, and I opened my eyes just as he pulled me in for a kiss. I leaned against his mouth, loving the feeling of his tongue exploring mine and his cock rubbing at my clit.

He grabbed my ass, rocking my body against him. He didn't show me any mercy, didn't leave me any reprieve. I exploded fast and hard, and I couldn't contain it. I groaned hard, clinging to him for dear life, pressing myself against him. I ground my hips back and forth until I was utterly and completely satisfied.

My entire body was shaking as I rested my head in the crook of his neck, which was when I realized he was still completely clothed while I was buck naked.

"You're so fucking sexy. You're everything I could dream of," he said into my ear.

"I was going to say that you just rocked my world."

"Happy to do it anytime."

"I want you so damn much," he said.

I swallowed hard. I'd managed to completely block out the fact that we were in his store. Sure, it was closed, the changing room was way in the back, and we'd closed the curtain, but still, this felt decadent.

Standing up, he moved the chair in front of the mirror.

Taking my hand, he led me in front of the chair. As he stared at my nakedness, he took his clothes off, which was a whole new level of erotic. He first removed his shirt and then pushed his jeans down. He didn't bother with his boxers; I simply freed his erection, pumping once.

He sat down and pointed at his lap. "Sit here, beautiful. I want to watch you, watch us."

Sitting with my back to him, I grabbed his cock at the base, but instead of sliding it inside me, I rubbed myself against the tip just the way he'd teased me before.

"Reese, fuck." His mouth was on my shoulder, so his voice was muffled. "Babe."

I swallowed hard, unable to reply.

Watching us in the mirror was insanely sexy. He cupped my breasts, touching them hungrily, before lowering one hand to my clit. My eyes lost focus for a few seconds, and I blinked rapidly to steady myself. I needed him inside me more than anything else, so I shifted my hips, taking him all in, grinding my back against his chest.

I stilled, unable to move. How could this feel so damn good? Had it always felt like this, or was today even better because we'd embraced all our fears and confessed our feelings? I didn't know, but I felt him so deep inside me that I could barely breathe. Then I started rolling my hips back and forth.

He didn't stop touching my clit, not even for a second. I was about to lose my mind. I wasn't in charge of my body anymore—Dom was.

He alternated between simply rubbing my center and slapping it lightly. Watching him do it was all I could take.

"You're beautiful when you surrender to me, Reese," he growled.

"Yes, God, yes," I exclaimed.

He shut his eyes, and I felt his mouth on my back in the shape of an O. He came a moment later, and then I completely lost sense of myself and gave in to him. The wave crashed over me without warning. There was no crescendo about it, just relentless pleasure from the way his fingers moved over my clit. I wasn't sure how I was still sitting on him when all my muscles seemed nonexistent.

My body felt incredibly relaxed, and I leaned back against him for support. I had no idea how long we stayed like that.

"Are you cold?" he whispered in my ear after a while.

"No, I'm only feeling an intense happiness. Is that normal?"

"It's the same for me, so I'm going with yes."

"So we went from defiling furniture to defiling your store."

He laughed, and I straightened on his lap before rising from it.

"Anytime, Reese. Just call me and I'll make it happen."

I blushed furiously, looking at myself in the mirror. "I should cover up."

"You're beautiful, babe."

I stopped in the act of reaching for my blouse because he cupped my face and kissed me slowly, tenderly. I sighed against his mouth, caressing his wrist with my fingertips. I loved feeling his pulse. It was racing—because of me.

Then I started to shiver. He must have felt it, because he stopped the kiss, looking down at me. "Now you're cold, right? I knew it. Let's get you dressed. We don't want you to get sick or something."

I immediately put on my clothes, as did he.

"Do you have a bathroom around here?" I asked.

"Yep, come on. I'll take you to it," he said.

I looked around the changing room. "I feel like people will know what happened in here."

"No, they won't."

He came with me all the way to the back. "Go in there." It was an employee bathroom. I handed him my trusty hand wipes, and we cleaned up.

"Okay, mission accomplished. Sexy crime successfully covered up."

Dom started laughing. "Sexy crime? That's what you call it?" he said as we returned to the front of the store.

"What would you call it?"

"Let's see... amazing sex?"

I chuckled. "We can go with that. I love you so damn much, Dom."

"I love you too. Now, there is one more thing we need to do before the story is complete."

"Hmm, and what's that?" I asked.

"You need a dress."

I frowned. "I don't understand."

"Remember our cover story? You came in to buy a dress."

"Oh, that's right. Duh, why else would I come here? But we never said that I actually ended up buying one." I smiled in the dark.

"The thing is, I have one you'd look amazing in."

I swallowed hard. "Really?" I was thrilled he'd chosen something for me.

"Yes. I'd like for you to try it on."

"Right now?"

"Yes." His voice sounded dangerous and oh so sexy. My lady parts were already paying attention. But honestly, was there anything this man could do that wouldn't turn me on?

He started to walk away. "I'm going to get it. Go back to the changing room. I'll bring it for you."

After going back in there, I glanced around with a smile. I could see us going down that rabbit hole again.

The store was silent for about three minutes, and then I heard his footsteps. When he came into view, my breath caught. He was carrying the dress in front of him. It was dark red with a small bow around the waist. The corsage was velvet, and the sleeves were organza. There were several layers in the skirt, of course, but only one in the sleeves, and I knew they would be see-through.

"This is beautiful," I said.

"Put it on."

"Okay, but you're not allowed to come in and watch."

"And why not?"

"Because I know you. You'll end up talking me into another sexy crime."

He grinned. "All right. Put it on and show it to me afterward."

"That's the plan," I said, taking the dress from him.

I changed in record time, and then I couldn't stop staring at myself in the mirror. The dress was absolute perfection. I'd never felt so beautiful.

"You can look now," I said to him through the curtain.

He pulled back the curtain in a fraction of a second.

He just looked at me for several moments, then murmured. "Reese, babe... you're the most beautiful woman I've ever seen."

"Thank you."

He walked right up behind me again and moved the chair back into its original place. Then he put a hand on my belly. "It looks amazing on you."

"It's as if it was made for me."

He darted his eyes away.

"Dom, what did you do?"

He flashed me his most charming smile. "I had it commissioned for you."

My eyes widened. "Wow! Why?"

"Because you described the dress in the car, and it stuck in my mind. I relayed it to one of our designers, and he came up with this. I instantly approved it. I knew it was you. Just you. It came back a while ago. I intended to give it to you as a Christmas gift, but this works too." He grinned from ear to ear.

"Yes, it does. Thank you." I turned back, glancing in the mirror. "God, I'm so happy. This is stunning." Dom was also looking at my reflection. "Dom..."

"What?" he asked in an innocent tone.

"I know that voice, that look. You're thinking about taking it off me, aren't you?"

"You're gorgeous in it. But my absolute favorite outfit on you is your bare skin."

My center started pulsing like mad at his words. I laughed, turning around so I could kiss him properly. I pressed myself against him, first kissing his Adam's apple and then his skin.

"You went through all this trouble to create my imaginary dress." I kissed his neck again, then pulled back. "But wait a second—how come it fits me perfectly? You don't know my measurements."

"No, but I took a page out of your own book and spoke to Kimberly about it."

I was giddy with excitement now.

I kissed the corner of his mouth and moved over to his lips, teasing him with a chaste peck, simply feathering my lips against his before giving him the dirtiest kiss ever. He deepened it even more, walking me backward until my back pressed against the mirror.

"Reese, I need you."

"I need you too," I murmured. I would need him every day for the rest of my life. I loved him so much that I wanted to live inside him. "We're not going to leave the store anytime soon, are we?" I asked playfully.

He smiled against my skin. "No, we're not. I'll make sure of that."

Chapter Thirty
Reese

On the twenty-fourth of December, I woke up at the crack of dawn. I had so much energy that I didn't even need coffee.

Next to me, Dom was sleeping soundly. I chastely kissed his chest before getting out of the bed as slowly as possible. I'd left clothes in the bathroom last night, anticipating that I'd wake up super early today. I'd always done that on the twenty-fourth and the twenty-fifth.

Today was a big day in my book. My tree was arriving in approximately two hours—not that I was counting. Then I could start decorating it. I'd packed my smaller fake tree back in its box yesterday.

Kimberly asked me more than once over the years why I didn't put up the big tree earlier. But Mom had always put up the tree on Christmas Eve,

and I wanted to follow her tradition. Although, I *was* cheating with the small tree.

I went into the kitchen, staring at the coffee machine before deciding I didn't need any. I was going to have a hot cocoa instead. It fit the holiday spirit, and I had a special recipe that included a few drops of vanilla extract and powdered cinnamon. It was like Christmas in a cup.

I opened the fridge and grinned as I took out the cream. *Oh yeah. It's not Christmas without a few extra calories.* I had zero regrets.

I stared at Chicago's snow-covered streets through the floor-to-ceiling condo windows as I sipped my cocoa, planning how I was going to decorate my tree.

About twenty minutes later, I heard sounds from the bedroom. I guessed Dom was waking up. I drank my last drops of cocoa and headed that direction. He was sitting upright in the bed, looking like God's gift to *me*. I liked seeing him first thing in the morning when his eyes were tired with sleep.

"Morning," he said, moving to the edge of the bed. "How long have you been up?"

"Not that long. I've had a hot cocoa."

He made a come-here motion with his finger, and I immediately stepped between his thighs, putting my hands on his shoulders. I loved mornings like this so much.

He kissed my belly over my top and then rested his head there, breathing in deeply before looking up at me.

"Come on," I urged. "Hurry up. The tree is going to be here in about an hour."

"Okay," Dom said, climbing out of bed and heading to the bathroom. He showered quickly, and then I did the same.

Back in the living room, I made an inventory of my tree ornaments. I could probably decorate at least three trees. I never managed to use all of them on one.

"I still can't believe I didn't get my tree," I said with a pout, remembering that I'd missed the lottery and had to settle with a different one.

Dom put an arm around my waist, kissing the back of my neck. "There's always next year, babe."

"I know, but I had huge hopes." I fidgeted against him, happy to have him here at my place. Ever since I bought this condo, it never felt like a proper home, but now it did.

The doorbell rang, startling us both.

"It's here," I practically screeched.

Thankfully, Dom pretended I hadn't just acted like a two-year-old. With a smile, he said, "Let's go bring in your tree."

I opened the door, smiling from ear to ear. A huge tree filled the corridor. There were four guys carrying it.

"Miss Reese Maxwell?" the one in front asked.

"Yeah, that's me. Come on in."

Every year, I was afraid the tree wouldn't get through the door. But this year, I was extra suspicious because the girth of it was even wider than usual. They carried it inside slowly.

"My, my," I murmured. I knew it had to be bigger than the one I ordered. "What size is this?" I asked one of the men.

"Fourteen feet."

I gasped. "But I thought mine was ten."

What if they'd accidentally delivered the wrong one and someone else was waiting for this gorgeous tree? I wanted my big-ass fir, but I didn't want to ruin anyone's Christmas.

Dom looked at me with a knowing smile.

"You did this?" I whispered as the men proceeded to the tree stand in the living room.

"Yes."

"But how?"

"I spoke to the owners of the nursery after I saw how upset you were when you didn't win the tree you wanted, and they put me in contact with a few other nurseries. One thing led to another, and you got your tree."

"Just so you know, if we were alone, I'd show my appreciation in all the ways possible." But we weren't alone, so all I did was step closer and give him a kiss.

"That is the best Christmas gift ever," I said.

We watched them put the tree up. It involved two huge ladders that the men brought from their truck and lots of strength.

"All right, ma'am. You sign here," one of the guys said after they'd successfully installed it.

I couldn't stop staring—it was absolutely gorgeous. I signed absentmindedly, and then Dom went with them to the door.

"I think I'll actually be able to use all my decorations this year. Where to begin?" I wondered as Dom returned. He was standing next to a pile of tree decorations, smiling at me. I had separate sets for the small and the big tree.

I put my hands on my hips. "Hey, don't look at me like that. This takes a lot of strategy. I had a plan in mind, but that one's no good anymore because the tree is larger."

"Only you could call decorating a tree a strategy. You want some pen and paper to make a sketch?"

"You're mocking me."

He grinned. "No, not at all. Just want to make things easier for you."

"I'll start with the red globes. I can't go wrong with that. I'll put all of them on the tree, then fill in the space with the golden ones."

"Sounds good."

I blinked at him, batting my eyelashes. "Want to be my helper? I promise to be extra feisty later on."

He chuckled. "I would have helped you anyway, but I won't say no to that."

I started putting on the biggest of the round ornaments. Dom was in charge of moving the huge ladder around the tree.

"All right. This looks good," I said after the first round. "Let's see what's next."

Dom cleared his throat. "I have one for you. It's special."

"You bought an ornament?" I was a bit stunned.

He nodded, handing me a beautiful box.

Oh, I was so excited. It had to be special if it was packed like this.

I carefully removed the lid, and my heart sighed. It was a hand-painted globe. I took it out of the box, carefully setting it on my palm. It had a pattern of red, gold, and white sprinkles that mimicked the snow. It was the strangest ornament ever, because it had a bit of a gap in the middle.

"It opens," Dom said, correctly interpreting my confusion.

"Why would it open?"

"Let's find out."

I was curious and nervous now. I carefully unclasped it, taking off the upper half.

"Oh my God," I breathed.

There was something inside—a ring with a gorgeous red stone in the shape of a rhombus diamond. It was absolutely amazing.

I opened my mouth, but my throat wasn't working.

Dom took the lower part of the ornament from my hand and then lowered himself onto one knee.

"Reese Maxwell, I can't imagine my life without you." He took the ring out, setting the ornament on the floor. I was still clinging to the upper half, barely able to contain my immense happiness.

"You have my love, Reese. My heart, body, and soul. You have every part of me, forever. On this day of the year that means so much to you, I want to ask you to give yourself to me forever. To trust me to make you the happiest woman for the rest of our days. To trust me to love you and take care of you."

"I do," I murmured, worried that no sound came out of my throat because it was so full of emotion. But Dom heard me. His eyes widened, just a bit, and his lips tilted up a lot more. "I love you so much, Dom. I'd love to be your wife."

With a wide smile, Dom pushed the ring onto my finger. It looked even better there than it had inside the globe.

Instead of getting up, Dom pulled me down with a yelp, and we both lay on the floor. I grinned as he held me against him, then kissed him, deep and dirty.

I touched my ring finger with my thumb, feeling the band. I was so giddy and happy.

"I'll always remember this day," I told him, pulling back a bit. "When you gave me a huge-ass tree and this gorgeous ring."

"I see. So you value those equally." There was a glint in his eyes.

"No, I didn't say that. Just that I'll remember both things with love."

We both rose to our feet at the same time. Dom picked up the bottom half of the globe from the floor and gave it to me. I put it back together, then set it on the end table by the tree.

"I can't believe you proposed like this," I whispered, looking up at him. "You go out of your way to make everything special for me."

"I do, Reese. And I promise I'll do it for the rest of our lives."

I beamed, looking at the tree, then at the globe.

"Where are you going to put it?" he asked me.

"I'm thinking right here, in the center. That way you can see it from almost everywhere in the room. What do you think?"

"You're the decorating boss."

I nodded, smiling. "That's right."

I hung the globe, then took a step back "Well, I think this is it. This is the place for it." Turning to the rest of my decorations, I tapped my chin, considering my options. "Now, let's see. Let's go on with the golden ones." I spoke more to myself than to him, but he moved the ladder in the direction I pointed.

I had a flash of us doing this together with two, maybe even three little ones, and I smiled at the image as I went up a few steps on the ladder. I could see our future crystal clear, and I couldn't wait to experience it alongside this amazing man.

First Epilogu
Rees

"Darling, you look so beautiful," Gran exclaimed.

"Thank you." Both she and Aunt Lena stood behind me. Lena was messing a bit with my veil under the pretext that she was arranging it under my hairdo. I suspected that she was simply busying herself to hide tears.

"Aunt Lena," I asked softly, "are you okay?"

She looked up at me, her eyes glassy. "Of course. I'm just emotional."

"Oh, Lena. Don't make the poor girl cry," Gran chastised, but her own voice was a bit unsteady.

"Why don't we all have a good cry now?" Kimberly suggested. She'd finished fastening her shoes and stood up. "That way we don't run the risk of randomly bursting into tears later. And by 'we,' I actually mean myself."

I turned around, looking at all three of them. "You know, you can cry all you want to. There's no reason to hold back. We all have waterproof makeup on." I was babbling. I was beyond nervous and full of emotions.

I turned around to glance in the mirror. My dress was amazing. The bridal collection was labeled Fairy-Tale Wedding, and I truly felt like I was in a story. The dress had short sleeves, and the detail in the lace was absolutely stunning. The same pattern crisscrossed all over the bodice.

The lower part of the dress had a different pattern, but it was just as breathtaking. It was interchangeable too: this one was tight around my body, but once the party started, I'd put on a wider skirt. It made me look like a princess, and it had the added benefit of allowing me enough space to dance. The veil was long, with a pattern of lace too.

"Aunt Reese, Aunt Reese. I'm here," Paisley said, and I heard footsteps outside the bedroom.

When Dom and I started planning the wedding, we both knew we wanted something small with just our friends and family. We both loved the lake house so much that we decided to do it here. Since the yard was huge, the wedding planner had no problem at all setting up a beautiful tent. Holding the party on our private property was also the easiest way to keep the press from butting in.

The fallout from that magazine article followed Dom for months. Reporters relentlessly pestered his PR team for a response, but they'd completely ignored it.

They'd written quite a few articles about the wedding, but both Dom and I were learning to embrace that. We hadn't heard from Malcolm in months, though I heard that Francesca had indeed divorced him and was going after him for every penny.

Paisley burst in, glancing at me. "Oh, Aunt Reese, you're definitely the most beautiful bride in the family." Then she pressed her lips together, widening her eyes in horror. "You were pretty, too, Gran."

Gran laughed. "Oh, I don't mind, Paisley. And I quite agree. Reese is the most beautiful bride I've ever seen." She gave me a quick hug, and then Lena and Kimberly joined her too.

My dad and his wife had arrived this morning. They'd left my sister back in London with her maternal grandparents. She'd come for Gran's wedding, but transatlantic flights and jet lag were hard on kids.

I'd invited my stepmother to help me dress, not wanting her to feel left out, but she insisted that it was quite all right if she just waited downstairs with everyone else. Kimberly, Lexi, Kendra, Liz, Megan, and Avery had fussed around me all morning.

"Are you ready to go downstairs?" Paisley asked.

I nodded. "Yes. Gran, Aunt Lena, you go first. Paisley and I will follow."

"Just like we practiced," Lena said.

"Yes, of course," Paisley replied as she grabbed the train with only the tips of her fingers.

"You're doing great, Paisley. I love you. And even if you drop it or something, don't worry, okay?" I assured her.

"I won't drop it," she said with so much shock that I barely held back from laughing. She was also holding my bouquet.

"Okay then."

We descended the staircase carefully, and I lifted my dress so I didn't step on it. The hardwood floors were a bit slippery.

My entire body seemed to pulse, not just my heart. I couldn't believe this day had arrived already. Dom and I debated getting married at once, but I took a page out of Gran's book—there was something extra charming about summer weddings—and we settled on August. Our wedding planner had transformed the entire house beautifully.

There were white and pink roses everywhere, along with matching bows. The french windows in the living room were open, overlooking the yard. Guests circulated around the tent, and the chairs were arranged for the ceremony. After it was over, the staff would put them around the tables.

"Reese is here," someone said. I thought it sounded like Uncle Emmett, but it might have been Dad.

A few minutes later, Dad walked toward me, beaming from ear to ear. Paisley gave me my flowers.

"My darling girl. You look absolutely beautiful." He had tears in his eyes.

"Thanks, Dad. I'm so happy you flew here."

"Obviously! I made it a point not to miss my girls' weddings, and by girls, I mean your gran too."

I chuckled as he gave me his arm.

"Are you ready?" I asked.

"To give away my daughter? No. I don't think any dad is ever ready for that."

"Uncle Harvey, that's not what you're supposed to say. You're supposed to say yes and wish her all the best," Paisley said in the bossiest voice I'd ever heard her use.

Dad looked over his shoulder. "Right you are, Paisley."

He glanced back at me. "Shall we?"

I nodded.

As the music started playing, I carefully put one foot in front of the other. The guests had all gathered at the side of the tent, making a tunnel of sorts for us. As soon as we stepped inside, everyone was in a flurry, moving to their seats. I took in a deep breath, trying not to see the mayhem around us.

My eyes locked on Dom's. He was waiting for me in front with the officiant.

Emotions bubbled up inside me. I could barely keep the tears at bay. I was determined not to break eye contact, but I had to because I needed to watch my step. There was a real risk that I'd step on my dress if I didn't pay attention, since I couldn't lift my dress now that I had to hold my flowers too.

I looked up again when we were only a few feet away from Dom. I'd never tire of watching those gorgeous eyes drinking me in. Fate found me a man who would love me forever. After everything I'd gone through, I couldn't believe that I was so lucky to have this man in my life.

"Dom," Dad said in a gruff voice, "you're a very lucky man, and I'm a very lucky father to have you as a son-in-law. Take good care of my girl and make her happy."

"I'll do my best, sir," he said.

Dom and I took our positions side by side.

Glancing over my shoulder, I watched Paisley arrange the bottom of my train on the floor the way Aunt Lena had instructed her to do. I wanted to pull her into a huge hug. She'd done so well. I gave her my flowers and taking a deep breath, I turned, looking at the officiant. Dom took both of my hands in his.

"Are we allowed to do this?" I was so besotted with him that I couldn't remember the dos and don'ts of weddings.

He grinned. "We've always done things our way."

The officiant started reciting why we were gathered here today. Dom interlaced our fingers, and I squeezed them very firmly.

She spoke about the importance of marriage and holding on to each other. I was drinking in every word.

We'd wanted to have traditional vows, but whenever we practiced, I'd burst into tears, so we decided against it. When that time came, the officiant gestured to us, and we looked into each other's eyes.

"I love you, Reese," Dom said. "I promise to love you every day for the rest of my life."

"And I promise the same in return, until my last breath."

A few tears streamed down my cheeks. He caught them with the back of his fingers, smiling at me.

"See, that's why I didn't want us to exchange vows," I said. We decided on simply saying "I love you," thinking I'd be safe from tears.

Apparently not.

The officiant smiled at us, her own eyes a bit watery, and continued the ceremony. "I've met with the bride and groom a few times before today, and it struck me that they are completely in love in ways I rarely see in other couples. And believe me, I've seen many. It's my absolute pleasure to declare you husband and wife." She turned to Dom. "You may kiss your wife now."

He looked at me and smiled before tilting toward me, pressing his lips to mine. He deepened the kiss for a few seconds before we pulled apart.

Everyone clapped enthusiastically, and there were even some whoops and catcalls—most likely from my cousins—which made us both laugh.

Dom interlaced our arms, and we slowly walked to our family. They gathered around, congratulating us.

Dom's dad was in the last row, and Dora sat next to him. He opened his arms wide, smiling from ear to ear. "Look at you. Come here, let me give you a hug."

I leaned down.

"Your veil," Paisley screeched from behind me. I heard her shuffle around me, probably trying to keep the veil from slipping under the wheel of the wheelchair or something.

Once she was holding it out of the way, I gave him a wholehearted hug, and Dom did the same.

"I'm happy for you, my boy," Theodore said. "For both of you."

While the family gathered around, congratulating us again, I heard the staff already moving the chairs, putting them at the tables.

"Okay, Aunt Reese, just stay like that while I take a few pictures," Paisley instructed.

"Just me and Dom or everyone else?"

"Hmm, you two first. Then I think everyone," she said.

She was determined to take pictures, which was probably why she'd stressed out when I asked her to also take care of the veil. She snapped a dozen pictures before the professional photographer we'd hired took over.

Liz came to me with quick steps and wide eyes. She was clearly tense as she stepped right up next to me, bypassing the veil.

"Liz, is something wrong?" I asked her.

She looked from me to Dom. "I've got a small problem. There are a few finger marks on the cake. I think one of the kids had a bit of fun."

I burst out laughing, and Dom chuckled, shaking his head.

"Liz, relax." I loved that she'd made our cake too.

"You don't mind?" she asked.

"No. As long as it's still standing and we have something to cut, it's all good."

Dom tilted toward me, kissing my temple. "I don't think anything can upset us today."

"Exactly," I agreed. It was the happiest day of my life.

Dom and I were still laughing as the photographer instructed the family how to position themselves around us.

I felt so blessed to be surrounded by my family. They'd taught me how to live, how to be strong, and, most of all, how to be myself. I'd learned so much from them, and I was beyond grateful to have them with us on our special day.

Second Epilogue
Reese

Six Years Later

"This is the best idea we've had!" Kimberly exclaimed.

"I agree," I replied, patting my belly.

We'd all decided to spend our vacation together. Since the family had grown by leaps and bounds in the last six years, it wasn't easy to coordinate so we all could get away at the same time. Finding a location was easier. The Maxwell Hotels was a large chain now with seven gorgeous properties.

"Aspen will always have a place in my heart," Kimberly said. She'd insisted on us gathering here. She, too, had a baby bump.

I loved being pregnant at the same time as my sister. It made our bond even stronger. She and Drake already had a baby boy as well.

"Let's join the rest of the group outside," she suggested.

"Good idea."

We'd booked adjacent suites on the ground floor, mainly because they also had small gardens and we could all gather in them. The staff removed the separators between the gardens, so the kids roamed around freely—and there were *a lot* of kids.

Tyler and Kendra had two sets of twins who'd been born within one year of each other. Talk about having a full house. But my cousin was thoroughly enjoying fatherhood. Tyler turned down a job to coach his old team, saying he wanted to spend time with the kids while they were babies and that he could always go back to coaching later on.

Tate and Lexi had a baby boy just last year. Liz and Declan had two adorable girls. Luke and Megan had twins three years ago. That's when we realized that somewhere in the family, we probably had a twin gene that had been dormant until our generation started having babies.

Travis and Bonnie had a second baby girl three years ago. Avery and Sam also had an adorable girl.

As for Dom and me, well, we'd been busy. He came up to me, holding Millie, our one-year-old daughter, in his arms and our four-year-old son, Harry, by the hand. I'd always wanted a large family, but my current pregnancy had been a bit of a mishap. I thought you couldn't get pregnant while breastfeeding. Turned out, I was wrong. But Dom and I were happier than ever.

Harry kissed my belly.

"Is the bunny ready yet?" he asked, making me laugh as Dom just shook his head.

We'd told him once that I had a bun in the oven, and ever since, he kept asking every few days if the bunny was ready. He was growing up fast, but sometimes I forgot he was still a toddler and took everything literally.

"Not yet, Harry. We still need to wait a few months," I explained.

"Babe, are you feeling okay? Want to lie down for a bit?" Dom asked.

"I did earlier," I said.

Kimberly laughed. "For like two seconds."

"Thank you for your support, Kimberly," Dom said with a grin.

"I feel fine," I cut in.

I'd been sick most of the time during the previous pregnancies—somehow I'd had morning sickness that lasted for the whole nine months—but I was doing better this time around.

"Can I go play with my cousins?" Harry asked. He spoke surprisingly clearly for a kid his age. It was one of the reasons why I sometimes forgot that he was still so young.

"Sure," I said. "It was such a great idea to remove the separators between the suite gardens."

"I agree." Dom kissed my cheek, putting his hand on my belly.

"She's sleeping." I'd never tire of this feeling of creating a human being inside me, feeling her every time she turned around and even when she woke up.

"You sure you don't need to lie down?"

"No, I slept on the plane."

"I know," Dom said.

"We *all* know," Sam added, coming up behind us.

I turned around to face him. "What do you mean?"

"Oh, nothing." He schooled his features.

I pointed at him. "Cousin?"

"You were snoring."

I clasped my hand over my mouth. "Oh my God. You think everyone heard me?"

"No... Maybe just half the plane."

"Oh God." I zeroed in on Dom. "Why didn't you wake me up?"

"You were exhausted. Of course I didn't wake you up."

I looked at Sam again. "Can you, I don't know, give me something?"

"For snoring?" He seemed stunned.

"Yes, so I don't terrorize everyone on the way back too."

Sam now looked at Dom in alarm.

"You opened this can of worms, man. Fix it," Dom said.

"There's nothing I can do here. Just relax, okay? Oh, I think I heard someone calling me," Sam said quickly, then darted off.

I saw right through his fib, but I'd let it slide—this time.

"Don't worry about it. You're gorgeous," Dom said, kissing my forehead.

I couldn't even come too close to him because my belly was pretty sizable even though I wasn't that far along. People kept asking me if I was having twins. I wasn't. I'd repeatedly asked the doctor.

We'd set up a huge firepit that we'd tried to babyproof as much as possible and placed lots of benches in a circle around it.

The only ones missing were my dad and his family, Lena and Emmett, and Gran and John. Gran wasn't flying much lately, and my aunt and uncle didn't want us all to be away from home at the same time, just in case she and John needed something.

Paisley hadn't wanted to come either. She had her own group of friends and declared that vacationing with her family was uncool. Tate was still processing that, even though he had his hands full with the little ones.

I sat down on a bench, unsure if I'd ever be able to get up again. Maybe I'd just roll off it.

"I'll bring you a plate of food," Dom said.

"Thanks."

Tate was sitting next to me, brushing his daughter's hair. My heart filled with tenderness watching this mountain of a man holding a bright pink brush and carefully running it through her silky strands.

"Still not happy that Paisley isn't with us?" I asked.

He grumbled, "I'm getting used to it, slowly."

"No, you're not."

He laughed. "No, I'm not. But that's fine. I'm glad we all came here."

"It's one of my favorite hotels," I said. Right here at the foot of the Rocky Mountains, life seemed easier, more serene somehow. We didn't have anything to complain about—except my snoring.

Dom came back with a plate of food and sat down next to me. Our girl had fallen asleep on him.

"You can put her down in one of those mobile cribs." We'd set a few of them around, knowing that at any given time, there were going to be at least a few kids sleeping.

"No, I'm fine like this. I like it when she's sleeping on me."

Oh, be still my beating heart. His love for us would never cease to surprise me. I'd never take it for granted.

"We've also got Maxwell wines circulating around. For those who can drink," Tate added, looking at me apologetically.

I laughed. "That's okay. I'm glad to see everyone else is enjoying it."

"You know, I think we were a bit too optimistic with all these benches," Declan said, coming to us, holding a glass of wine. It was the first break he'd taken since we arrived. He seemed to constantly be chasing one kid or another, even those who weren't his. "It's not like we can all sit down at the same time."

"No, we can't," I said, glancing around. I was looking for Harry, but I needn't have bothered. Dom was already following him with his gaze, never letting him out of sight.

Luke came up to us, and he, too, was carrying a sleeping baby. Just then, Tate jumped up from the bench, chasing his girl, who'd hopped off from his lap.

We were all definitely busy, but we managed to enjoy our afternoon snack out in the garden. The weather was perfect for the week ahead, and that wasn't always the case in June in the Rocky Mountains.

A few hours later, the kids had run out of energy, and we were all relishing one of those rare and brief moments of silence when Dom suddenly got up with a glass and lowered our girl into a crib.

He cleared his throat. "Everyone, I'd like to say a few words."

"We're listening," Tate said from next to me.

"I'm very happy that we're all here today, and that we managed to take time off as a family. When I met you all six years ago, I instantly realized that you were a special group by the way you rallied around Reese and also accepted me into your ranks. I'm proud to have married into the Maxwell family and to be here with all of you. I couldn't have wished for a more loving wife or a more caring family, and I want to toast to that."

There was a chorus of "Hear, hear" and the sound of clinking glasses.

Dom sat down next to me, and I kissed his cheek. "Have another glass for me, will you?" I whispered. "And thank you for the beautiful words."

"You're welcome, love."

Travis joined us just then. He'd been inside the hotel, chatting with the staff.

"That sounded like a toast," he said.

Dom blinked. "Man, I didn't realize you weren't here."

Travis started laughing. "That's fine. Plenty of Maxwells to go around. Now, I'm starving, so you can fill me in later."

We all stayed out in the garden until the sun set, then went back to our respective suites. We had a full schedule tomorrow; today was just to relax and enjoy each other.

The suite was eerily quiet. Somehow we'd managed to get both our kids to sleep in record time. I slipped under the covers, and Dom moved right in behind me. He turned onto one side, propping his head on his elbow and putting his other hand on my belly. He kissed my neck lightly, and I squirmed against the sheets. Just then, the baby turned around.

"You felt that?" I asked.

"Yes!" He smiled widely. "I'll never tire of you being pregnant."

I grinned. "I love it, too, especially because it's easy this time around."

He wiggled his eyebrows. "What do you think? After she's here, should we go for number four?"

I smiled, putting a hand on my belly too. "I think you can talk me into that by using the legendary Waldorf charm."

I'd loved growing up in a huge family. And I loved even more that we were creating our own.

Printed in Great Britain
by Amazon